seeking
Alice

seeking
Alice

a novel

CAMILLA TRINCHIERI

excelsior editions

AN IMPRINT OF STATE UNIVERSITY OF NEW YORK PRESS

Published by
STATE UNIVERSITY OF NEW YORK PRESS, ALBANY

Printed in the United States of America

EXCELSIOR EDITIONS IS AN IMPRINT OF
STATE UNIVERSITY OF NEW YORK PRESS

For information, contact
State University of New York Press, Albany, NY
www.sunypress.edu

Production and book design, Laurie D. Searl
Marketing, Fran Keneston

Library of Congress Cataloging-in-Publication Data

Trinchieri, Camilla.
Seeking Alice : a novel / Camilla Trinchieri.
pages ; cm. — (Excelsior editions)
ISBN 978-1-4384-6128-1 (pbk. : alk. paper)
— ISBN 978-1-4384-6129-8 (e-book)
I. Title.
PS3553.R435S44 2016
813'.54—dc23
2015030786

10 9 8 7 6 5 4 3 2 1

IN MEMORIAM

Memory believes before knowing remembers.

—WILLIAM FAULKNER, *Light in August*

ONE

CAMBRIDGE, MASSACHUSETTS—JANUARY 1956

Our house is creaking, settling in for the night. David is in the den typing up a paper he's been working on for at least six months. I sit in the armchair in my study, feet propped up on the windowsill, needing to pee, too tired to get up, too busy caressing my belly, bidding the life growing inside me goodnight. Twelve weeks old. The size of my palm, Dr. Page says.

With the baby, Mama has come back into my head. I need her, want her here to guide me. David is loving, attentive. He is willing to shop, cook, wash the dishes, sweep the floors. He'll do anything to keep me happy and rested and I love him all the more for it, but I ache to say, "Mama. I'm expecting a baby," and pour my happiness over her, to keep her warm, to make her face shine with pride. My baby, her grandchild.

I am filled with questions. Did she dream that her baby would be born with a hole in its heart for lack of love? That the weight of her body, tossing in sleep, would suffocate it? When does the fear go away? With its first kick? When it meets the world and screams?

I picture scenarios in which I ask her to place her hand on my belly and tell me the sex of the baby. She was always good at guessing. A girl, she says, and we start spouting possible names. I paint her laughing with joy, hugging me, telling me not to fear, all will be well.

The old Mama dream has come back.

We're rolling down the mountain surrounded by snow and rock. A black bed of pine trees waits below. Above us the barbed wire of the Italian-Swiss frontier plays its thousand bells, announcing Christmas, warning the German guards. I hold my baby sister against my chest and feel Mama's hips embracing mine, her arms locked round my waist, her chin hooking my shoulder. A human avalanche, we roll to what we perceive as safety.

Romantic. False. Wishful thinking.

Since that night on Mount Bisbino, twelve years ago, Mama has drifted in and out of my landscape. Sometimes I've felt her presence like the phantom limb of an amputee, and in my dreams I've asked her countless questions, both serious and silly. Should I cut my hair? Is it okay for my boyfriend to touch my breasts? If I get married, will my love, his love last? For how long? Why aren't you here to help me? What happened to you?

Other times I've reduced her to a pinpoint in my heart, pretending that not having a mother was just fine, nothing to go on about. I had Papa to take care of me. I wasn't an orphan like so many other kids after the war.

Papa always maintained Mama was killed the night of Christmas Eve, 1943, trying to escape Nazi-infested Italy with two of her children. Me and Claire. I believed the story in my teenage years when I was too absorbed in the now of my life to question it. But even then, when someone would ask about my mother, I could hear doubt unfurling as I answered, "She was killed in the war." As an adult, I cannot help but think her death is the easy, neat explanation, the one that leaves everyone guiltless. Everyone except me, that is.

Maybe Papa knew the alternate ending to Mama's story. Before he died, I plied him with questions, but his answer never changed. "Alice is dead. Please, Susie, let your mother rest in peace." I'm left swaying on uncertain ground.

Is her death a lie? Did she die, or did she decide her life would be better without us and walk away? What will I tell my baby about the grandmother she will never have? I want my child to grow up without doubts. I need to search for the different truth that I believe is there. I need to free myself of the guilt I feel. Let go of the past. I have only six months before the baby leaves the cradle of my belly. She will need all of me then. I promise her that. I was a bad daughter. I will be a good mother. I promise.

I have no proof Mama is still alive, but I was there that night on Mount Bisbino. If the Germans had killed Mama, I would have heard the shots. No one fired a single shot.

I'm horribly late, but here I am applying another layer of lipstick. Fuchsia. My mouth looks like a wound. "Obergruppenführer," I mouth at my reflection in the gilt-framed mirror Marco bought me as a welcome-to-Prague gift. "Obergruppenführer." This time out loud. It sounds funny, silly even. It means superior group leader. The new governor of Bohemia and Moravia, Reinhard Heydrich, is an Obergruppenführer, and there isn't anything funny or silly about him. Giorgio Scarditti, the Italian consul, is honoring him tonight with a reception downstairs. As the wife of the vice consul, I'm expected to show up and be gracious. What I feel is anything but gracious.

I smile at Susie's reflection in the mirror. Looking at her makes me feel better. She has her father's looks. Sharp cheekbones on a narrow face, thick, long black hair I braid every morning, and wide dark eyes that never seem to get enough of the world. "Germans do that, string a bunch of words together," I say. Susie is sitting on the bed, playing with the buttons of the gown I should already be wearing. Her hands are probably dirty with the chocolate Marco gave her before going downstairs. Tonight I don't care. "They're doing it with countries too. Stringing them into one."

Susie giggles. "*Donaudampschiffahrtgesellschaft*. That means Danube Steamship Company." She's only eleven and learned to speak fluent German after only a few months. Andy too. It's easy for the children. Seventeen months have gone by and I still barely understand it. I refused German lessons. At thirty-two I'm too old, the language is too difficult. After years of living in Rome I manage in Italian, although I can't get rid of what Marco teasingly calls my "chewing gum" accent.

A Handel adagio drifts in from Andy's bedroom. Handel is my favorite, and with eyes closed, I tilt my head forward and wait for the soothing notes to wash over me, but the clock on the bedside table clicks the passing seconds too loudly. It's no use. I have to move, get dressed, face the evening.

"Help me with the buttons, please, Susie." She slips off the bed and holds up the gown. I step into it and suck in my stomach as Susie reaches my waist. I've gained weight since the last time I wore

3

this gown, a smoky blue satin I bought at Bonwit's in New York before sailing to Europe.

"The eyelets are tight," Susie complains.

"Why can't we see Heydrich too?" Andy, my sweet talented boy, is standing in the doorway, a shock of hair covering one eye as always. He too has his father's lean dark looks except for his eyes, hazel and deep set like mine.

"He's just a man like any other," I say. Why does power excite? Marco came home early from the office today, his face flushed and taut, his eyes brimming with anticipation. It turned my stomach. "There's nothing to see, Andy."

"He's the snake and the devil," Susie says and flops back on the bed. "You're done, Mama."

"Thank you, sweetie." I slip one of my evening gloves on, tug it up my arm. The snake and the devil is what Jitka, our Czech housekeeper, calls Heydrich.

"I think it's unfair." Andy's voice cracks. "I told everyone at school I was going to meet him. What am I going to say now?"

Susie starts jumping up and down on the bed. "Lie."

"No lies. Susie, please stop jumping." I offer Susie my gloved arm and the sapphire bracelet Marco gave me as a wedding present. "Help again." As Susie bends over to close the catch on the bracelet, I kiss the top of her head. Her hair smells of the lemon juice I rinse her hair with to make it shine. I must remember to ask Jitka not to say anything more about Heydrich in front of the children. Jitka, who told me that horrible story. I had heard rumors about Heydrich. That he had been behind the burning of the Reichstag, that Hitler had picked him to govern the German protectorate for his ability to destroy any resistance. That in the few months since he'd come to Prague, he had ordered the torture and killing of many men. They were only rumors until last week when I found Jitka sobbing in the kitchen. She kept repeating the same Czech words, getting louder and louder, trying to make me understand. I poured her a glass of brandy and ran downstairs to get one of the consulate secretaries to translate.

The day before, an old man, a widower who lived on the floor above Jitka, sang the Czech anthem from his window as Heydrich's open car passed in front of their building. That morning she found his broken body propped against the doorway.

My heart froze. I had to pour myself some brandy too. Thank God the children were in school. I told Marco when he came home for lunch, told him that I wouldn't, couldn't, go to the reception. I asked him to stay home with me, to find some excuse not to participate in honoring a murderer. He said that was impossible. There were going to be many other receptions; he couldn't always come up with an excuse. Doing his job did not mean he was endorsing Heydrich's methods. Ugliness was part of war and there was nothing we, as individuals, could do to put an end to it. Resigning from his job wouldn't save a single person. In fact, his job was keeping the family safe. We had children to think about. The war would be over soon.

I can hear him now.

"We're stuck in a bad situation, and all we can do is make the best of it. I need you to be on my side. We both agreed a diplomatic career was a good idea."

That's true. With the Depression reaching Europe, his career as a civil engineer had petered to nothing. Marco is good-looking, charming, persuasive, with a knack for listening intently to the most boring guest, and an ability to quickly assess a situation. The perfect diplomat, I thought naively, when a life lived in different countries seemed exciting, when I still judged Mussolini just a pompous windbag, when I still believed diplomacy had some relevance in world affairs. That the Italian state wasn't likely to go bankrupt was an added incentive.

Andy is still leaning in the doorway, looking forlorn. "The adagio was beautifully played," I tell him. "You've made enormous progress." If I stay, I could read a bedtime story with Susie, listen to more Handel.

Marco expects me to meet this Nazi murderer, shake hands with him, smile even. If I don't go downstairs, I'll get a week's worth of simmering anger from him, another stifling round of lectures on the duties of a diplomat's wife from Giorgio's wife, Lilli, and probably a scolding behind closed doors from the consul general himself. Staying upstairs will not change the course of the war or save anyone's life.

I push myself to the door. "I'm proud of you, Andy. You'll have to play it for Papa." Andy moves aside to let me pass—at thirteen he's at the do-not-touch stage—but I manage to sneak in a quick kiss on his chin. Both my children are tall, something that fills me with a pride I'm slightly ashamed of. I blame it on my own height, five foot two. "Tell your friends the truth," I tell Andy. "Your father wouldn't let you." The one thing we had agreed on—keep the children away from Heydrich and his cronies.

"I made tons of mistakes in the adagio," Andy says.

I smile. My son was never any good at accepting compliments. I blow both my children a kiss. "Good night, sweeties. Don't let the bed bugs bite."

Heydrich and his party are in the front hall when I walk in, only a few feet away, saying goodbye to Giorgio and Lilli. The huge Bohemian glass chandelier Lilli is so proud of dribbles light on his head. May it fall on him, I think, and then the snake and the devil looks at me. I stop, one arm half sheathed, the glove hanging limply from my hand. I find myself unable to take a step in any direction. Waiters hold up open overcoats. He is tall, thin, with a never-ending forehead, jutting ears, a prominent nose. Small eyes that suck me in. I could scream at them and there would be no echo. The sound would simply be snatched from me, swallowed.

Heydrich plunges his arms in the armholes of his coat.

For a moment the man is defenseless, but I do nothing. Can do nothing.

Then Marco is at my elbow, pushing me forward. "This is my wife, Alinka." Alinka, the name everyone has adopted for me here, making me sound Slavic. Alice is so American. I don't mind. I some-how feel safer, less like a woman straight out of a Henry James story.

Heydrich nods and I curtsy like a silly school girl.

When Heydrich leaves, I sense an audible release of tension. Louder voices, laughter, the clinking of glasses. Marco kisses my fore-head. "Good for you. The curtsy was a charming touch." I feel only shame.

My head fills with all the foolish actions, the insidious compro-mises I've made to please, to be deserving, to keep love. I tell myself I'm being a good mother, keeping my children happy, safe. That gives me a warm little glow for about ten seconds. What choices do I have? When Mussolini entered Hitler's war last year, I begged Marco to take us back to the States. He refused, convinced no American company would hire an Italian. If the children and I went back without him for the duration of the war—no one knew, knows, how long that might be—I was afraid it would end our marriage. Marco kept repeating that he needed my trust, my support, my presence to give him ballast. For better or for worse, I had vowed.

I love him, the children love him. We are a happy family. We are safe. All I have to do is pretend the war doesn't concern me. Keep my opinions to myself. Be Alinka, not Alice. Fold my conscience and tuck it out of sight like the lace handkerchief I keep in my purse in case of a sudden gust of tears. Be like Lilli, wrapped in the importance of her husband's career, facing each day with a smile permanently etched on her powdered face.

I'll try. For Andy and Susie. For Marco, who still makes my heart dance. I take a glass of champagne from the tray a waiter offers, walk over to Lilli and say, "The flower arrangements are gorgeous." At least that's true.

CAMBRIDGE, MASSACHUSETTS—JANUARY 1956

It's a cold night and the squirrels have gotten into the attic again. They're having a grand old time—playing soccer with pebbles from the sound of it. David is oblivious, his steady breath adding a comforting warmth to my neck.

Half an hour goes by. An hour. I'm still wide awake. The squirrels have quit their game. The only sound is David's breathing and an intermittent gurgle in my stomach, another call for food, or hormones doing battle.

It's always been hard for me to go to sleep. Dropping into a void where I have no control. As a child I made a pact with Mama. On the nights she went out, I promised I'd go to bed without a fuss, but when she came back, she had to stop in my room and, if I was awake, tell me everything.

The night of Heydrich's reception I was waiting for her. I remember her looking more beautiful than ever. The gray blue of her long dress had turned her eyes the same color. She had pinned back her red, curly hair, but strands now straggled down, framing her soft round face. Pearls dangled from her ears. Her neck was bare.

"Don't you sometimes wish you were back home?" Mama asked me.

Home where? Newport Beach, where we lived for three years while Papa commuted back and forth to the Italian consulate in Los Angeles? Rome, where I was born and lived the first seven years of my life? Rome was ages ago. Newport Beach I missed vaguely. My letters to my best friend Judy never got a reply. I stopped writing. My American friends were becoming goodbye poems in my friendship book. The maple syrup and peanut butter my mother kept sending for never arrived either. Europe was at war. We couldn't go back.

"Home is here," I said. Where the family was together again, all of us in a fat circle in which I could roll to my heart's content. Papa had come to Prague before us, while Andy and I finished the year in the red school-house on the beach. For those six months I thought I'd lost him forever.

I asked her, "What did you do to the snake and the devil?"

"I put pepper in his champagne and a toad in his sock."

When she bent over to kiss me goodnight, I saw that her eyes, those eyes that seemed to look at you from somewhere deep inside her, shimmered. She'd been crying, but I said nothing, afraid that it was Papa who had made her cry.

Why would I think Papa had made her cry? Had he made her cry before? Papa had a temper; he used to yell if he couldn't find the shirt he wanted to wear, or Mama wasn't ready on time, or Andy didn't study. His outbursts were part of the background noise of our lives. We didn't mind them very much, which probably made him angrier, but his anger petered out quickly, a flare quickly doused by Mama's calm response. I don't think he ever made her cry. Not then.

PRAGUE, THE GERMAN PROTECTORATE OF
BOHEMIA AND MORAVIA—OCTOBER 21, 1941

I wait in Marco's bed to hear his footsteps down the hallway. He's on duty downstairs until the last guest leaves. Since we've moved into this Prague apartment with too many rooms, we each have our own bedroom. His idea. Marco likes to read well into the night, which keeps me up, and he's started snoring. I do sleep better, but I miss the inconsequential chitchat before turning out the light, the weight of his body next to mine, closing my eyes to the sight of his profile as he reads, reaching out with my foot and finding him in the dark.

I'm hungry, wet with wanting him.

I wanted Marco from that first night in Baltimore, when he appeared at Eliza's eighteenth birthday party, on his way to South America to build a bridge on the Magdalena River. He was bent over Eliza's mother. She was showing him how to crack a crab. He'd never eaten one before, he was saying in heavily accented English. His foreign looks—jutting cheekbones, a long straight nose pointing to his smile, intense dark eyes, black hair smoothed back from a high forehead—made me instantly greedy for him. His gaze was direct, different from the bungling glances I'd sometimes caught from the Johns Hopkins boys. I stared back, my usual shyness gone, thrilled by the thought of him as an exotic stranger, telling stories, opening vistas.

Marco was passed around from girl to girl, mother to mother, like an hors d'oeuvre they hadn't tasted before. He kept up his end— kissing hands, never losing his smile, telling jokes that made everyone laugh too loud. He finally noticed me, a freckled awkward eighteen-year-old in a hideous little-girl dress my mother had forced me to wear. He held me in his gaze, and the smile left him. I felt chosen by his sudden seriousness, beautiful enough for my mother to unpurse her lips later that night and my father to hold his gaze on me for more than two seconds. When Marco walked over to me, I was so wet I had to run to the bathroom. Later, behind a tree, spiking my lemonade with his gin, Marco accused me of running away from him.

What if I had? So many twists and turns possible, with no map, no outcome specified. It's the fabled three doors. Behind which one waits the tiger?

I turn off the lamp by the bedside and wrap my arms around the pillow. I would never have found anyone to love as much as I love him. Anyone to love me back the way he does. I wouldn't have my beautiful children. I opened the right door.

The snap of the lamp wakes me up. Marco leans over me. "How nice of you to visit." He is usually the one to come to me.

I clasp his neck and draw him to me, kiss him. With my free hand I pull at his shirt, reach my hand underneath to his skin. I breathe in his smell—tobacco, cologne, alcohol and something else, something I can't place. A sweet smell that I like.

Marco slips the straps of my nightgown down to my waist, nuzzles his head between my breasts. "Thank you for tonight," he mumbles.

"Come inside me. Wipe tonight away."

I should get up, go back to my bedroom, wash myself, but Marco's fallen asleep on my shoulder. My arm is all pins and needles, but the weight of his head grounds me. Like the burn in my nipples, the rawness between my legs.

Two weeks after Eliza's party Marco leaned out of the bus window belting *Voglio bene a Alice* all the way to Fort McHenry. Excessive emotion is what I called it then, loving every second of it. Excessive emotion that I still need to cover myself with nightly, using it like a cream to keep me young.

From the beginning we couldn't keep away from each other. We eloped a month after Eliza's party and went to live in Colombia while Marco finished building his bridge. Andy was born a year later in Bogotà. After keeping us and the doctor waiting for ten days, he came in the dank basement of our rented house. Marco still insists it was the goat that brought Andy out. A flayed, gutted goat peering at me from a butcher's hook supposedly frightened me into letting him go. He makes me laugh with his operatic stories.

Marco turns. My shoulder is suddenly free and I kiss the back of his neck, the dip between his shoulder blades. I love you, Marco Alessandrini, but sometimes you are wrong. It was the heat and the flies that kept Andy in the darkness of my belly. I was resting with my feet up in the cool basement when my water broke. The goat I saw weeks later, covered with blue green flies, so shiny they would have made a pretty necklace.

I reach down under the covers and retrieve my nightgown.

CAMBRIDGE, MASSACHUSETTS—FEBRUARY 1956

I learned to adore my father by watching Mama. His presence brought a softening of her posture, a thickening voice. Her chin lifted to reveal the whiteness of her neck, her fingers stretched open. Her nose quivered as she inhaled his scent. If he touched her, her lips parted like the lips of the women at Sunday Mass who lean against the altar railing, waiting for the body of Christ to rest on their tongues. At first I wanted that love from Mama. I would imitate him and run my fingers down her face, follow the curve of her hip with my hands, kiss her in the dent behind her ear, smell her. She would laugh and push me gently away, offering me a doll instead.

After losing Papa for six months, I turned to him. In Prague I made sure to be the first to reach the front door when I heard the jangle of his keys. I interrupted whenever my parents spoke to each other. His lap was my chair. If they touched, my hand would slip between theirs. I would listen for his slippered footsteps outside my room long after the sounds of the apartment had shut down. Her door opening and taking him in. Closing me out.

I made a pest of myself, Andy kept reminding me. Papa seemed to enjoy the attention. Mama said she was happy there was so much love in our home.

The night of Heydrich's reception I slipped out of the apartment and waited in the stairwell for Papa to come home. I wanted to show him a drawing I had done in school that day. On the floor below, the consul general's door finally opened.

"*Danke schön und gute Nacht.*" A large man came out on the landing in a thick overcoat, a hat in his hand. A reedy woman walked out backward, a silver fur jacket flung over her shoulders. Her hair was slipping out of a low bun. Hair with so much henna it looked purple.

The marble stairs were cold. There was no heat in the stairwell, and I had to go to the bathroom.

Papa came out, in his black uniform, a cigarette burning in his hand. I crouched not to be seen and watched the woman move into the chandelier's light, next to him. The silver fur fell from her shoulder. Papa's hand caught it at hip height.

They walked down, out of sight, and their mingled footsteps stopped. I heard the rustling sound of silk; the same sound Mama made with her nightgown when she got in and out of bed. I bumped down a few steps, holding my thighs tight to keep from peeing. The woman's fur jacket lying on a stair, like a dog sleeping. I couldn't hold it anymore and ran home. In the rush, I forgot my drawing.

I woke up with a sore throat the next day. Mama insisted I stay home. Jitka probably fed me her capon broth and Mama read to me. That's what they always did when we got sick. When Papa came home for lunch, he shooed Mama from my bedroom and dropped my drawing in my lap.

"It's good. You caught Mama's unruly hair. And my long nose." He laughed. "But you're prettier than that."

"No, I'm not." I had drawn a circle with our four faces.

"What were you doing on the stairs last night?"

"I wanted to say good night."

"I bet you weren't wearing your slippers. That's why you caught a cold." Papa sat down on the bed, his palm on my forehead to test for fever. He was warmer than I was. I waited for the scolding that was sure to come.

"Do you know what I used to do to stay home from school?" he said instead. "I'd hold the thermometer against the radiator until the mercury boiled like pasta water. I'll show you my armpits. They're so burned up they're hairless."

I laughed.

PRAGUE—DECEMBER 6, 1941, THE FEAST OF SAINT NICHOLAS

We're having a dinner party for Marco's new friend, Karl Müller, and Jitka's mayonnaise has curdled twice, which prompted Marco to storm off to his bedroom with whatever is necessary to start a new batch. He's convinced that the mayonnaise curdled because Jitka is having her period. I look in and laugh. He's sitting on the bed, dish towel tucked in his undershirt, whisking frenetically as Susie pours a thin stream of oil into the bowl on the night table. "You really are ridiculous, Marco, straight out of the Dark Ages. Please, Susie, don't believe your father's superstitions." Seeing her standing resolute, proud of her role in saving tonight's dinner, fills me with tenderness, and I kiss the top of her head. "You're doing a great job, sweetie." I feel light tonight, blessed, despite the guest, a German munitions expert I haven't met. I've promised myself not to think of how many people his expertise has killed. Not tonight. I'm brimming with good feeling and Kay and Rudolf Vlasek are coming. Kay is American and Rudi is Czech. They're the only people I consider friends here.

I check in with Jitka in the kitchen. She's leaning her formidable body against the stove, arms folded across the balcony of her chest. She looks exceedingly grumpy. I ask if I can help, English words she understands. She shakes her head, knowing how useless I am in the kitchen.

"Tereza!" Jitka points to the kitchen clock. Tereza, her niece, whom she recruited to help her serve dinner, hasn't shown up yet. "Pstruh!" Her finger pans to the huge steamed trout, our main course, lying on a Meissen platter on the table. It's missing an eye and it's much too large and fragile to turn it on its other side. "Susie will fix it," I say and go back to Marco's bedroom to tell Susie she's also needed in the kitchen. She's the food decorator, the flower arranger, the aesthete in our household.

The bowl now holds a glistening pale yellow mound. "It's coming," Marco says.

"Alleluia," I shout and leave them to lay out Susie's dress on her bed. It's her favorite, burgundy velvet with a cream lace collar and cuffs. Andy struts in to show off his new lederhosen. He's slicked back his hair with his father's hair cream, but his cowlick sticks up anyway. I pin it down with a bobby pin. "Very handsome," I tell him, "but your knees need a good scrubbing. Go on. It won't kill you."

In my bedroom, I choose an apricot silk gown with a low neckline. I want to look my best tonight. Not for the guest. For my husband. For me.

"*Zlaty Da'zd* it is called—golden rain," Rudi says, handing me a small gold branch tied with many red ribbons. "It is a traditional gift on Saint Nicholas." I kiss his cheek, still cold from outside. The smell of alcohol prompts me to squeeze his arm. He's a quiet man with exquisite manners and not a drinker. "Thank you," I whisper. His and Kay's presence is a great act of friendship. Together we form a secret alliance against the Axis powers at the table.

Giorgio, looking his pompous consul general best, arrives with his wife, Lilli, glittering with jewelry. The guest of honor comes late. His date is Milena, a regular at diplomatic parties. Usually alone. She's a skinny, sinuous woman with small teeth, gray with lack of calcium. Not beautiful in any way, but what Marco would call "a type." I barely know her, but I'm fascinated by her deliberate movements, the smooth whiteness of her skin, the dark almost purple hair. Most of all by the sadness in her face. She seems to have that special strength that grief can give women. I've noticed them in the streets of Prague, their heads covered in black kerchiefs, each feature of their faces emphasized, underlined by the loss they're bearing. A son or a husband lost in Russia, maybe. The faces seem drawn in charcoal, the kerchief worn as a mourning edge, like the black frame of a death announcement. Milena has some of the same emphasis on her face. All anyone seems to know about her is that she's a Polish refugee lucky enough to have found work as a translator for the German command. Refugee. The word alone explains sadness.

"Welcome, Milena." I kiss both her cheeks, and am left with the sweet smell of her perfume and two bags of chocolates for the children.

13

Marco takes over the introductions and offers spumante. Susie, glowing in her dress, tosses her braids and passes hors d'oeuvres. After everyone is settled on sofa and armchairs, Andy plays the Handel adagio he's been practicing for weeks. He's removed the bobby pin and his cowlick trembles in rhythm with the movement of his bow. "It's been raining for a week," he says afterward to excuse his mistakes. "The damp affects the soundboard." He's always good at shifting responsibility, not unlike Marco. "Did you know Schumann went *wahnsinnig*?" Andy asks all of us. He likes to show off the bits of information about composers that his Czech maestro feeds him. Last week it was Smetana's political problems with the Hapsburgs. He's also good at deflecting.

Karl Müller laughs. I have no idea what *wahnsinnig* means, but I'm not about to admit it in front of Lilli and Giorgio or this tall, large German with a square face and wheat-colored hair, who could easily pass as a farmer from the Midwest.

"And did you know, young man," Müller asks in English, "that Obergruppenführer Heydrich is an excellent violinist?" The conversation has been proceeding in a jumble of English, German, and French. "Perhaps you would like to play for the Obergruppenführer? When it stops raining, of course."

I sit up. "Never!" Marco sends me a warning glance meant to shrivel my tongue. I beam him a reassuring smile. I will not let this evening be spoiled.

Karl Müller's eyes dart to my cleavage, stay there. I feel myself blush. "I respect your wishes, Frau Alessandrini. Children must stay innocent."

Milena is watching us. Her hair is loose on her shoulders. Her sleeveless sheath is the color of oysters, with the same wet sheen. Her skin is so white I will call her the swan. Turning people into animals is a game I play with the children. Müller is the bear.

Tereza announces dinner and I tell the children it's time to say good night. Andy bows, Susie curtsies and passing by me, whispers, "Schumann went cuckoo." I smile my thanks. My clever girl, she knows her Mama's shortcomings too well.

We move to the dining room. The table is covered with my favorite tablecloth—a white Florentine linen we bought on my only trip to Florence. The gray embroidered forget-me-nots are so delicate they look drawn in pencil. Susie's carefully written place cards sit next to the three glasses for each guest. In the center, I've placed Rudi's gold branch with the red ribbons on it. Lilli launches a begrudging smile at me. The table setting has passed muster.

Müller pulls out my chair. I thank him and sit as Marco pulls out Milena's chair. Kay sits down on her own. I watch Milena sink down in one floating motion, see Marco's hand brush the length of her arm. I unfold my napkin, place it on my lap, take a sip of water. Her skin is inviting. It's only a gesture.

Müller, to my right, is spooning his soup when he tells me I look like golden Prague. *Zlata Praha*. He's flirting with me, which doesn't flatter me. "I have just discovered that *Praha* means threshold in Czech," he says. "The beginning, the possibility of change. I like that idea."

"The possibility of an end to the war?" Milena asks.

Kay leans over her plate, spoon high in front of her. "If so, who's going to be the victor?"

Marco quickly proposes a toast to his guests. Müller counters with one to his hosts. Kay's question gets buried under long drafts of wine.

"When my train pulled into the Prague station this morning," Müller says, after Tereza has cleared the soup plates, "I had to make my way through a large, silent crowd of men, women and children."

Lilli tilts her impeccably coiffed head. "Why would any person wish to leave Prague? After Rome, it's the safest place in Europe."

"These people were not leaving or coming. They were waiting. I had a strange feeling, almost of fear. The uncanny silence of so many people."

"What were they waiting for?" I ask him. My eyes are transfixed by Milena's arms poised on the tablecloth, comparing them against my own, muddied with freckles.

"They were waiting for the trains from the eastern front that bring in the wounded. It has become a favorite pastime to watch dying German soldiers."

I shudder. For the soldiers. For Marco's hand skating Milena's bare arm.

"Cruelty is to be expected," Müller says. "What I find frightening is the passivity of their hatred."

"It's dread they're feeling," Kay announces in a shrill voice. "Dread that not enough Germans have died."

Before anyone can comment, Tereza breaks into the dining room holding up the trout on a silver platter. The fish's head is intact, body skin replaced by a smooth coating of yolk-bright mayonnaise dotted with slivers of black olives and lemon slices Susie has meticulously substituted for scales and fins. She's restored the missing eye with a caper. The *pstruh* is now perfect.

The guests applaud and I announce, "I also have a Saint Nicholas present to give. A lovely one. On Saint Nicholas we should have only good news." I make sure everyone is looking at me. The inauspicious start will have a happy ending.

"Marco and I are expecting a baby."

I sit on Marco's bed, still in my evening gown, waiting for him to come out of the bathroom across the corridor.

"That was quite a surprise," Marco says, walking in.

My thumb traces different shadings against the velvet of the duvet. "You're not angry I told them before you knew?" My hands feel cold and heavy.

"I would have preferred to be the first one to find out."

"I'm sorry. I hadn't planned on it, but I had to stop things."

Marco drops his bathrobe on the armchair and sits down next to me. The bed shifts with his weight. "Stop what?"

I'm not sure. More ugly stories from Karl Müller? Kay saying something irreparable? My doubts? I'm too tired to know. "I wanted to talk about happy things, that's all. Are you happy?"

"Not the best of times to bring a baby into the world." Marco clasps my hand. I've been rubbing the velvet thin. "And three will be a handful for you, but I think it's great." He kisses my forehead and I lean into him. He smells of toothpaste and soap, and the banality of those smells acts like a balm.

"It was a good evening," Marco says, getting into bed. I feel his long legs slide behind me under the duvet. "Everyone got tight with too many toasts to us and the baby."

"Except Milena."

"Can you blame her for claiming she wasn't feeling well? Karl didn't take his eyes off of you the whole time. I think he's *ein Bisschen* in love with my wife." The thought seems to please him. I'd rather he were jealous.

"Milena is very attractive."

"She's too skinny." He reaches for my shoulders, runs his hands down the length of my arms. "Flesh is what I like." Goose bumps appear on my skin, and I laugh.

I wake up to a glorious morning, with the sun pouring into the room and the sky wearing only a few ragged clouds. Marco has already gone. His bedroom window faces a garden covered in gravel and ivy, and dotted with billowing stone statues of half-clad beauties, a garden that could just as easily be in Rome, especially with today's golden light. Wisps of Roman memories scud across my mind: Marco's coffee-stained kisses in the morning, our afternoon lovemaking while baby Andy napped. Pinching pennies. All we could afford were beans and pasta. We got fat. On Sundays, Marco plunged us into Roman history—museums, ruins, the cool, musty interiors of countless churches, the surprise of a new piazza or a half-open doorway to a Renaissance courtyard, the city awash in apricot light. I was enchanted.

Romans made me feel that being an American was something special, prized. Everyone welcomed me, filled me with anecdotes about saints, popes, politicians. Shopkeepers cheered my terrible Italian with extravagant hand gestures. On the street men and women alike looked me over as though I were worthy of appraisal. The attention embarrassed, then thrilled me. I began to feel sensual, even beautiful. I miss that.

I slip on Marco's bathrobe. I have to get back to my bedroom before the children wake up, but I look at my reflection in the window glass first and tell it, "I'm still happy."

CAMBRIDGE, MASSACHUSETTS—FEBRUARY 1956

The morning after the Saint Nicholas dinner was a Sunday, a day when Papa usually cooked us an American breakfast: eggs, pancakes, French toast with caramelized sugar instead of molasses. By the time Andy and I came back starving from Mass with Jitka, Papa had gone to Kolín for the day on business, which meant we got stuck with the usual—*caffè latte*, bread, and jam. After breakfast Mama asked me if I wanted to go out with her, just the two of us. I was thrilled. A special girl-to-girl privilege.

We were paying a sick call, she said as we crossed the Charles Bridge with its statues black with coal soot. It wasn't far, a twenty-minute walk along the Vlatva to the Josefov quarter, the old Jews' Town.

"Last night Milena wasn't feeling well." Her words came out in puffs of smoky air. I kept warm by jumping puddles. Mama looked cheerful, at ease under her fawn hat, one arm clutching the fern that she'd taken from the bathroom at the last minute.

"Ah, so you are here." Milena opened the door a few inches so that we could see only a narrow slice of her.

"I hope you're feeling better," Mama said.

"What is it you came to see? How I live?" She let go of the door and walked around the large square room. "Not like you. One room, barely a kitchen, a closet of a bathroom." The one window had no curtains. Clusters of flower prints covered the wall behind the unmade bed. Some were shiny and looked as if they had been cut out of magazines.

"This is not a fancy quarter. Cheap. Even cheaper now." Her strong accent made her words stick to the roof of her mouth like toffee. She was wearing a paisley bathrobe belted tightly around a waist which didn't look much bigger than mine.

Mama stopped just inside the threshold, but I went to the one empty chair and sat down. The place smelled of tobacco, wet coal dust, and sandalwood. The white ceramic stove in one corner gave off too much heat.

"I should have brought flowers." Mama took a step inside the room and held up the fern.

"For me?" Milena clasped the plant to her chest and laughed. "Take off your coats." She pointed to an armchair piled with pillows and slipped behind a flowered curtain. "I will make tea."

I asked to use the bathroom. It had lavender walls and a cracked bath tub. I had a need to search, but didn't know what I was looking for. I turned on the faucet, sniffed Milena's perfume bottle—the smell was icky sweet—opened her powder box. When enough time had elapsed, I pulled the chain. Back in the room, I stepped behind the flowered curtain into Milena's kitchen.

"What is it?" Milena squinted at me. Behind her, cups and sausages hung from a rod above the sink. Stacks of jars filled with food sat on the floor.

"I want to help." There was barely room for the two of us. She sent me back out with the sugar bowl.

Mama, now sitting in the armchair, whispered, "You should thank her again for last night's chocolates."

"Andy ate them all."

"I should be making tea for you," Mama called out.

"It's a simple grippe. I am fine." Milena appeared with a tea service on a tray. "The water will boil in a moment." She placed the metal tray on a chair and bent over to drag a long bundle wrapped in brown packing paper out from under the bed. "This is why I laughed when I saw the plant you have brought me. This is a gift which I received also today. I have a little cold and in one morning I receive two gifts." She unknotted the string.

"I must show you." Milena unrolled a deep blue Persian prayer rug covered with stylized flowers and leaves. "It is a gift from a good friend. Very valuable."

Mama rubbed her fingers on the rug. "It's lovely."

I heard the tea kettle rattling and started to get up, but Milena's hand on my arm stopped me. "Today you are in my home."

She poured the tea sloppily, spilling it on the tray. With her slipper, she flipped back the tip of the rug. "It's pretty, but cheap these days. Prague is a treasure chest of bargains. Giving a carpet is not a sign of love. A baby is different. That is love, is it not?" She offered both of us a dripping cup. "Of course, to make one is only a few minutes and then he turns away, lights a cigarette, and leaves. Maybe a baby is not love."

Mama gave me a quick look and put her cup down. I think she was sorry she had brought me along.

"Do you not know"—Milena let her hair slither to one side with a tilt of her head—"that the Germans have warehouses full of furniture, paintings, silverware? Ask your husband, if you do not believe me. From where do you imagine all my belongings arrive?" She waved her arm. "Examine this tea service. It is lovely and fine, you agree?" She held her cup against the lamp. "It is as transparent as skin. Do you see? Do you see?" Her fingers showed through the porcelain, looking like shadows. "Can you believe it was buried in a garden? An entire service. For twenty-four people."

I didn't learn until after the war the significance of those buried objects. Whole families, mostly Jews, leaving family history—the physical measure of who they were, how hard they had worked—to what they thought was the safety of a soil to which they would return.

As Mama gulped down her tea that Sunday morning with the church bells ringing six times across the old Jewish quarter to sound the noon *Angelus*, I didn't think about the beautiful objects my father brought home, how he must have known, or at least guessed, their provenance.

After the Allies won, the Czechs shaved off Milena's hair. She was jeered at and spit on in St. Wenceslas Square, along with hundreds of others who had collaborated with the Germans. Then she was shot.

"Don't say anything to Papa about our visit," Mama said when we got home. "He'll worry you'll get sick, too."

Part of the family's Sunday ritual was to eat dinner together in the dining room, a long yellow room with black and white prints of Prague on the walls. I used to run into that room to watch an enamel nightingale pop out of the gilt clock on the sideboard to sing the hour. I made countless drawings of that clock, a clock that stayed in Prague along with the prints.

That Sunday Mama told us she was expecting a baby while we ate a tart Jitka made with the pears Papa had brought back from Kolín. I immediately decided I didn't want a sister or brother. We were fine just the way we were, but at least Andy and I got to drink half a glass of spumante and polish off the tart. Papa must have told at least one of his silly jokes:

"Does anyone know what hell is?"

A chorus of nos.

"Hell is eating a meal cooked by an Englishman, matching wits with a Frenchman, waiting for an Italian, and disobeying orders from a German."

I'm sure we laughed.

Because of the time difference, my parents couldn't have known about the Japanese attack on Pearl Harbor.

PRAGUE—DECEMBER 8, 1941

Jitka is trying to teach me how to roll out strudel dough when Marco appears at the kitchen door with a stunned look on his face. My heart dips. "The children?"

"No. Oahu." I don't know what that is. He explains. "No one knows the exact death toll yet, but it's bound to be immense." I go on rolling. The dough is almost transparent. Just a few more rolls. Steady, repetitive movements I can do forever. Jitka takes the rolling pin out of my hands. The dough is in tatters. I cover my face with my hands and dread pours over me. So many of our own dead. What will happen now? More war. More death. Everyone has gone mad. It will never end. How can I bring another child into this world? They will kill us all.

Jitka cleans my face with a corner of her apron. Marco comes and wraps his arms around me.

"How will we tell the children?' I ask.

I pick up the children at school in the New Town, across the Vlatva, which the Germans now call the Moldau. We plan to tell them about the Japanese attack after lunch, minimizing it as much as possible not to frighten them. Congress has already declared war on Japan, Marco told me before I left.

"How was school today?" I ask. Susie has her nose glued to the streetcar window as usual, taking the world in to better reproduce it later in her sketchbook. "Was it fun?" Talented like her brother, she will be a wonderful painter one day if this war will let her grow.

"I have to memorize another poem," Susie says to the window. The words leave a halo of steam.

I fuss with the buttons of my coat. I will not start tearing in front of my children. Or on a streetcar with everyone gaping at me. "I'll help you."

"In German!"

"I may not speak it, but I can follow the text. Andy, please stop."

Since the beginning of the ride he's been flipping the latches of his school bag back and forth, back and forth. I clasp his hand. He looks up at me with a look of satisfaction, and I think for an instant he's going to tell me about receiving a ten on a test or winning a game of soccer. Something nice.

"The States will have to go to war now," he says. He knows. A teacher. A schoolmate. A glimpsed-at newspaper headline.

"We'll talk about it at home."

Andy tugs at Susie's braid and tells her in a rush. Japanese planes spitting bombs. The American navy destroyed. Everybody dead. Blood everywhere.

"Stop it!" I put my hand over his mouth and with my other arm hug Susie. She's started crying and asks if her friends in Newport

Beach will be bombed next. My assurances don't stop her tears. A woman getting off the streetcar drops a candy in Susie's lap and is gone before I can thank her. Susie unwraps it, pops it in her mouth, and continues to cry. I kiss her head, smooth her hair, hold her. Andy has gone back to flipping the latches of his school bag. The woman's kindness has broken down my resistance to tears.

As soon as we're home, I let Susie open one of her Christmas presents, a set of colored pencils. When Marco comes up for lunch, Andy is pestering Jitka for food in the kitchen and Susie is in her room, immersed in her favorite pastime. We don't mention Pearl Harbor again.

The children are having their midafternoon snack in the kitchen when Lilli comes up with a box of dates the Spanish consul has sent her. "I know how much Marco enjoys them," she says with her usual insincere smile. After I ask Jitka to make some coffee, I usher Lilli into the vast cream-colored living room furnished with Biedermeier furniture Marco finds elegant and I think is unwieldy. I glance at the grand piano in the far corner with longing and fortify myself with the thought of Andy's sweet music filling the room while I accompany him on the piano. Lilli sits at the very edge of the green damasked sofa so that her tiny well-shod feet can touch the floor and lights a cigarette. She's only a few years older than I am, with a pudgy face and body, silver hair cut short and perfectly coiffed, wearing too much jewelry, always dressed in the latest style her Roman dressmaker copies from the French designers. Today it's Chanel, I think, a gray tweed that matches the rainy day and the grim expression on her face.

Lilli's visits are rare. She dislikes me and I resent her. It doesn't help that she reminds me of my imperious mother, who will never forgive me for the bad taste of eloping with an Italian. Lilli has tried hard to shape me into the diplomatic wife she thinks Marco deserves. My sins are many: no language skills, an atrocious accent, shifting my fork from one hand to the other to bring food to my mouth, eating fruit with my hands, inappropriate attire, disheveled hair, taking my shoes off any chance I get, even in front of the Italian foreign minister. She doesn't realize her lectures provoke me, make me want to irritate her all the more. At a cocktail party I sat in a corner to finish

Gone with the Wind. Another time I warned the Japanese consul that his fly was unzipped.

I pour coffee.

"Three, please," she says. I drop three cubes of sugar in her cup and offer it to her.

"This new turn of events is tragic." She gargles her *r's*, which makes her sound affected.

"It is tragic. So many dead." I know she is not talking about the Japanese attack, but I can't stop myself from turning into the rebellious child Mother never managed to harness.

"It was very foolish of your president to declare war. Very foolish." She peers at me with blue eyes large with anger and goes on and on. Roosevelt is just an entitled rich boy, his ambitions will ruin my country, he doesn't know what he's up against. Mussolini and Hitler will put him in his place. "You Americans are very naive."

I eat a date, then another. I don't like dates, but they keep my mouth full.

"There will be consequences," she adds.

"Of course," I say. The Germans will be defeated.

"There will be disastrous consequences." Lilli leans forward. I picture her falling off the sofa. *All the King's horses and all the King's men*—"You will be careful, Alinka. Very careful." It sounds like a threat. "Now, more than ever, is no time to be disrespectful." She's referring to my greatest sin.

I had been in Prague about six months when she put me on tour duty. I had to take the wife of a visiting Italian dignitary around the city. I knew it was a test. That if I passed, I would finally be in her good graces and be assigned more and more tour duties. The first stop was the Old Town Square across the Vlatva to see the famous Astronomical Clock in the City Hall tower. Every hour on the hour Christ and the twelve apostles file past a row of windows. Then the windows close, a cock flaps his wings, a Turk shakes his head, a miser watches over his sack of gold, and a man admires himself in a mirror. After the cock crows, the clock strikes the hour. Everyone always applauds when the figure of Death shakes his hourglass.

I pointed at Death and told Mrs. Wife of Important Dignitary—I don't remember her name—that if she squinted, she'd see the swastika on his scythe. She squinted, saw nothing, then gasped. I was so proud of my splendid bad behavior that after I walked the lady back to her hotel, I bought myself a huge ice cream cone with whipped cream.

Marco forgave me only after many nights of fierce lovemaking on my part and a promise that I would truly behave from then on. Which I have. Acting out my thoughts accomplishes nothing. Lilli has yet to forgive me.

"Remember,"—she stands up and kisses the air around my cheeks—"you're Marco's wife. An Italian."

"Of course," I say just to get her out of my home.

PRAGUE—DECEMBER 11, 1941

Marco has gathered us in the studio—he insisted the children be with us—to listen to Hitler declare war on the United States. "Mussolini will be next," Andy says, aiming an imaginary rifle at the window and making gunshot sounds with his mouth.

"Andy, please," I beg. He sneaks a look at his father, then stops, the excitement on his face replaced by boredom. He's still a child, a sweet boy who thinks of war only as a game.

"What am I?" Susie asks. She's leaning against Marco's knee. "American or Italian?"

"Italian," Marco says. "We're all Italians. There's nothing to worry about."

A spurt of ill-timed pride makes me blurt out, "I'm a hundred percent American." Susie's face crumbles as if I've punched it. I quickly try to turn my outburst into a joke. "With my accent, I'll have to keep my mouth shut as long as the war lasts. Won't the three of you just love that?"

Marco lifts Susie onto his lap. "Peace at last."

I'm trembling inside. God, don't let my children suffer because of me.

As I'm washing up, ready for bed, I hear Marco go into my room. I quickly dry myself and join him. We have not yet talked about the United States' entrance into the war, of what may be in store for us, for the world. I need him to reassure me or prepare me for the worst. He knows that.

I find him searching in my top bureau drawer. "What are you looking for?"

"Your American passport." He holds it up. His face is tired, taut. This is not easy on him either. As his wife I travel with an Italian passport, but I'm still an American. I'm now the enemy, married to my enemy.

"It's best I lock it up in the consulate safe." Marco comes over and gives me a hasty kiss. "Goodnight. See you in the morning."

I can't find words. The door closes behind him and something in my chest tightens into a sharp-edged rock I don't know how to dislodge.

CAMBRIDGE, MASSACHUSETTS—FEBRUARY 1956

I remember a story Mama told us after Hitler declared war on the United States. I can see her now, sitting in the study, on the bubble-gum-pink chair she had brought from California, her outstretched arms calling us to her.

"One morning when I went to school," she said, "I was in third grade then—my teacher, Mrs. Grout, was standing by the flagpole out on the front lawn, clanging the school bell high above her head and crying buckets. All the girls gathered around her. Some of us started crying too. Maybe the school was on fire, or maybe someone had died. We didn't know what to say, what to do.

"You know what it was? Why she was ringing the bell and crying rivers of tears?"

Maybe I shook my head.

"When Mrs. Grout finally put her glasses back on and saw the whole grammar school standing around the flagpole, she yelled, "God be praised, the war is over!"

The next day Papa brought home a brass bell the size of a pineapple and said we'd all ring it together when the time came. Soon, he promised.

The sun has set, and outside my bedroom window the sky turns lavender gray.

Fairy light was what Mama called twilight in Prague, a city filled with magic and legend. From her bedroom window, with the consulate doors open during the day, we could see a rectangle of Nerudová, a sloping street whose walls held jutting gas lamps that hadn't been lighted since the

Germans marched in. Nerudová led to the Hradčany Castle and had been part of Coronation Way when the city was still ruled by kings and emperors. Below a mullioned window a curlicued wrought-iron bar hooked out over the street. It had once held a wooden sign painted with gold grapes to advertise the wine cellar—*vinarna*—just out of sight. Prague had been full of these colorful signs before the Germans took them down.

In the distance we could see the upper edges of Baroque palaces, the turquoise dome of Saint Nicholas. Spires of churches whose names I never learned pierced the sky, giving Prague the moniker of city of a hundred spires. On the sharply-angled rooftops, tiles curved around dormer windows like sleepy eyelids. After the United States entered the war, Mama caught Andy sitting on the sill with his legs dangling in space, trying to reach the "eye" across the street with his slingshot. He said he was Ulysses fighting the one-eyed monster, Polyphemus. I don't think he knew which side he was on. I know I didn't. It must have been heartbreaking for Mama.

I have a strong memory of us, the family, from not long after the United States entered the war:

It is morning. Andy, Papa, and I are out in the terraced garden in the back of the consulate, with the Hrad, the castle overlooking the entire city, looming over us. A fortress more than a fairy-tale castle, the Germans have made it their headquarters. It must be a Sunday since we aren't in school. Andy and Papa kick a soccer ball around. I'm looking up at Mama at the open kitchen window. She is wearing her American bathrobe, a red plaid that clashes with her hair. It's a present she gave Papa on our last Christmas in Newport Beach, which he didn't take with him when he left. Now she won't give it back.

Mama waves. "Aren't you cold, Chipmunk?"

Papa hears her and yells "Catch" as he kicks the soccer ball up to the window. Mama leans over the windowsill with her arms outstretched. Two feet short of her hands, the ball falls back down and lands in a rose bush. Mama's arms stay outstretched, her hands empty. For what seems a long time she doesn't move, her face blank.

Remembering, my heart aches for her. Papa, Andy, and me, even the ball, were out of her reach.

TWO

CAMBRIDGE, MASSACHUSETTS—MARCH 1956

I come back from the supermarket drenched by a sudden shower to find Kay Vlasek's letter from Chicago, where she has been living since the Communists took over Czechoslovakia. I had found her address among my father's papers. I let the letter lie, unopened, on the linoleum countertop while I put groceries away. I've been waiting for this letter, but now that it's here, I'm suddenly afraid of what's written inside. I check my other mail. I go upstairs and change my clothes. Dry my hair. I walk into what used to be my study. My mind clings to the baby. What color will she like for her room? A new leaf green or a buttery yellow? David likes the green. I can't make up my mind. Even the simplest decision now carries a disproportionate weight. Should I read Kay's letter now or save it for when David gets home in case I can't bear what it says? Did my mother write to Kay that she didn't want to take care of us anymore, that she wanted to be free of me, her ungrateful, spiteful daughter? These are questions I've kept at the periphery of my thoughts, questions that now won't stop swirling in my head. If she left us, how much of the blame is mine? If she died, I'm the one who got her killed.

The Vlaseks lived out in the country, just outside the village of Mcely. To a black and white photograph I add color to the stout eighteenth-century house with peeling yellow paint, brown shutters that always made me think of dark chocolate bars, and a roof of shiny slate tiles half-covered with snow. Rudi bought the house, once the summer residence of a Hapsburg noble-man, as a wedding present for Kay. Above the entrance was a chipped, undecipherable coat of arms and the front door had a lion's head brass knocker which hadn't been polished in years. I kept painting MGM above the lion's mane, but the rain always washed it away. Every chance Mama got, she took us there after school on Saturday to stay overnight, with Papa often coming only in time for dinner.

Kay was hulking and bony, with broad swimmer's shoulders and fine blonde hair. Always smiling eyes, chapped lips, fingernails dirty from the garden. Around her neck, a choker of large pearls that was her only inheri-tance from her once wealthy family in Lenox, Massachusetts. Rudi called Kay "the sunflower" because she could find the bright side of any situation.

Before the war Rudi had been a guide, taking groups from all over Europe and the States through the famous forests of Czechoslovakia to hunt for grouse, pheasant, deer, and wild boar. On one hunting trip Kay had accompanied her father. Six months later she had snuck back to marry her father's guide. "With not a second of regret," my mother added when she told me the story. "Just like me."

In the kitchen I make myself a cup of tea and open Kay's letter. She congratulates me on the baby, tells me I must send pictures. She fills me in on the daily details of her life: Rudi's recurring bronchitis, the three dogs they picked up at the pound, the dismal winter weather. "I wish I knew something that would give you hope. If Alinka is alive, she has not contacted us. She loved you, Andy, and Claire very much, and I cannot imagine a circumstance that would make her leave you, disappear without leaving a trace.

"Your mother is often on my mind. I remember so vividly the first time we met her back in June of 1940. It was on a Sunday and two days earlier the Germans had invaded Paris, which had put both Rudi and me in terrible moods. We had gone for a long outing at the deer park, on White Mountain, to cheer ourselves up a bit. She was sitting on a blanket, barefoot, plucking bundles from a picnic basket. When we approached she looked up with an expression that was both defiant and lost at the same time. Marco, Andy, and you were off picking flowers, I think. Old Hus, the Vlaseks' pointer, picked up one of her shoes, dutifully brought it to her, hoping to get some food, which helped start up a conversation. She had only just arrived from the States with you and Andy a month before. When

Alinka told us her husband was the Italian vice consul we made some lame excuse about having to get back to Mcely. We didn't fool her. 'The cassock doesn't make the priest,' she said flat out. 'And I'm desperate for friends.'

"Please come and visit when you can with your husband and baby, and we'll reminisce until the wee hours of the morning. Perhaps next Christmas? I can't promise the spread we had for our last Christmas together, but Rudi still roasts a delicious goose."

I walk upstairs to the study with Kay's letter still in my hand, and I open the wooden trunk filled with David's and my memorabilia to find Papa's Prague picture album. I open it to Mcely, Christmas, 1941. He recorded most of it. Christmas Eve was the big event. We all stand in the living room, in front of a tree that grazes the ceiling, covered with wooden fruit baskets filled with red apples the size of raisins, stubby mushrooms covered with white polka dots, sleighs, dwarves, gingerbread cookies, white candles, and sugar candy canes that had come from the States and were carefully saved from year to year.

I'm wearing my velvet dress with lace collar and cuffs, Andy his first pair of long pants, Papa his tuxedo, and Mama a shapeless black dress. At my feet, Old Hus has bells on his collar. Dr. Paroch, Mcely's only doctor, and his wife are also in the picture. The doctor wears a morning coat. His head is bald, a shiny globe that reflects the light from the brass chandelier, his cheeks look like goblets full of red wine. His waistcoat is too tight for his belly.

Kay wears her wedding dress—a Bohemian costume from Pilsen that had belonged to Rudi's mother. It has a fringed shawl that crosses over her chest and huge balloon sleeves that could float her up to the ceiling. We're all smiling.

After the photos, the adults hustled us into the long dining room. Red candles ran the length of the table covered in a white lace tablecloth. On the four walls hung a row of pine wreaths covered with the nuts I painted red during that summer's weekends. The flatware was mismatched. Kay had donated her silver to the Czech Defense Fund set up when the Czechs still thought they could defend their borders with the help of France and England.

We waited a long time to eat. Rudi made a rambling speech about his homeland and hard times ahead. Papa tried to lighten the mood. "By the way, did I ever tell you the story about my incredible Christmas in Colombia when a python gobbled up the Virgin Mary from the crèche and lost his evil ways?" No one urged him on. There was a lot of toasting with Czech wine from Mělník. When the traditional Christmas carp finally arrived at the table, Dr. Paroch flourished his fork in the air. "Ah, good! I fear this fish he escaped back to the pond." Most of my carp I hid in my napkin.

After dinner the villagers came with their children. Andy and I helped pass around hot cider and cinnamon-covered dumplings. We kissed and hugged, wished each other *Krásný Vánoce*. Then we all sang *Stille Nacht* with Mama at the piano and Andy playing the violin. Dr. Paroch waved a glass of wine and with his operatic bass voice sang loudest of all. Kay and Rudi distributed presents to the village children. Afterward, everyone trooped a snow-piled mile to attend Mass in the village church.

Kay's words intrude into the memory, take over. She loved you, Andy and Claire very much, and I cannot imagine a circumstance that would make her leave you.

MCELY, THE GERMAN PROTECTORATE OF BOHEMIA AND MORAVIA—CHRISTMAS MORNING, 1941

I turn off the alarm Kay lent me. It's six-thirty in the morning, time to slip quietly downstairs to put the children's presents under the tree, hang their stockings on the fireplace mantle. I turn over in bed, weighted down by morning sickness and a swelling sadness. This may be our last Christmas with Kay and Rudi, in this haven where we've spent so many wonderful weekends. Marco says he's bound to be transferred soon. Not to Germany. Germany is a plum post and an American wife is a liability now. They'll send us to some minor post that I hope won't attract Allied bombs. It's the one small advantage to our situation. It may not be good for Marco's career, but the children's safety has to come first.

The door opens with a slight groan, followed by the click click of Old Hus's nails on the floor. He nuzzles my shoulder with his cold nose. I scratch behind his ear and get up.

With the help of a candle, I shiver my way down the cold, creaky stairs as quietly as possible. Old Hus trots ahead of me, eager to go out. I open the front door and a slap of icy wind blows out the candle and leaves me stunned, without nausea for a moment. The trees are covered in hoarfrost. The world outside looks made of glass. Just as fragile.

I've walked down the narrow corridor that leads to the kitchen so many times I don't need a light. The presents are in the broom closet. I open the door. It is warm in here. Embers still glowing in the fireplace give off a weak light. The smell of fish and cinnamon hangs in the air, which brings my nausea right back. I'll be quick. I turn to switch on the light and a hand stops me. "Don't," Kay says. Her face is barely visible.

A chair scrapes. Kay quickly shuts the door behind me. Something dark crosses in front of the fireplace. The back door to the vegetable garden opens. Wind feeds the embers and a small flame spurts up. The door clicks shut. I understand nothing.

"Who was that?"

"No one."

"The back door opens and closes by itself?"

Kay lights a candle and cups her fingers over it. On the table a round of cheese, a loaf of bread and a coil of sausages sit on a spread-out shawl.

"Go back to bed, Alinka." The candle flame haloes her fingers. "The children won't wake up for ages."

I can't understand why my best friend is dismissing me. "What's going on?"

The sound of tapping makes me turn to the narrow window above the sink. Kay pushes the candle into my hands and knots the ends of the shawl over the food. "Do you have any money?"

"I'll get some from Marco."

"No! Swear on your children's heads you won't say anything to Marco." Kay reaches up and pushes one side of the window open.

Who is outside the window, and what can't I say to Marco?

She whispers something in Czech. A man's voice answers. I recognize Dr. Paroch's deep voice. An arm juts into the room and quickly grabs the bundled shawl. Kay comes back to the table and fills a handkerchief with a heap of coins and paper money she takes from the drawer. She removes the pearls on her neck and places them on top.

"Talk to me, Kay. Please."

"We're helping someone." Her eyes look down at my wrist. "Jan, Dr. Paroch, has gotten word that the Gestapo is rounding up Jews today."

I stare at her pearls sitting on top of the meager pile of money. Pearls which have never left her neck since I've met her, and I realize that Kay wants me to give up the sapphire bracelet still on my wrist. It belonged to Marco's mother; it was my wedding present. He would never forgive me. She doesn't trust my husband.

"Marco would never, never betray a human being to the Nazis. How can you not know that?"

"It's all right, Alinka. I understand. Go back to bed."

"How would I explain the missing bracelet to Marco? I'm no good at lying and the truth is too dangerous for him. He works for them." Helping Jews escape is punishable by death. "I can't. I'm sorry."

"It's all right." Kay hands the bundled handkerchief to Dr. Paroch, closes the window, and leaves the kitchen. I stand in the middle of that emptied place, my nausea gone, and listen to the silence stretching out its limbs, taking over the room. As the minutes pass, the silence turns into fear pushing against the old, thick walls, and I'm reminded of the times when Mother would shut me in the basement, in the dark, for being a bad girl. I was convinced the dark would last forever like a death, or if the light came back, I would find my parents, the house, the garden, the neighbors gone. I would be the only one left.

CAMBRIDGE, MASSACHUSETTS—MARCH 1956

For the past two years I've been volunteering as an art teacher at a senior center in Brookline on Saturday mornings. Today I've brought bananas, apples, and a blue bowl from home for them to paint. After setting up the still life, I tell my students, seven women whose ages range from sixty-eight to a healthy eighty-seven, that because I'm pregnant I can no longer work with oil paints and turpentine. The fumes can harm the baby. "We can focus on drawing with graphite or colored pencils, or if you prefer, watercolor."

There's a chorus of "watercolor."

Mrs. Pennock, beige felt hat permanently attached to her head, disagrees in her raspy voice. "I don't like watercolor. You can't paint over."

"I know watercolor is hard," I say, "but we'll learn to plan ahead, to think of the whole picture before we start."

Mrs. Stein, the oldest student, who escaped Germany in 1937, starts to clap her gnarled hands. Her arthritis is so bad I have to bandage the paint brush to her hand. "Planning ahead, that is good, not that for me I have much ahead," she says in her accented English. "But you," she grins at me, every tooth of her own still in place, "what good news you give us. Mazeltov. I wish you and the baby good health."

The others join in the congratulations, except for Mrs. Pennock, who does not like the fact that I am half Italian. She lost a son in the battle of Monte Cassino.

As I distribute new brushes and cakes of watercolor, I explain how, with watercolors, we have to map out the white areas first. How we must start out with light brush strokes of color, wait until the paint dries to continue, slowly build the picture, add the darks last.

After class, while I'm removing the bandage from Mrs. Stein's fingers, she tells me she will knit the baby a sweater. With her arthritis I know that's impossible, but the thought is all that matters and I start to tear. She clucks her tongue and strokes my arm. "You will see what good will come. You think you know love, but wait, wait until the baby is here." She presses her hand against her chest. "You cannot believe what you feel. The heart explodes, it is so much with happiness. Believe me. Enjoy."

I give her a hug. She's my favorite pupil—eager, optimistic, in spite of having lost all her relatives. In the past few months, during that quiet time after class while we wait in the emptied room for her daughter-in-law to pick her up, I've been tempted to tell Mrs. Stein about my own years during the war, about my need to find out if my mother is still alive, but the thought of her suffering always stops me. My need, my grief, is small next to hers.

Driving back to Cambridge, I think of how less than a month after our last Mcely Christmas, Reinhard Heydrich went to Berlin and held the Wannsee Conference to secretly set in motion "the final solution of the Jewish question."

The yellow stars had first appeared in Prague in September of '41. Three weeks later, when school started, my bench companion Olga, who liked to chew on garlic cloves during recess, didn't show up. My classmates said she must be a "*Jude.*" Before Prague I didn't know "Jew" in any language.

"Why can't they go to school?" I asked Papa when I came home.

"They have their own schools now."

"Why do they have to wear stars?"

"Don't you remember in first grade," he said, "your teacher asking the class to wear a white ribbon the first week of school so she could recognize her pupils during recess? In Newport Beach, don't you remember?"

"Hogwash!" Mama declared and marched Andy and me to her bedroom. She shut the door in Papa's face. "They have to know the truth."

Hitler was the purest definition of evil, she told us. "Don't listen. Don't believe a Nazi word."

Andy asked if it was true the Jews had killed Jesus.

"Pontius Pilate, a Roman, and his Roman laws killed him," Mama said, "and you don't see Hitler persecuting his Roman pals, do you? They're the best of friends."

I wanted to know if Jews ate raw garlic.

"Italians do that," Andy said, which made me laugh with relief. Papa's favorite dish was spaghetti with oil, hot peppers, and lots of garlic.

In my sleep that night I dreamed my German teacher was sewing blue and white striped stars on our clothes, over our hearts. Only my father was exempt. "That's what you get for knowing the truth," Olga whispered in my ear.

The next morning in class I recited a Schiller poem and the teacher complimented me on my good German diction. After Christmas I got a new bench companion, Ilke, who became the envy of the classroom because she wore a bra and claimed she had been menstruating for over a year. I forgot Olga.

After the war, during the three years we lived in Rome, we never talked about the horrifying events the Nazis and the Fascists had unleashed. That Papa had worked for the Fascist government was relegated to the bottom drawer of history, something to be forgotten. If I had questions, I didn't voice them. Probably I was too busy studying, partying, worrying about boys.

It wasn't until I was eighteen and leaving for an American college on a scholarship that I brought up the subject. Papa and I were on the ship in the Bay of Naples, drinking warm spumante in my second-class cabin, when I asked, "Did you believe in Fascism?"

"When I joined the diplomatic corps, Mussolini seemed to have all the right answers. Nationalism, order, increased employment." The words were spit-polished, whatever he really felt well hidden.

"When it became wrong, how could you stay with it?"

"I was only a low-grade civil servant, and I had your mother and you children to think of."

"You knew what was going on."

"I heard what I wanted to hear," my father said. "Not unlike being in love." The motors turned on. The ship shuddered. "I wish for you a good American man," he said. "Loyal, kind. Who will take care of you and bring a smile on your face. With love, forgiveness."

"It's not going to bring Mama back."

With my mother gone, my father had become the lightning rod for my anger, my sense of deprivation. The guilt I felt for having fought her, for perhaps causing her death, fueled the anger. I stopped trusting his love or mine for him.

On my seventeenth birthday I had announced that I wanted to go to the States—I believed that discovering how to be American again would bring me closer to Mama, dead or not. The States was where she had always wanted her children to be. Papa didn't fight my decision, but I would catch him looking at me, disappointment and sadness creasing the corner of his eyes. The same expression he had now as we stood on the ship's deck, an expression that made me think of a sheet of crumpled paper someone had retrieved and smoothed out with the palm of her hand.

We hugged quickly, both of us incapable of saying how much we would miss each other, that, after all, there was love between us. With a dry throat I managed to say, "I'll write and let you know how things are going."

"I did the best I could." He handed me a parcel. "*Bon voyage*." Before I could thank him he was halfway down the deck.

With the unopened package under my arm, I watched my father walk the gangplank. His gait was still young, cocky. There still would be women in his life.

On land, everyone waved at the passengers. The passengers waved back. Except my father and me. In the space of twenty minutes his figure shrank until he was a tiny mark on the hot Neapolitan wharf.

Once land was no longer visible, I opened my *bon voyage* present and discovered letters my mother had written to him during the war, drafts of letters he had written to her, pieces of their married life. Just looking at them made me feel like an intruder. I was able to read them only after Papa's death.

After the first exciting weeks at college, I wrote to Harriet, Mama's mother—I couldn't think of her as my grandmother—then a widow. I was in the United States, in Boston, could I visit her in Baltimore? I included my address, added the dorm's telephone number. I had tried, in the years right after the war, to keep in touch with an occasional scribbled postcard, the dutiful Christmas letter filled with my teenage activities, as if we had a relationship, as if she cared what happened to me or I to her. She never answered. She didn't answer this time either. A few weeks went by during which I tried to make new friends, learn to play bridge and study between long nightly discussions in one room or another about the existence of God, the need or not for a boyfriend. I saved dimes and when I had a jarful, I sneaked a beer into my room, drank it quickly, burped my heart out as the operator found Harriet's number and connected me. With the wall of that long dorm hallway holding me up I fed my dimes into the slot. I listened to the ringing, my chest flooding with expectation: Mama answering, "Hey Chipmunk. I've missed you."

Harriet didn't sound anything like Mama, and she let me know I wasn't welcome. I should have stayed across the ocean with my father, the man who got her daughter killed. She hung up.

On Thanksgiving Day, armed with a turkey sandwich, I took the train down to Baltimore.

At the front door of a row house painted blue, Harriet told me she had suffered enough and to please go away. The door closed in my face before I had a chance to call out, just in case Mama was there and could hear me.

I stayed at the YWCA over the weekend and went back on Sunday morning. I remembered Mama saying that Harriet Wheeler never missed a Sunday service. Off she went with her white gloves, a navy blue coat that reached her ankles, her hat held on with a black elastic band under her chin. I almost stepped out from behind the tree to snap that elastic band hard and see her teeth fall out of her mouth. Her teeth and her meanness.

I watched Harriet mince down the street. What if Mama was in the house? What if my mother was better off without me? What if she told me that it was my fault she left us? What if she refused to talk to me? What if? What if?

The only thing keeping me from knowing was a wooden door and my own frightened thoughts. My last time with Mama, she had held my face close to hers until my eyes filled with her, despite the darkness. Her hands were cold and she smelled of rubbing alcohol. "Don't be scared. I'll be right behind you." Then she pushed me under the barbed wire.

I rang the doorbell, listened to the sharp sound arrow to the back of the house. I rang again. I knocked until my knuckles got red. I called out. "Mama!" "Alice!" "Alinka!" I silenced the birds. Squirrels stopped leaping. With each name, a dip in my heart, a wrenching in my stomach.

I picked up a pebble and drummed at the kitchen window. No one answered.

PRAGUE, THE GERMAN PROTECTORATE OF BOHEMIA AND MORAVIA—FEBRUARY 17, 1941

I am finally facing Kay in the *vinarna* on the corner from Saint Nicholas Square, down the street from the consulate, a place Marco calls the Crypt because of its vaulted ceiling and two-feet-thick walls. Outside it's raining "rats and frogs," another Marco coinage. It has been raining all week. We're sitting at a corner table, a curtain of lace breaking the gray day outside into a pretty pattern. After I refused to take Kay's calls for over a month, I found the courage to ask for this meeting. I want to apologize, to explain that some people commit unspeakable acts and keep their sanity and even happiness. Then there are people like me, whose every misstep turns into a drop of poison. We exchange banal pleasantries. The weather is awful, the children are growing, the husbands are busy. I'm ashamed, but also cautious. I don't know what has been lost between us. In my pocketbook, a package holds money I have saved since that Christmas morning and Marco's bracelet.

A woman comes to take our order. The photograph of a young man's face is pinned to the front of her apron. A son, a younger brother. Dead or missing. Kay orders tea and ham sandwiches for us, and I hand over my diplomatic ration book.

"Did the woman get away?" I ask while we wait, keeping my eyes on Kay's large, lined hands.

"I don't know."

I look up at her square chin, her broad cheekbones that give Kay a mannish, capable look; at her plain brown eyes with laugh lines shooting out from the corners; at her wide chapped lips. Her signature welcoming look is gone. Her cheeks are flushed. Her hands sweep across the tabletop brushing off nonexistent dust.

"You don't want to tell me?"

"There's no way of knowing." Her tone is patient.

"I don't deserve this, Kay. I was surprised, scared, unprepared."

Something I can't read flickers across Kay's face. "I'd tell you if I knew, but I don't. Not even Dr. Paroch has access to the network. We only know the one person ahead of us."

I hate lies. They dismiss me, make me feel expendable. I've been added to the Do Not Trust list, because I kept the bracelet, because I'm married to a man who works for the Fascist government. Maybe the drop of poison is spreading, making me paranoid. I can't stop myself. I have so little to hold on to beside Marco and the children. Kay was the one person I thought understood, as another American, what dispossession feels like, in the midst of a world war, in a country where Americans are the enemy.

"That's all I know, Alinka." Her face is now impassive.

"I understand." Marco and the children are all I need.

The woman appears with the tea and sandwiches. I clasp my pocketbook and leave.

CAMBRIDGE, MASSACHUSETTS—APRIL 1956

One Monday morning—Dr. Page examines me and says all is well with me and the baby, now eighteen weeks old. He asks if I'm still brooding about my mother. I resent the word brood and tell him so. He shakes his head and says it's the future I have to think about now, not the past. I leave in a bad mood—there's truth in what he's said—and when I come home the past is begging for my attention in the form of a letter—this time from Lilli Scarditti, the consul general's wife, now the ambassador's wife in Berlin.

Short, pudgy, stuck-up Lilli didn't like Andy and me. We made too much noise, we left fingerprints on the stairs, we had bad manners. We didn't like her either and called her *The Toad*.

"Marco was talented, full of ambition," Lilli writes. "He had no way of knowing before the war that an American wife would become a difficult weight to bear, but Alinka seemed to get pleasure out of worsening the situation. I don't wish to be insensitive, but you did ask for the truth. I did the best I could for her. I helped her with Italian grammar. I taught her about teas, lunches, dinners, which fork to pick up when, where to go with visiting wives."

It was always I-I-I with Lilli.

I drop the letter on the kitchen table and go upstairs to do some work on Caravaggio. On the way to the bedroom I pass what was once my study, now empty of furniture, with walls David has diligently stripped.

Our house is small with a front porch that creaks when you walk, I tell the baby inside me. From the window you'll see the backyard, which barely holds two elm trees and a hammock. It's a house we love, with this bedroom just for you. If you want brothers or sisters, we'll have to move. Hold off for a little. David is an associate professor of archaeology at the university, on a tenure track, publishing as much as he can, but he won't be up for review for at least two years. I'm only an adjunct lecturer, with miserable pay, but once I get my PhD, I'll make you and David proud. Except I can't seem to work, to concentrate. Music as depicted in Italian Renaissance paintings—my work of the last year and a half—seems a frivolous subject now that you've come. Only you and Mama swim in my head. I sit at my desk, now in the bedroom, and instead of stringing sentences together, I string memories to help me be a good mother. The memories follow me as I wander through the house and in the classroom. They replace dreams at night.

Outside the window one of the elms is showing its first April leaves, and I decide that David is right, leaf green is the perfect color. A decision has been made. I'm making progress.

Hours later the phone rings while I'm fast asleep in my armchair, in a sea of index cards. It's Andy. "Is everything okay?" I immediately ask. Transatlantic calls are expensive and reserved for Christmas and birthdays. He says he just wants to know how my pregnancy is faring. He and Priscilla, his wife, have no children, which may or may not be their decision. I feel the subject is too personal to broach, even for a sister. Claire has been living with them since Papa died two years ago. Maybe she's all the child they need.

"Baby and I are fine," I tell him. "David is working too hard." Claire is fine, Priscilla is fine. Everything is fine, he says and then adds, "What did Papa do to you?"

"Nothing."

"Why would Papa lie to us about something this big? Come on, that makes no sense."

"I'm sure he believed Mama was dead."

"Of course she's dead. Why can't you get that in your head?"

"Papa didn't look for her. He took her death as accepted fact."

"Why shouldn't he? The passer said she was shot dead."

"Maybe that's what Mama told him to say. When Papa was in the hospital after his operation he started to tell us something, remember?" I can't stop myself from grasping at straws. "He mumbled, 'You must know,' and then stopped. I asked him, 'What Papa? What must we know?' But he just shook his head. Maybe he was trying to tell us about Mama."

"He was dying, that's what he was trying to tell us. I know why you're doing this. You want her to be alive so you can stop feeling guilty."

He hits a home run with that one.

"Let it go, Susie. Keep mourning her, if you need to, but set your heart facing forward. What you're missing is the ritual of grieving. Go to your local cemetery, pick a grave and put flowers on it. Tell yourself that's where she is."

"Is that what you've done?"

"Once."

"Where?"

"A country cemetery in Tuscany. A place I thought she would have liked. It helped. You should try it."

"One day," I answer.

Andy gives me good news about Claire, and I ask to speak to her.

My fourteen-year-old sister has just won the piano competition for a place in the Rome conservatory. She gets on the phone and accepts my congratulations with her usual coolness. She has not forgiven me for coming to the States. She was too young to have any memory of Mama, and for the time I lived with her, I filled Mama's shoes awkwardly.

"When are you coming to Rome?" she asks.

I haven't been back since Papa's death. "It won't be possible for a while. How about you coming here when the baby's born?"

"You want me to?" She sounds disbelieving.

"I'd love it. Come, please. The baby's due August 25th."

"Maybe." She doesn't like to commit to anything. "If it's a boy, you have to call him Fabrizio."

"That's a mouthful in America."

"At least think about it."

"I will." After we hang up, I realize she has just told me about her first crush. Fabrizio.

PRAGUE, THE GERMAN PROTECTORATE OF BOHEMIA AND MORAVIA—MARCH 1942

I'm bone tired. My back hurts constantly. My moods are never-ending roller coaster rides. I alternate between bursts of love for the baby and sullen worry that no one should bring a child into the world now. I'm so big, I joke that I'm carrying a baby elephant. I've stopped taking the children to school, picking them up. I've begged poor Jitka to take over. She has enough to do, but she loves the children. I only stick my nose outdoors for our ritual Sunday afternoon outing. The family together, with the rest of the world out of my thoughts. We take a walk on Kampa, the small island park on the Vlatva just off the Charles Bridge. Marco has his favorite bench, where he smokes a few cigarettes away from my now overly sensitive nose. If he has the newspaper with him, he folds a sheet into a sailing boat, which Andy and Susie float down the Devil's Brook. I sit on another bench and wait for the baby's dances. A girl, I think. Marco plays soccer with Andy. Susie steals the ball and wants them to chase her. Afterward a stroll across the Charles Bridge into *Staré Město*, the old town, to wind the afternoon down. When it's too nasty, we end up at the Crypt.

Every day, Andy studies a Mozart violin concerto for the entrance exam at the conservatory in June, with me at the piano.

On overcast days, I like to play a specific Schubert rondo. Andy, a folded red bandana under his chin, follows with the violin. The rondo brings the sun into the room.

At snack time, in the kitchen, while the children sprinkle sugar on buttered bread and I sneak spoonfuls in my mouth of whatever is plop-plopping on the stove for dinner, Jitka entertains us with Czech folktales which Susie translates for me. Dalibor, who, imprisoned in a tower of the Hrad, carved a violin out of the wood his jailer gave him and enchanted a whole city with his music. Zhito, the magician, who swallowed his German rival whole and then spit out first his boots, then the man, in King Václav's spittoon. Charles IV, the Holy Roman

41

emperor, who asked his countrymen to contribute all the eggs of the empire to add to the mortar to build Prague's Charles Bridge so that it would withstand the fierce changing currents of the Vlatva. With tears in her eyes, Jitka tells us the bridge has withstood six centuries, and will withstand at least six more.

While Susie does her homework, I sit on the bed, my swollen feet tucked under the *perina*, the down comforter. Her movements reassure me—the careful way she dips her pen in the inkwell, then removes it without spilling a drop. The graceful swirl of her letters on the lined sheets of her notebook. As soon as she's finished, I hand her the paint box. My bedroom walls are covered with her watercolors.

Whenever the baby kicks, Susie wants to rest her cheek against my belly. We both laugh when the kick comes. Andy is sure I'm carrying a boy. "He's playing soccer." A ballerina is Susie's guess. I think she's just a girl in a hurry to get out.

I am full of love for my children. I can't get enough of them. I listen to Andy as he scratches notes on the violin until he produces seamless chords. I sharpen Susie's crayons, supply her with colored pencils, cakes of watercolors and art books from which she copies Gainsborough's refined ladies and Redon's flowers. When I wonder out loud where my children's talents come from, Marco is quick to claim paternity.

"Papa, you can't draw a straight line," Susie protests.

"You're tone deaf," Andy declares.

Marco insists. "One New Year's Eve, I refused to go to bed, so, to teach me a lesson, my mother proceeded to throw my considerable artistic talents out the window with the broken crockery!"

I laugh with the children. "Your mother left you the ability to make up the most ridiculous stories."

Our favorite one is Marco going to a party in Colombia with an eel around his neck because he couldn't find a tie.

After dinner, if their homework is done, the children sit with us in Marco's study, a wood-lined room filled with old German books that came with the apartment. We read or listen to the radio or the record player, me in my pink California chair, Marco next to me on the sofa. When the baby kicks, he taps made-up Morse code on my belly. When, near the end of the month, our ration book is almost used up, he taps wished-for menus. "Tomorrow, penne all'arrabbiata, veal cutlets wrapped in prosciutto, and chocolate ice cream with double whipped cream with a maraschino cherry on top. If not tomorrow the day after. If not then . . . there's a Czech saying—everything has an end. Except a sausage. That has two."

We are a privileged family in a world filled with misery. That privilege weighs on me when I let myself think about the war, but I bask in it too, and sometimes I worry that I will pay for that basking. That I deserve to pay for it.

CAMBRIDGE, MASSACHUSETTS—APRIL 1956

Hours after Andy's phone call, I pick up Lilli's letter and hear her thin voice with its underwater *r's*.

"You must understand, Susanna, it was a difficult time for all of us. For Alinka more so, of which we were only too aware. Giorgio and I were very concerned. The war destabilized her. We did the best we could. Whatever we did, you have to know we have always had your family's best interests at heart."

I'd like to ask Lilli, "What did you do to her except make her feel she didn't fit in?" Instead I write to thank her for her letter, and then toss her words in the garbage pail.

THREE

The German command had invited the diplomatic corps to a concert at Wallenstein Palace in honor of Hitler's birthday. Mama refused to attend.

Papa kissed her goodbye, gave me a hug. I stuffed dry bread in the pocket of his uniform for the swans.

When Papa came home from the concert, he woke up Andy, made him get dressed quickly, and took him downstairs to Giorgio and Lilli's apartment to play for Heydrich and his pregnant wife. Milena and Karl Müller were there, too, Andy told me afterward. He played Schubert's rondo for them and he boasted that Heydrich shook his hand and told him he would one day be a fine violinist.

That night has come back to me many times, and I fantasize that I had woken up in time to go downstairs with Andy, that I brought Papa back home. Maybe nothing would have changed.

In the morning Jitka brought breakfast on a tray.

"I'm not sick."

"A treat for being a good girl. Breakfast in bed like a grownup. Two eggs cooked in goose fat, you always like that. Food keeps you happy." Food had made Jitka big. Andy named her the Hippo.

"Careful, don't burn yourself." I touched the handle of the iron skillet to make sure and scorched my finger.

45

Jitka sat down on the chair, on the clothes Mama had laid out for me. Normally, when Jitka sat, she was as unmoving as a monument that had been in place for hundreds of years. This morning she couldn't sit still. She rubbed her felt slippers together, tugged at her apron, kept turning her head to the door.

"Where's Mama?" I asked. She was the one who always woke me up on school days.

"You eat."

I scrambled out of bed.

"Suzinka, where are you going?"

"Pipi."

The bathroom was at the end of the corridor. I went the other way, toward the closed study door behind which my mother was shouting. I heard the clang of the big bronze bell, then the crash on the floor, then the name Milena. "You're sleeping with her," she shouted.

Thanks to Andy I knew what "sleeping with her" meant. Not the details, but the fact that it was bad. In Newport Beach, a friend of Mama's had divorced her husband for "sleeping" with someone else.

Jitka took me back to my room, tucked me in bed, put the tray on my lap. "Eat your eggs, little one."

I tried to concentrate on my plate. The goose fat was glazing over, but the egg yolks were still a deep orange, clean, thick. I put my fork down. If the eggs stayed whole, nothing would change.

"There's a war going on," Jitka said. "Thousands are starving."

I explained why I couldn't touch the eggs. "Eat them whole," she suggested and put the fork in my hand. Together we carefully cut the whites from the yolks with the edge of the fork and ended up with two yellow rounds sitting on the plate like cakes of watercolor. I scooped first one yolk then the other in my mouth. I held them on my tongue. "I want them both," I told God.

When my father came to my room, I was already dressed for school. I didn't know what to expect, a scolding or an explanation.

Papa pulled me to him. The usual smell of aftershave, a sharp scent that tickled my nose. His hair was a shiny black cap ridged with comb strokes. I studied his Roman nose, a long straight ridge ending with an inward tuck that I used to pull when I was smaller. The tuck was still there. The yolks had worked their magic. Nothing had changed.

"Mama is all right," I declared.

"Mama will be fine in no time," said Papa.

When I came back from school, Mama had locked herself in her bedroom. She wasn't feeling well, Papa told us. She needed peace and quiet. We tiptoed. We spoke in low voices. Andy practiced in Papa's office across the courtyard.

The next morning RAF planes dropped bombs on Pilsen, but missed the Skoda munitions factory. Pilsen was only fifty-four miles from Prague, and the bombing was the closest we had ever come to experiencing the danger of war. Papa took us down to the cellar to show us where we would hide in case the RAF came back to bomb Prague. Lilli had Pino, the driver, drag down mattresses. Jitka prepared baskets of food, filled empty wine bottles with water.

After the visit to the cellar, Papa took us to the movies. The newsreel showed planes dropping bombs on Exeter and Bath. "The enemy has lost a thousand lives," the announcer declared. "One more victory for the heroic German Luftwaffe." They came to be known as the Baedeker Bombings, after the English guidebook the Germans used to pick their targets. I don't remember the movie, but afterward I wanted to go shopping for a net to hang across the cellar ceiling. At the circus in Los Angeles we had seen Savetti, the human cannonball, shooting across the white sky of the tent. The net caught him each time.

Andy told me I was dumb, that a net wouldn't stop a bomb. "Your brain's already bombed out," I yelled back. Papa distracted us with a visit to the Europa Hotel for hot chocolate. When we came home, Mama's door was still closed.

I began to write notes in my best calligraphy, notes to go with the meals that Jitka brought her and Mama barely touched. Notes with white lies.

"The lamp on my desk won't turn on and I can't finish my homework."

"I got a five in drawing yesterday. Papa can't help."

"Andy is sick and coughs all night. He keeps me awake. Don't you hear him too?" I signed them, "I miss you, your daughter, Susan."

I blamed Andy. "You played for Heydrich. You played her sun music. She hates Heydrich." We began kicking and punching each other in silence until Jitka separated us. Andy knew about our parents' fight from me, but I had left out the reason. I preferred to let him think he was to blame. I couldn't rat on Papa.

Four days went by. My notes didn't work. Peace and quiet didn't either. "What if she never comes out?" I thought. On the fifth morning, I told Andy he had to play in front of her door. "The rondo."

"She'll think of Heydrich."

"She doesn't know about Heydrich."

"Liar! You told me she did."

"I'll give you two weeks' allowance."

"I don't want your allowance, stupid. I want Mama to come out."

"Play the rondo."

When Andy finished playing, we waited soundlessly in front of her door until Jitka dragged us off to school.

For at least a week after the bombing, Andy and I yelled "*Notfall, Notfall,*" at the night sky. *Notfall* was the German word for emergency.

PRAGUE, THE GERMAN PROTECTORATE OF BOHEMIA AND MORAVIA—APRIL 30, 1942

I roll up the blackout cloth to let the air in. I'm wet with perspiration. How many days have I been in this room? The baby kicks a lot. I sing to her to keep her quiet, to keep from crying out. Jitka comes often. I unlock the door when I hear the shuffle of her felt slippers. She brings food to keep me healthy, food as a remedy for pain. I can't eat. Think of the baby, Jitka says by pointing to my belly, but I can't put anything in my mouth. *Dekuji*, Jitka, *dekuji*. Thank you is all I can say to her, but she understands. One time she hugged me. The folds of her neck smelled warm and damp, like freshly ironed towels, and I clung to her and wrung my heart dry of tears.

I breathe in the fresh air and keep my eyes closed, not to see the courtyard below, not to bring back the vision of that night. A useless attempt. It's in my eyes and ears even when I sleep.

The rumble of car motors being turned on in the courtyard below woke me up. It was past midnight. Who was out there? I went to the window and saw Heydrich being driven off in his open car. Milena's hennaed head appeared next. Karl Müller and Marco trailed her. All three got into Marco's car. He's taking them home, I told myself. He'll be back soon.

I settled down on the armchair by the window, covered myself with a throw and waited. Why did I wait? I knew. I knew since the night he ran his hand down her arm in front of everyone, as if he couldn't keep away from her.

I dozed off. This time I was jolted awake by the shrill scrape of the iron bolt of the consulate doors against the cobblestones. It was almost dawn. The skyline had faded to gray. The blue Fiat, headlights hooded in black, inched through the doors and crawled to the far corner of the courtyard. Marco got out in his shirt sleeves, tieless, uniform jacket flung over his shoulder, his face a momentary pale blur. With a few long strides he disappeared from view, and the denied truth took shape, became clear, crisply painted, every detail dropping into its proper place with a heart-puncturing snap.

I let the blackout curtain drop back down. I feel exposed, split open like a blister. I keep asking myself why did he go to her? Because I'm seven months pregnant and afraid making love will harm the baby? Because I despise the government he works for? Because I don't give him enough love? Because he loves her, not me?

I wanted to be the center of Marco's life, his marrow, his warm humid core that makes almost anything bearable. How else can a woman measure herself, if not in the importance she has for her husband, her children?

I try to picture myself going on with my family life as if Milena hasn't happened. Marco and I meeting anew, starting over. The thought repulses me.

CAMBRIDGE, MASSACHUSETTS—APRIL 1956

The morning after Andy played the rondo, a hand tickled me awake. Mama was leaning over me. She looked like a scarecrow. Her curls—so thick my hand would get lost in them—were twisted stubbles. I started crying.

"You lose a lot of hair after a baby, Susie. I didn't want to wait."

First chance I got, I stole into her room. The window was shut, the blackout curtains closed. There was a lingering smell of stale air and sweat. I turned on the light. The silk on Mama's headboard now hung in ragged strips. Strands of red hair dusted the toilet seat. The rest she must have flushed down the toilet.

My parents' fight, Mama's retreat into her bedroom, were never mentioned. For one week our family routine fell back into place, with a variant: Papa went courting. Whenever Mama left the room, he followed; he filled her with compliments; he brought home presents for her, for us. He wore the blue sweater she had bought him for his birthday in November, the argyle socks she had given him in Newport Beach. His fingers always reached for her.

He talked about the near future. "Next Sunday, if the weather is good, how about a boat trip to Slapy Lake? The Sunday after that, we could go see the Przewalski horses at the zoo. Would you like that? Is that a good idea?"

He talked about the long-ago past. "Do you remember our last Easter in Rome, driving to Tivoli and hiding the eggs in the Villa D'Este gardens? How hot it was, how Susie squealed when she put on her new knitted gloves? We had a wonderful time. Don't you remember?"

"In Newport Beach," I added, "Papa hid the eggs in the sand, and when we couldn't find them, he told us the eggs were hatching and the chicks would grow scales instead of feathers so they could go for a swim. Papa couldn't find the eggs either, but you made more and you hung them from the ceiling, Mama. Remember?"

"Always look up," Papa said. "That's the happy place. Your words, Alinka."

"Easter is over," she said. She was still angry. I saw it in the way she held herself still when he was near her, the way a rabbit does when a hawk flies overhead. At night her bedroom door stayed shut.

PRAGUE, THE GERMAN PROTECTORATE OF BOHEMIA AND MORAVIA—MAY 9, 1942

Marco is drinking his after-dinner coffee. Andy is repeating a bar of music over and over in his room. Susie is helping Jitka in the kitchen. The stupid bird peeks out of the clock on the sideboard and chimes the hour with a few shrill notes. I resist the temptation to fling my spoon at it. Tonight is the first time I've let myself be alone with my adulterous husband. He has skinned me alive, smashed my heart against a rock, but I have to go on. He's leaving. His new post has come through.

"When did it start with her?" I ask after I've closed the door and sat back down across the table from him.

"I'm sorry. It will never happen again." His voice is soft, his expression contrite. "I'm sorry." Since I've come out of my room, Marco's been producing charm as if it were an emergency limb, something to help him slide back into grace. I want the excessive emotion he showed when we first met, wild declarations of love, tears of contrition. His charm unnerves me. It seems so calculated.

"You and the children are all I have." He speaks to his coffee cup. How can I trust him? "When did it start?"

"I don't know." He throws his wet spoon on the tablecloth, and I watch the coffee spread into a pale brown circle on the yellow linen. "These things just happen,' he says. "She was there like a glass of champagne. That's all. Not a good glass at that."

"Insulting her doesn't help." I empty the salt cellar on the stain, tap the crystals down with my finger. "I could understand you falling in love."

"Really?" His tone is mocking. I keep tapping.

"Love just takes over, makes you powerless. I know that. At least it would have given you an honorable reason. Not just the itch in your groin. I really need to know when it started."

Marco turns off the light and walks over to the window. "She never questioned me. Never stood in judgment."

I wipe my fingers clean with the napkin and turn to his back. "When, Marco?"

"What difference does it make? It's over." He opens the window. The days have lengthened and a mauve light still clings to the garden. That color brings back a memory. A silk dress spread on grass on a hot day, the folds of the mauve skirt shaded, looking like clusters of violets.

"Remember the picnic we had at White Mountain two summers ago?" I ask. Of course he remembers. "It was June. I had arrived with the children only a month before. You had made your famous Russian salad. It's when we first met Kay and Rudi, remember?" His back stiffens. "After they left, suddenly there she was, in her silk dress, alone, laughing at the coincidence of running into you, a man she said she had seen a only few times at cocktail parties. You introduced us, and I remember thinking she wasn't the fresh-air-and-sun type at all. You were already lovers, weren't you?"

Marco's silence tells me I'm right. It had started while I was in the States, missing him every minute. It had started after four wonderful years in California. It had started before the baby. It continued after I conceived.

He turns to look at me. "I'm sorry, Alinka."

I'm straining to recover love for him. I was convinced I knew everything about my family. I thought love gave me that clarity, that sureness of foot. I'm stumbling in the dark now. I see clearly only when it comes to the children.

"Will you wait for me in Rome?" he asks.

"Send us to Switzerland. We'll wait out the war in Switzerland."

"The Ministry won't like that. It would look like my family is defecting."

"The children will be safe only in Switzerland." I've earned the right to make demands. Earned! What an absurd word in this situation. Loss gives me rights—reparation rights. "And I want my American passport back."

Marco thrusts his hand in his pocket, clenches and unclenches his fist against his thigh.

"How do I know you won't sneak them off to America as soon as you can?"

"You're asking me to trust you. Trust me back."

He takes his hand out of his pocket and finally nods. "Switzerland then. The consulate will take care of the permits and all the other details."

CAMBRIDGE, MASSACHUSETTS—APRIL 1956

For one week Papa tried to win her back. Then time ran out. At lunch one day he told us he was being transferred to Osijek, in Croatia, another German puppet state, at the end of May.

I wanted to know if we would live in a house with our own garden so I could have a dog. Andy asked if Osijek had a good music conservatory.

It didn't matter what Osijek had to offer us. We weren't going. The Serbs were ferocious resistance fighters. It wasn't safe.

I could feel my nose getting snotty. I pinched my arm not to cry. "Will you be safe, Papa?"

"Of course. I have immunity. I'm a diplomat."

"What about us?" Andy shouted.

I stared at Mama. How long had she known? Why wasn't she crying, protesting? Didn't she love him enough to stop him? "I won't let you go," I said.

"I don't have a choice, Chipmunk. I'll visit often."

"Where? Here?"

"In Switzerland. Lugano," Mama said. "They speak Italian there."

"What about the conservatory?" Andy asked.

"I'm sure there's an excellent one in Lugano," she said.

I ran out and hid in Papa's closet.

Later Andy and I met in his room to hatch plots.

"We could throw away Papa's clothes at the very last minute," I suggested.

"That won't stop him." Now, at fourteen, his voice was deep, without cracks, in this moment soothing with its strength. "I'll slash the tires of all the cars." He still had his "Be Prepared" Boys Scout knife from California.

"He'll just call a taxi," I said. "I'll paint you red and you'll stick the thermometer behind the radiator. Scarlet fever! They'll have to quarantine all of us."

We argued; we hugged. I finally bawled my heart out onto Andy's argyle vest.

"Nothing is going to happen to Papa," Andy said, "and I'll take care of you and Mama."

"You're going to the conservatory. I'll probably never see you again either."

Andy offered me the front tail of his shirt to blow my nose on.

The grandfather clock behind me chimes nine o'clock. David will be home any minute now from teaching his Wednesday evening seminar. His dinner is drying out in the oven while I wait for him in his armchair by the lit fireplace, my nose picking up the faint scent of his Old Spice, thinking of how Papa's wish for me came true.

My last year of college I helped out in the Student Center, put out the food for an event, hung posters, sent out invitations, ran the slide projector during the monthly talks. That's how I met David, in his last year of graduate school. He was giving a talk on his summer trip to Egypt. I liked his looks—a lanky man with sandy hair and a soft voice that would have put me to sleep if his slides and his talk to the mostly empty room hadn't been wonderful. I remember odd details. Camels are considered the ships of the desert. In Luxor, at the temple of Karnak, brides run around the sacred scarab stone seven times in hopes of getting pregnant. *Aruusa* means bride in Egyptian. The native bread is tan, round and squishy like a camel's foot. The Egyptians paint tattoos on their hands to ward off the evil spirits. The patterns are handed down in families from generation to generation.

At Abu Simbel, Ramesses II built a temple on the shore of the Nile so that twice a year—mid-February and mid-October—the sun reaches directly into the innermost chamber and shines on the god-king Ramesses and the gods Amun-Ra and Re-Horakhty as they sit through eternity together.

"What a spectacular sight it must be," I said when David came to the back of the room to pick up his slides. "For three thousand two hundred years, twice a year, the light has penetrated the darkness of the chamber and lighted their faces in a kind of resurrection."

It's an image that has stayed with me. To come out of the darkness and bask in that warmth, to shine again in Mama's light. Me and the baby. That's my dream.

I hear David at the front door, and I call out to him, too tired to get up. I didn't fall in love with him right away. I was afraid of being hurt, deceived. Most of all, I didn't trust my own ability to love. David wore down my diffidence with humor, patience, friendship, with a quiet honorable strength that made me feel whole again. Discovering love allowed my anger to dissipate. Papa and I made peace with each other before he died.

David kisses the top of my head and I start to tear. I cry a lot these days. A side effect of being pregnant, Mrs. Stein has assured me. David hunches down in front of me, his dear face filled with love. I know he silently worries that my plunge into the past will end up hurting me rather than helping. It might, but I can't stop. I don't want to. Not with the baby coming in three and a half months. I ask David to hold me. I snuggle against his neck and thank him for loving me, for wanting our baby, for understanding, for not asking me to leave Mama in her unknown grave. He stands, lifting me up with him. We lean against each other, and I feel myself and the baby melt into him, become one with him. I'm awash in peace, happiness.

"I'm still all yours and the baby's," I say. "I always will be." He takes my hand and walks me upstairs to bed. For the time it takes us to make slow, delicious love, Mama, dinner, even the baby are forgotten.

With the good weather, David and I take long walks along the Charles River before dinner. We watch the rowers on the water, the forward glide of the sculls as the light deepens. These walks were David's idea, for my health and the baby's. Sometimes my back hurts too much and we sit on a bench. I've started remembering out loud. David holds my hand and listens.

"Rows of trains stretched out beyond the station exit. Above us, soot-caked wires dropped black dust over us. The smell of coal was overwhelming.

"We huddled in front of the open door of Papa's car. Our parents faced each other, Mama saying she'd make sure we wrote, she'd send photos.

" 'Every day,' I promised. In my eyes Papa was the hero going off to fight ferocious Serbs with dripping black mustaches and flashing knives spouting from their yellow teeth!

" 'Don't forget my American passport. Last night you said you'd give it to me now.' Mama's face was upturned, expectant. I wanted Papa to kiss her. "There's not much time. Give it to me.'

"The conductor blew his whistle, and Papa climbed up onto the carriage step, still holding my hand. 'God, Alinka, I'm sorry. I packed it by mistake.'

" 'Get it, please.' She was holding up her belly, enormous now, and I kept hoping the baby would come out right there so that Papa would have to stay.

" 'I don't know which one. There's no time. I'll send it to you.'

" 'Throw it out the window!' Around us people turned their heads. 'You have no right to keep it!' She was shouting in English. 'God damn it! You said you'd give it to me now. I believed you.' She hit the side of the car with her fist.

" 'Don't get hysterical. I'm sorry, I've got a lot on my mind. Leaving you and the children isn't easy, you know. I'll send it to you the minute I get to Osijek. I promise.' The train moved backward a few feet. 'Trust me.' Papa slipped out of my reach. I waved at his window as the train moved away. All I saw was painted blue glass."

The scullers have gone from the Charles River. Evening traffic streams down the road. I notice that David has his arms around me now. "Let's go home," he says. "I'll make dinner and I'll even clean up."

This is a first. "You're not feeling sorry for me now, are you? I'd hate that."

"No. I want you to sit with me in the kitchen, feet propped up, maybe with an eye out to watch that I don't burn anything, and keep talking. It's the first time you've included me, and so far I don't like what I've heard, but I do like you telling me. I've wanted to be part of this piecing together of yours from the beginning."

"I'm sorry. There's so much I'm ashamed of."

"Don't worry. Whatever you did, I'm keeping you."

Back at home, while my archaeologist husband opens up a can of soup and makes an omelet, I continue remembering out loud.

"After Papa left, Kay telephoned, but Mama wouldn't come to the phone. Karl Müller, the munitions expert, sent an armful of yellow roses and kept leaving messages with Jitka. 'Is he in love with you?' I asked Mama.

"'He's your father's friend, not mine,' she said.

"'Why did he send roses?'

"'To clean the gun powder from his hands.' I hugged her. She didn't like him.

"The following week the diplomatic pouch brought a letter from Papa and Mama's American passport. She took us out for ice cream to celebrate.

"'Now you can take us back to the States,' I said with the red passport in my hand.

"'The minute the war is over.'

"'The second it's over.'

"'Even sooner.'

"'All of us.'

"'All of us.'

A few days after the passport came, on May 27, two men threw a bomb at Heydrich while he was being driven down a street. The details I got from reading his biography. What I do remember is Pino taking us out of school before closing time, driving us home. We could see posters being plastered on walls. The German Reich offered a reward of five thousand crowns for information leading to the apprehension of an enemy of the state.

I wondered if my American mother was an enemy of the state. Would the police come to search our apartment, find her American passport, take her away? Mama had diplomatic immunity, Andy said, trying to reassure me. Papa would never let anything bad happen to her. I thought of Milena and didn't believe him. Milena, Mama locking herself up, Papa leaving us, now the attack on Heydrich—they were like small bombs being thrown at us, at me, at my safe, complacent world.

When Heydrich had first come to Prague, he boasted, "A German has nothing to fear from a Czech." Now he was in Bulovka Hospital, the same hospital where Mama was going to deliver the baby.

That evening we clustered around the radio cabinet in the study to find out more. Frank, the interim head of the Protectorate, declared a state of siege. A calm baritone read the ordinance every ten minutes. The reward was increased to ten million crowns. We kept waiting to hear how serious Heydrich's wounds were, if he was going to die. We were never told.

Mama sat very still as she listened, outwardly calm. That's how I remember her. Andy says she kept offering us food every few minutes, bringing in milk, tea, biscuits, slices of ham, repeating that we were perfectly safe. That's his memory. Mine is of Jitka crossing herself all day, Andy swallowing the news with ghoulish curiosity, Mama quiet. I stayed scared, only thinking of what was going to change for us, the four of us, giving no thought to what anyone else would suffer.

The state of siege meant no one could come or leave the city, and I thought I would never see Papa again. The following morning I pestered Mama until she agreed to let me send him a telegram. I was allowed ten words, which I took as an enormous responsibility. "Do you love Papa?" I asked her while she was braiding my hair. "Do you?"

"Say it, Mama. Say, I love Papa very much."

She waited until my long braid was done before answering. "Yes, Susie." I barely heard her.

Before leaving I showed Mama my ten words: "We are safe and love you lots Chipmunk Goat Gingercatmama."

Mama declared them perfect. Jitka would go to the post office after she took us to school. I slipped the sheet of paper into my pinafore pocket. At the steps of the school I handed Jitka a second sheet on which I'd written: "We are safe I love you very much kisses Mama."

That telegram was among the letters Papa gave me when I left for the States. He had pencilled in a note at the bottom of the telegram for my benefit.

"Your mother never signed Mama."

PRAGUE, THE GERMAN PROTECTORATE OF BOHEMIA AND MORAVIA—JUNE 1, 1942

The obstetrician has ordered daily walks. I get tired easily and stay close to the consulate, walking only as far as the Kampa, the Charles Bridge, up Nerudová to the castle. Today is a cool, clear day and Susie has offered to come with me. With her by my side I venture farther, across the river, all the way to Wenceslas Square, the half-mile-long hub of the city. It's more a boulevard than a square, crammed with all kinds of shops, with traffic streaming through on each side of a grass aisle filled with roses and pansies. Sunlight glints off the Art Nouveau bas-reliefs of the Hotel Europa, giving a Hollywood-like sheen to the square. A welcoming scene until I look toward the upper end, where four German tanks squat, caked with mud. Between them the statue of an armored St. Wenceslas, the patron saint of Bohemia, looks helpless on his horse.

Wenceslas Square—a vast meeting place, to cheer, to protest. After the Czech government handed over the Sudetenland to the Germans without a fight, thousands of people filled it, waving the flag, crying, singing the national anthem, screaming they wanted to fight. Today the only sound is of cars trickling by. An old man walks by, chewing his lip to stop it from quivering. A woman presses a handkerchief to her mouth, and I imagine her holding back a scream. Then I look again. The man and the woman are just people going about their business. Lately, my thoughts have turned morbid.

We resume our walk. After a few steps, Susie tugs at my sleeve. "Kay's friend," she says. Dr. Paroch, the Mcely village doctor I last heard outside Kay's kitchen window that horrible Christmas morning, is walking toward us. He sees us, waves, hurries his step. It's too late for me to change direction. He stops in front of us and before he can speak, I start blathering. "What a surprise, what are you doing here, imagine, what an incredible coincidence, how have you been, and your lovely wife, Irina? You remember my daughter, Susie?"

"Yes. Susinka, I do not forget. We sing Christmas music together. She has a good voice. And Zdena is well."

"Of course, Zdena. She's well? Good. I'm glad." I don't know what else to say. I'm sure my face has turned scarlet. He must know I refused to help.

"Forgive me, Pan'i Alessandrinova, you should be home. The streets are not safe."

He looks sincerely concerned, and my shame ebbs. I see that he looks tired. His bald head is shiny with sweat and his eyes are wet, the whites yellowed and opaque like Old Hus's. Maybe he's sick. "You are well?"

He shrugs. "I do best I can."

"How did you come to Prague?" He lives in Mcely. "Isn't the city sealed off?"

"There is Czech saying that if you go the length of Wenceslas Square, you will meet someone you know. So we meet." Dr. Paroch takes the wool scarf bulging out of his jacket pocket and wipes his head with it. "I have been here a few days. But you should be home."

I explain about the obstetrician's orders.

"It is too far from the consulate." He stretches out an arm. "May I?"

I let him rest his palm on my belly. His short puffy fingers splay across my navel.

He taps. "I want him to kick."

"She's quiet."

Dr. Paroch removes his hand and smiles. "I do not dispute boy or girl with a maminka. It is not a time now to make noise. In a week, ten days, your new daughter will come." He offers me his arm and leads me away from the sight of the tanks. Susie walks ahead, looking into the shop windows.

"Is the woman safe?" I ask. He tilts his head, looks puzzled.

"I heard you at the window Christmas morning."

"I left her in honest arms."

"Many people will be killed." I am thinking of Heydrich now. We walk at a slow, even pace, steps synchronized, as if we are an old married couple. "But he is evil, he deserves to die." Hitler, Heydrich, and Himmler, the three H's of Hell.

"Pan'i Alessandrinova, one has to remember the price."

"If we think only of the possible price, then nothing good would ever be done." I hear my voice rising. "Prudence is cowardly."

"Personal sacrifice is one thing, the killing of hundreds is another. One must always remember the price. Even to oneself." He reaches inside his breast pocket, holds up a leather-covered flask and unscrews the top. "Becherova, a national bitter herb drink that will give breath to the dead." He offers me the flask. "Guaranteed to make the baby come."

I laugh. "I think I'll wait."

He takes a quick drink. We are walking on Národni now, going toward the river. I ask him why he's in Prague. There's no one else on our side of the street. Susie is skipping twenty feet ahead of us.

"Are you involved with the attackers?" I picture him taking care of the wounded one.

"No, no, no, no. What are you saying?" He looks scared, disarmed, a turtle caught without its shell. I was foolish to ask. If he is involved, why, how could he tell me, the Italian vice consul's wife?

"I have something for you, Dr. Paroch. A package I was going to give to Kay. Something I should have given you Christmas morning. It has weighed on me ever since. Come back to the consulate with me. There's a sapphire bracelet, some money and other jewelry, use them as you see fit."

"Out of question." Flask still in hand, he is looking up and down the street.

"Please let me help."

Dr. Paroch strokes my arm, readjusts my straw hat. "Pan'i Alessandrinova, the city is under martial law. They search every corner. Jewels on a country doctor . . ."—he brushes his hand over his rumpled clothes—"I be shot without questions." He licks the side of his mouth as if a drop of the herb drink has caught in the crease. "You keep and wear in good health." He takes another drink. His arm trembles with a quick spasm. "To wear in good health is a Jewish wish. Keep it in your heart. Do not repeat it.

"I come to the city to help my daughter and son-in-law move to his parents' house in Lidice. She has become afraid of the city, he does not like Mcely, so they go to Lidice, a small town, nothing there, but that is what they chose. That is why I am here."

Dr. Paroch stops under the Bridge Tower that leads to Charles Bridge. Susie has been waiting for us. "Pan'i Alessandrinova, tell Kay when the baby arrive and I come to see you. Forget differences. She is good friend to you. She miss you. And do not worry. There is health for your baby. Please go home now, the street is not safe."

He plants a kiss on Susie's forehead. "Take care of your maminka and I promise, your sister will not be so terrible." He shakes my hand, then, as an afterthought, kisses both my cheeks. Close up, the veins of his cheeks look like a jumble of tangled red threads.

I watch Dr. Paroch, with his rumpled trousers, his gray scarf trailing from a pocket, hurry back along the bank of the river. He's rebuffed my offer of help, for good reasons that don't make me feel better, but he's made me realize how much I miss Kay.

FOUR

CAMBRIDGE, MASSACHUSETTS—APRIL 1956

Packers moved in for a few days. We weren't leaving Prague until the end of July, but with the baby coming, Mama wanted the packing over with, repeating, when anyone questioned her hurry, that there was nothing wrong with sitting on crates and eating off borrowed plates.

Several days after the packers left, Andy and I came home from school to find Mama in the living room prying open a crate with the forked end of a hammer. All the other crates the packers had nailed shut sat pried open, straw and crumpled newspapers spilling out of them. The antique dressing table mirror with the gold leaves which Papa had given her as a welcome-to-Prague present stood against the wall, still half covered in straw. She had unpacked the inlaid *vetrine* too. The enormous "peace bell" we were all supposed to ring together when the war was over sat on a corner crate. They were all things Papa had bought in Prague, and seeing them again filled me with hope.

"Is Papa coming back?"

"No, your father is not coming back." She lifted out the blue enamel clock that had sat on her night table and put it on the window sill. "These objects don't belong to us." She started hammering the lid back on the crate.

"You are so mean," I spit out, with all the venom I could muster. She was going to throw Papa's beautiful presents away. Suddenly I was sure my mother would never let me see him again. I ran from crate to crate, tearing off the destination labels and throwing out stuffing.

Mama let me be and I eventually got tired of my temper tantrum. I remember sitting under the piano, straw prickling my legs. Mama sat on the piano stool. All I could see of her were her bare feet. They were swollen and dry. Cracks cut across the skin. The ugliest feet I had ever seen, I decided.

"What if Papa bought what once belonged to people forced to run away?" she said. "After the war they'll come back and claim their belongings. If we take them with us, they'll never get them back."

"Papa would never take anything that belonged to someone else."

"Maybe he didn't know."

"You don't know!"

"It doesn't matter. It's the right thing to do. Kay is going to store these things until the war ends."

"You don't like Kay anymore."

She said we were going to stay with them when school was over and the siege was lifted. They had made peace. I don't know how or when exactly.

Mama let me hold her ankle for a long time, her patience and my cradling a kind of truce.

Heydrich died on the fourth of June of septicemia. The next day schools were closed; all of Prague shut down. Flags hung limply at half mast. Andy and I wanted to watch Heydrich's coffin being brought up Nerudová to lie in state at the Hrad, but Mama wouldn't let us. Jitka shut the windows to the apartment and told us she knew for sure that a Czech orderly had spread Heydrich's own shit in his wound. "Killed by his own poison," she said and whistled the Czech anthem—"Where Is My Home"—as loud as she could. Then she went to make strudel.

A few days later Heydrich's body was leaving Prague and Mama let us stand in front of the huge consulate doors, kept half-closed in mourning, to watch his coffin inch down the steep slope of Nerudová, on the first leg of its journey to Berlin. The military band played Siegfried's funeral march.

Andy complained they were out of tune, then started whistling loudly to correct them, which got him yanked back behind everyone. I played "good girl" and made the sign of the cross as the coffin went by.

After the procession was over, Mama took us to the Church of Our Lady of Victory. She told us to kneel in front of the Prague Infant Jesus—a sumptuously dressed wax doll that had been dispensing miracles for three centuries. "Give thanks," she said.

I didn't know what I had to thank him for. I asked the Infant Jesus to bring Papa back.

I'm swinging in our hammock, between two elms that keep the small garden in the back of our house in constant shade. I want to cut them down, plant a cherry tree when the baby is born, and fill the garden with flowers. David hesitates. He loves his hammock naps and suspects that most of the gardening will fall on his shoulders. Today, a Sunday, we celebrated the first warm day of spring with a barbecue. David is scraping the grill clean while I lie in the hammock and munch on a cold hot dog. Next week I've got to spring clean the house, write at least twenty pages of my thesis, buy paint—new-leaf green—for the baby's room. Next week. Now I luxuriate in the sun, in the life inside me, in David's love, and in this cold, still delicious hot dog.

"Papa used to rub Mama's stomach when she was expecting Claire," I tell David, "invoking food that wasn't available any more. I wonder if that's why Claire is such a good eater."

"If that's the reason, he must have done that with you, too."

I hold my hand over my belly button and list the food I've eaten today. The baby should know what she got. "Hamburger, two hotdogs with only one bun, a little potato salad, and a very thin slice of chocolate cake."

"Don't believe her," David calls out. "It was a thick slice." And then I feel it, a movement against my hand. "Oh God, David! She's moving. I swear. Come here." He runs over and I take his hand, place it next to mine. "Do you feel her? Him? Do you?" The baby obliges and we both start to laugh with joy.

The afternoon is fading. David and I are still sitting in the backyard, on chairs this time, wallowing in contentment, waiting for another communication from our child. Without the sun the air is cool. David has brought out sweaters, carefully wrapped my belly and legs with a throw. We hold hands and look up at the elms, listen to the birds make their end-of-day racket.

"It's been a perfect day," I say, and a moment after the words are out, a line of poetry pops into my head. " 'There through the broken branches go the ravens of unresting thought.' Who wrote that?"

"Poetry is not my line." David turns his head to study my face.

"Mama used to quote it sometimes when she saw us looking glum. 'Flying, crying, to and fro, cruel claw and hungry throat.' That's all I remember."

"What's the unresting thought?"

"How difficult it must have been for Mama those last days in Prague. She was left by herself, pregnant, taking care of us, knowing her husband had cheated on her. She didn't know when she was going to see him again or whether he'd get killed by Tito's men. She ached to get us out of the war zone. And I was just awful to her."

"You were eleven years old."

"Twelve by then. And now here I am, feeling so incredibly lucky and happy, my heart is going to explode. I don't deserve this, but I want it. You, the baby, this house, my work. I want it all, but I know I don't deserve it."

David chuckles. "You might change your mind when the baby is in his second hour of unremitting howling, and there are a hundred stinky diapers needing to be washed, and you can't find your research notes—they'll be buried under the diapers—and I've had a bad day at the university and demand my dinner pronto."

"Very funny. I know exactly where my research notes are and I'm hiring a diaper service and you can get your own dinner and our baby will be so happy she will cry, if at all, only ten minutes a day."

On June 10, 1942, year XX of the Fascist Era, exactly two years after Mussolini declared war on France and Great Britain, my sister arrived. Bald and mottled like a sausage, with all her toes and fingers and one eye she kept closed for several days. She had too many names at the start. She was Claire for Mama, Chiara for Papa and the Fascist government, who did not accept foreign names, Clarinka for Jitka. Andy called her "little sis." I nicknamed her Pstruh, after the one-eyed trout I had decorated the night of Saint Nicholas.

PRAGUE, THE GERMAN PROTECTORATE OF BOHEMIA AND MORAVIA—JUNE 11, 1942

The sun from the window covers us while my sweet little mouse sucks at my breast. The pink fuzz already curling across her tiny head makes me dumbly proud. I slip a finger in Claire's curled hand and close my eyes. A feeling of lazy contentment overwhelms me. I could be lying on the hot sand, listening to the thrust and pull of the Pacific. I can hear it here in Bulovka Hospital. I'm dozing and Marco covers me with our dark blue beach umbrella. White light streams down the edges, surrounding me like a waterfall. He takes the children digging for steamers in the wet sand. As always, they will be too big. Marco wants the clams of his Italian beaches, no larger than Claire's little toe. He's always complaining that everything is enormous in America, but we'll go home with the children's pails full of steamers anyway, and he'll cook them in oil and garlic and pour them over spaghetti. At the last minute he'll add two tablespoons of ocean water "to give it life."

This morning I wrote Marco a letter.

Your daughter Claire weighs three kilos, six hundred grams. She is very beautiful. I have a sense of accomplishment, and I feel suddenly released. My house is in order. With our new baby and Heydrich dead, Milena is gone too. I am still filled with sadness for life not being that wonderful rosy romantic thing that loving you made me hope for. I did not deserve Milena. Nor did the children. I wish you were here to hold your new daughter. The children and I miss you. Keep safe.

Your wife,
Alinka

There's a knock on the door. Kay walks in with many plumes of dark purple lilacs that fill the room with their perfume.

"Oh, Kay, thanks. They're spectacular."

"These are the last of them."

"How did you get here? I thought no one could enter or leave the city?"

"Giorgio pulled strings. I had to see your baby."

I blow her a kiss. "Look at this beauty." Claire is still feeding and I have to lean forward to show her off.

Kay bends over and traces a finger over Claire's head. "She has your hair. How sweet." Kay looks up at me with a sudden grimace of pain. I hug her, knowing she has always wanted a baby. She leans away and says, "I have horrible news."

It's afternoon. The room glows pink from the setting sun and the air is filled with the sweet smell of Kay's lilacs and Lilli's white roses. I look at Claire asleep in her crib next to the bed and try to summon this morning's happiness. Susie and Andy are coming any minute for their second visit. I would give anything to keep them unaware of what has happened, what *is* happening around us every day, but to do that I would have to lock them up, surround them with silence. Their teachers, the newspapers, will tell them only lies. My children need to know the truth. Truth, ugly as it may be, will help them grow. Arm them. Sear right and wrong on their hearts.

They come in with Jitka. Susie presents me with daisies, "I picked them from the garden," she says with pride in her voice. "Lilli didn't see me."

"It will be our secret. They're beautiful. Thank you." Andy has brought his violin and wants to play for Claire. I wrap my arms around them both, kiss their cheeks, their ears, their hair. My precious children. I will keep them safe in Switzerland. We'll leave as soon as I get my strength back. As soon as Claire is strong enough to travel. I will convince Marco to join us. We'll be a family again, all of us together in Switzerland.

Jitka mumbles something at the door. I look up. Her devastated face tells me she knows.

"Something very sad has happened today," I say as soon as Jitka closes the door behind her. "In Lidice. It's a town not far from here. Have you heard about it? The Germans call it Liditz."

Andy shakes his head.

"That's where Dr. Paroch's daughter went to live," Susie says. She remembers from our walk in Wenceslas Square.

"He was helping her move." I clasp my lips for a moment to stop them from trembling. "Yesterday German soldiers surrounded Lidice because of a rumor that one of Heydrich's attackers had taken refuge there. When they didn't find him, they started shooting people." I don't tell them that by the time their sister was born, the soldiers had executed all the men, more than a thousand, and sent the women and children away in trucks. That Kay heard that the blond, blue-eyed children have been transported to Germany. That no one knows or is telling what has happened to the rest of the survivors. That Lidice has been razed to the ground and Mrs. Paroch and her daughter have simply disappeared.

"Did Dr. Paroch die?" Susie asks me.

"Yes."

"There are posters all over town listing the people they've killed," Andy says in a bored voice.

"Hundreds of people," Susie adds with an impassive face. Death doesn't yet mean much to them. The closest they have come to it was watching Heydrich's coffin parade down Nerudová. The Pilsen bombing happened fifty miles away. At school, if a student's father dies, they're made to sing *Ich Hatte einen Kamaraden*, in which a comrade, a friend, is killed by a bullet. It's a sentimental, morbid song that makes them cry and absolves them of any lack of true feeling. I wish I could believe that for children not knowing is a blessing, but I can't help thinking that ignorance is a luxury no one can afford anymore.

Andy wants to know who Dr. Paroch was. At least Susie remembers him.

"He was a good man," I tell Andy. "Now play our sun music for your new sister."

CAMBRIDGE, MASSACHUSETTS—APRIL 1956

Our last week of school, a few days after Mama and Claire came home, Andy walked into school and went directly to the bathroom, where a big gangling German boy, Walter, the son of an officer in the Gestapo, told him something that prompted them to stay locked in a stall to wait for the class bell. Ten minutes after the bell, with the teachers and students safely in their classrooms, Andy and Walter walked through the empty entrance hall and back out onto the street.

I didn't find out that Andy had played hooky until Jitka showed up to take us home and we couldn't find him. Where was he? Why hadn't he told me anything? Why wasn't I with him? I sorted through my collection of revenges: salt in the sugar bowl, a short-sheeted bed, mustard in his underpants, pebbles in his shoes. By the time the taxi dropped Jitka and me off at the consulate, I still hadn't made up my mind which revenge would be the worst.

Mama was breast-feeding Claire in her bedroom when Jitka told her about Andy. "He probably didn't study for a test," I added. She handed Claire over to Jitka and ran out of the room. The front door slammed, and I remember being worried that she would forget to button her blouse and everyone would see her breasts.

Jitka tried to feed me lunch. I called Kay in case Andy had taken a train to Mcely. The siege had been lifted the day before. Rudolf offered to come and help in the search. His voice was so grave I started getting scared too. Jitka kept crossing herself.

When Mama came back, her face looked smashed.

The Gestapo was still looking for Heydrich's attackers. Hundreds of people had been arrested. Entire families had been shot for the flimsiest of reasons. In her head, I'm sure Mama saw her only son bleeding in an alleyway.

The first thing we heard were the metal tips on Andy's shoes clicking on the stairs. By now it was past three o'clock in the afternoon.

Alinka, Jitka, and I had been waiting on the landing. I leaned over the railing. Now I could see Andy's head, his knees, his feet taking the stairs two at a time. I skipped down the stairs, greeted him with a pinch in his underarm, where it hurts the most. "Boy, are you in trouble! Where did you go?" I whispered. "You nearly killed Mama. Why didn't you take me with you?"

"You're too sissy."

"I am not!"

Mama just stood on the landing. She didn't look angry.

Andy stopped two steps from the top and announced with his new deep voice, "They got Heydrich's killers! They were hiding in the crypt of a church. The Gestapo brought floodlights, fire trucks, machine guns, loud-speakers. Everything!" Andy wiped his nose with his shirt cuff. "I saw it all."

Mama hugged him. "The Gestapo could have killed you."

Andy squirmed out of her grip. "They didn't!"

She grasped his shoulders and started shaking him.

"Mama!" I pleaded. "It's a just a crazy story to get out of trouble."

It was as true a story as Lidice was. The three resistance fighters who had been parachuted in from England and four other men had sought refuge in the Karel Boromaeus Greek Orthodox Church. One of their friends had turned them in. Three men were shot right away, dragged out of the church and their corpses put on display on the sidewalk. The remaining four resisted the Gestapo from the crypt.

"The fighters had tons of ammunition," Andy said. "No one could get near the window. The firemen tried with a mattress, with gas bombs. Everything got thrown back."

Mama put her hand over his mouth. "God, you sound like you enjoyed it! You can't enjoy it, it's gruesome." She was shouting now. "You could have been shot through the head, through the chest. Dead!"

Andy pushed her away and yelled back. Nothing had happened to him. Why didn't she leave him alone? She was getting hysterical over nothing. "I'm not a baby anymore!"

"Don't you have a four o'clock music lesson?" Lilli asked, peering between the railing a few steps below us. "If you don't hurry, you'll be late."

Andy stomped into the apartment on his metal-tipped shoes, his rebellion linked to making as much noise as possible.

PRAGUE, THE GERMAN PROTECTORATE OF BOHEMIA AND MORAVIA—JUNE 18, 1942

Andy is standing on the landing with his violin case, ready to go to his music lesson. I stare at him, my heart kicking my ribs, horrifying thoughts hammering my head. My son arrested and tortured, or kidnapped and sent to Germany. My son shot dead in the street.

He says, "I'm sorry."

I'm sorry? Is that all he can say? Sorry? He sounds just like his father. I snap open the case, catch the violin before it falls on the floor. "I'm sorry. So sorry. I'll never do it again. Promise. Cross my heart and hope to die. Honor and obey until death do us part. Words. Letters jumbled together. They don't mean anything." I hold the violin, a Testore, by its scroll out as far as my arm can reach.

I dangle the violin over the stairwell. Andy watches me with a fierce face. "'I'm sorry' only means something if you feel it, Andy." His eyes flick to the violin. "You have to feel it." I open my hand.

The violin spins head over heels down the three flights and lands with a loud crack. Below me someone cries out. I stare at the shattered violin at the bottom of the stairwell and feel a great sense of satisfaction. I turn to face Andy and watch the stunned surprise in his face give way to anger, the same anger that sometimes vibrates just underneath Marco's skin. He closes the violin case and walks away, back to his room. His shoes barely make noise.

I look down at the violin again and a memory intrudes. The day Andy turned twelve. We were roasting marshmallows on the beach for the first time, the Pacific at low tide, almost quiet. I'd tied Andy's present to the spokes of our blue beach umbrella. Andy, at Marco's asking, had opened the umbrella and the Testore, his first full-sized violin, had dangled down on his head. Marco and I raised our beers and shouted, "To a glorious career."

I run after Andy, my heart shattering, my thoughts whirling. How can he ever forgive me? How can I say I'm sorry after the scene I've just made? "I'll buy you a new violin," I shout after him. "A better one." He has shut the door to his room. I don't knock. "I love you, Andy. Please forgive me." I would give anything to reel backward, the violin still in its case, with me only relieved and grateful that Andy is home. What frightens me most is that my children have only me now and I have lost all sense.

When I turn back, Lilli is in the front hall, wearing her pious face. Marco has specifically asked her and Giorgio to watch over his family, she tells me. Andy deserves punishment for his bad behavior, but my reaction was far too extreme. "You need to calm down."

Ashamed of how right she is, I tell her, "Mind your own business." Her faces freezes in shock. She retreats without another word, and I'm sure she'll rush a letter off to Marco the minute she gets downstairs.

CAMBRIDGE, MASSACHUSETTS—APRIL 1956

After Lilli left I ran downstairs to pick up the violin. The strings still held some of the bigger pieces, and I hoped that by some miracle they could be glued back together, but Mama took the pieces from me, threw them in the trash and went to Andy's room. I listened at the door, but could only hear her murmur. If Andy said anything, I didn't pick it up. He wouldn't come out of his room for dinner. I think I ate every last crumb that had been on my plate, the way Mama always wanted me to. I was sure she was going to lash out at me next.

After Mama and Jitka went to bed, I brought Andy some buttered bread, which he threw across the room.

"She was scared, Andy." He told me to get out, his jaw looking like a fist he was going to hit me with. I told him he wasn't being fair, that he didn't know everything, and I told him about Milena. He called me a liar. I was making up excuses for Mama. He wasn't going to forgive her. Not even if she bought him a Stradivarius, he was never going to forgive her. The strength of his fury, an echo of hers, frightened me.

Until that afternoon, my brother had been someone I could hug, kick, pinch, someone I knew intimately, whom I could count on to stand in my corner against the world of grown-ups. On the streetcar on the way to school we had played our usual last-letter-first-letter word game, a different language for each word: schatz, zoo, onore, enshuldigen . . . Then we walked into school through our separate entrances. He walked out again, without me. And now I felt he was someone separate. Unpredictable.

We sat in silence, in the dark. Andy was in bed, me by his feet, twitching under the covers. He started to cry, small hiccups of torn sound. I cried too, but we each cried on our own, never acknowledging the other's tears. Then he told me how the four surviving men in the crypt, rather than surrender, had shot themselves with their last bullets. All together. One big sound. "They must have counted," he said.

Three days later Mama came home with a new violin, a valuable Amati she had bought from the maestro—provenance untainted by the war since he had received it from the grateful parents of a pupil many years before. Andy played a few strands of music and said the Amati had a beautiful sound. Everything seemed all right again.

We celebrated the last day of school with vanilla ice cream and a chocolate sauce that Jitka made from what was left in the cocoa tin. Mama

71

said she didn't feel like ice cream even though vanilla was her favorite. She wanted to leave more for us, even though she could not have known this would be our last ice cream until the end of the war. I dribbled chocolate sauce down my blouse and Mama, after dabbing a dish towel against the faucet, which always dripped, cleaned me up, slowly, meticulously.

"I will always take care of you," she said after the chocolate stain was only a brown shadow trailing down my chest.

"There's no more chocolate in all of Czechoslovakia," I said, thinking she was talking about my blouse.

"I'll make sure you're safe," she added. "All my children safe."

"No chocolate in all of Germany," Andy said, the spoon still in his mouth.

"What about Switzerland?" I asked.

"Mountains," Andy decreed.

"With powdered sugar for snow." I clapped my hands and laughed. The school year was over. No more German declensions ever. I had exchanged hugs with the few friends I had made. They had written goodbyes and poems in my friendship book, but I was already looking ahead: to Mcely, to a visit from Papa. Mama's protection I took for granted.

The next day Rudi was waiting at the train station in his old Skoda and drove us through the village, past low stucco houses with sharply angled roofs. Each house, painted in pastel colors, had a carefully tended garden filled with dahlias and marigolds. The air was steeped with the sweet scents of hay and flowers. No more school. No more Lilli, the Toad, watching us. No more emptied apartment. There were secret nooks to be discovered in the forest with Andy and Old Hus, trees to be climbed, a stream to be waded in. Even the whiff of manure was exhilarating.

Outside the village, birches flanked the road. Behind them, flat fields with rows of apple trees and a distant, craggy line of dark woods. At a wooden signpost with *Vlasek* painted on it, Rudi veered the Skoda onto a dirt road. At the end of the road, a steep driveway led to his yellow house with its chocolate brown shutters.

My first memory of our last Mcely summer is of being surrounded by a sweep of sunlit green and yellow with Old Hus watching me crawl through the tall grass, looking for four-leaf clovers. My knees were permanently stained.

The few times Andy hung around, I would race him and Old Hus down to the stream at one end of the property. Andy always got there first.

Old Hus, eighty-four years old in human years, trotted instead of running, always mindful of his dignity. Andy and I tore off our sandals and jumped in. The cold water burned my legs red and now reached only to the bottom of my knees. I had grown since the year before. Already tall, I wanted to be taller, as tall as the Mcely church steeple that I could always see in the distance, a periscope keeping watch.

I ran back to Mama the first time I made the connection between the water's depth and my own height. She was reading in the living room, Claire in a basket at her bare feet. I stood in front of the open French window. "I've grown an inch." She continued reading. "I've grown a foot. I'll become a giant. I'll get a goose that lays golden eggs."

Mama rested the book on her lap and laughed. "I'll have to get you new clothes, then." She seemed happy.

After breakfast, except for the two mornings a week that he went to Prague for his violin lesson, Andy stuffed the pockets of his shorts with his Boy Scout knife, bread, and an apple and headed for the woods on Rudi's bike. It wasn't far—four kilometers. Mama didn't object. After smashing his violin, she let him do whatever he wanted. I tried following him once, crouching in the high grass so he wouldn't see me. When the grass met the first stand of chestnuts, Andy turned around. "Go home," he shouted.

When Rudi needed the bike, Andy stayed close to the house and looked for frogs, silverfish, grass snakes, which he cut up while I, with clenched teeth, volunteered as a surgical nurse. Watching him sink his knife into a frog's white underbelly made me sick, but I held on to that squirming frog as if it were my brother trying to slip away.

After dinner one night, Mama asked Andy to get the Amati. He played Bach with Mama accompanying him on the piano. In the middle of a sweet passage, he lifted his bow and put his violin back in its brand new case. He gave no reason for stopping. Rudi and Kay supplied their own. "Our piano needs tuning." "The boy's on vacation. He needs a rest." I offered "It's too hot."

Mama sat on the piano stool, her fingers still curled over the keyboard. "It's my fault. I'm sorry, Andygoat." Andy proposed a game of Monopoly.

A few days later Andy announced he didn't want to study with the maestro anymore. "What's the point? We're leaving."

"What about your love of music?" Mama asked him. "The conservatory in Switzerland, the concert stage? Don't let anger dictate your life. It's wrong, it doesn't help. Please, Andy. I know."

"You always exaggerate, Mama. I just want a month off. Thirty days free of music, that's all."

Weeks later, with our suitcases in the hall and Rudi honking from the car, Andy called the bakery on the maestro's street. "Tell Maestro Korchak Andrew Alessandrini is going to come back to Prague one day and play so well it will knock the whiskers off his face!"

Without closing my eyes, I see pictures. Mama sitting under the lace shade of the one cherry tree, writing a letter with her face half hidden under her California beach hat. Claire is in the basket on top of the picnic table. It's hot and Mama keeps her feet in an enamel basin filled with water. Every few minutes she stops writing to reach down and dip her hand in the basin. She leans away from her letter and splashes water on herself. Then wipes her wet hand on Claire's brow. I watch as the drops of water spread, larger and larger across the front of her dress. When it dries, the water leaves a puckered imprint on her chest.

Mama has lost weight since the baby came. Her rigid diet has convinced me my father is coming for Claire's christening one week away. Except that she is writing to him now. Does that mean he isn't coming? No letters from him in the two weeks we've been with Rudi and Kay. Are they lost? Has he written? I don't ask, afraid of the answer.

MCELY, THE GERMAN PROTECTORATE OF
BOHEMIA AND MORAVIA—
JULY 4, INDEPENDENCE DAY, 1942

Kay and I are determined to celebrate the holiday despite being impossibly far away from the ideals of independence and equality. A dinner of würstel, potato salad, Kay's apple pie. Lots of beer for us, sugar water for the children as Kay hasn't been able to find any lemons to make lemonade. After we close all the windows and shut the doors, we might even belt out a few American favorites. "My Darling Clementine," "On the Sunny Side of the Street," "Swanee," "My Old Kentucky Home," "If You Knew Susie." There are so many, we might end up singing all night. I think we should. The bright light of our hopes and dreams will be our fireworks.

Tomorrow, as every Sunday, we're going to the village church to light candles for Dr. Paroch and the other Lidice victims. It's a helpless gesture and yet it soothes. Since the massacre, the church is always ablaze with candles.

I do feel safe here and try to rest as much as possible for our upcoming trip to Switzerland.

My packet of jewelry and money, which Dr. Paroch refused, Kay has passed on to friends in the Czech underground. She won't say who these people are or how the network functions. "Wars never end, only the enemy changes," Rudi has said. I know he wasn't thinking of me.

Rudi—placid, sad, with a pale face that seems to fade in the sun as Kay's gets darker, blue eyes hidden behind glasses, a thin mouth, a newly grown Van Dyck beard the color of pinewood. Every morning he marches off to patrol the boundaries of his property.

I can see him from the guest bedroom, a tweed cap on his head, a stick slung over his shoulder to replace the hunting rifle the Germans confiscated after Heydrich was attacked. Old Hus follows him, visible in the tall grass only when he raises his snout to sniff the air. Every fifty yards or so Rudi whistles and waits for the dog to catch up, until they disappear from view.

While most of the world is going to pieces, these days are good ones for us. Every day I write to Marco. In each letter I ask him to quit his job, to join us in Lugano. We're leaving the middle of August.

His letters ask about my health, remark how the baby must be tiring me out, how the children need special guidance in these harsh times. He's suggested I hire a governess to look after the children. I can hear Lilli's voice in his words.

I have always thought of Marco as my essence and have loved him at times even more than my children, but he cannot accuse me of not being responsible, of not having their best interest at heart. They don't need a governess. They need a father.

CAMBRIDGE, MASSACHUSETTS—APRIL 1956

David tells me Claire called this Saturday morning while I was teaching at the Senior Center.

Claire never calls. I'm the one who calls. I study David's face for the tight look that precedes bad news. He is perfectly at ease. "She's okay?"

He nods. "She found something in your father's papers. She wants you to call her, but not when your brother is around. She suggested Monday morning between nine and ten. I told her that would be in the middle of the night for us and tried to get her to tell me more, but she wouldn't. She did sound pretty excited."

"I'll call her now."

David envelops me in his arms and kisses my forehead. "It's past midnight in Rome."

"Tomorrow then." I snuggle into his embrace. "I can't wait until Monday."

At night, with David asleep, I feel my heart racing. What did Claire find in our father's papers? I cannot sleep and go to the kitchen for ice cream. In the den, Papa's photo album is waiting to lull me into memories again. It helps the time go by, time until I can call.

The day Claire was christened the rain clattered on the roof of the Mcely church. The scent of Kay's flowers blended with the smell of candle wax and the previous Sunday's incense. Lilli brought white carnations. Rudi took me to meet Jitka and her niece Teresa at the train station. When Jitka lowered herself off the train, big pillowy Jitka in her Sunday blue and white polka dot dress with a veil bobby-pinned to her hair, I burst into sobs. Jitka squeezed me to her chest and, from her pocket, fed me cookies which got stuck in my throat. I coughed cookie crumbs and tears and forgot why I had started crying in the first place. When, after the party, it was time for her train, she was the one to cry. She blamed it on the cake she had brought. She hadn't been able to find enough butter or eggs. The cake was too dry. Mama said it tasted of sadness.

Papa had planned to come, but Tito—the leader of the partisan movement—had bombed the railroad tracks leading out of Croatia. With gas not available for personal use, Papa was stranded. Two nights before the christening, he made an expensive trunk call. Mama kept repeating, "Are you going to give it up? Are you? Are you coming to Switzerland?" She never asked him if he was safe and she hung up before I could talk to him. I told her she was selfish.

We got all dressed up for Claire's big day. I fussed and whined until Mama dug out my burgundy velvet dress with the lace collar. It was too short, too hot, and I loved it anyway. When I took the dress off after the party, my slip had turned pink with perspiration. Claire wore my old embroidered batiste christening gown. Giorgio was godfather, Kay godmother. The priest dripped water over Chiara Claire Alessandrini and welcomed her into the Catholic Church.

After the christening Kay and Rudi served apricot jam crêpes along with Jitka's cake. Mama poured sugar water for Andy and me and Giorgio offered the grownups the spumante he had brought from the consulate. Everybody kept toasting Claire. I kept thinking how Papa would have toasted me too. At a certain point I slipped out into the hallway for a few private self-pitying sniffles.

"Poor Susanna, no one is paying any attention to you today."

Stung, I wiped my face quickly and swung around. The Toad was standing by the door. "That's not true!" She was wearing her usual smirk. "I just wish my father was here."

"Of course you do." She handed me her handkerchief. "Wipe your face and let's take a little walk," Lilli said, giving my back little pats as if I were a dog. "It has stopped raining and I have a little secret that will make you happy."

I took her to the old kennel that Rudi had turned into a chicken coop. While her wedged shoes sank into mud and chicken shit, she told me her secret. In the fall, I was going to a school run by nuns, an exclusive school at the edge of Villa Borghese Park. It was all set, my place reserved. We were going to Rome, not Switzerland.

"Does Mama know?"

"If Andy passes the entrance exam, he'll go to the conservatory of Santa Cecilia, the best in the world." Friends of Papa's had already found us an apartment in Parioli, the best residential area.

"You'll be closer to your father," Lilli said. "He'll be able to visit you much more often."

"How close?"

"A puddle jump away, just across the Adriatic Sea. Your father has a right to see you."

"Does Mama know?"

"I told you, it's a secret just between you and me. You mustn't tell anyone. A letter from your father will explain everything."

We walked back to join the party, and I forgot to thank her for the secret.

After everyone left, I whispered "I have a secret" in Andy's ear.

"Girl secrets are stupid."

77

I whispered it in Old Hus's ear and got a lick in return. I told no one else.

My grown-up secret exhilarated me at first. At night, I shut my eyes and tried to remember what Rome had been like. Most of my memories came from photo albums and anecdotes my parents had repeated. Andy and I slept together in the tiny apartment on the Janiculum Hill. In the summer we ate on the small terrace in the shade of a sycamore tree and squashed the ants parading across the railing. When our parents took their afternoon naps on Sundays, Andy sometimes made a loose paste of water and flour, climbed out on one of the sycamore branches and dropped "bird doo" by the teaspoonful on hapless passersby. For my sixth birthday someone had given me two parakeets: Blue Sing and Green Song. One night—it must have been in the spring when the nights were still cold—I forgot them on the terrace. The next day I went to kindergarten with Sing and Song in my sweater pockets to keep them warm. The birds survived, but the sweater didn't.

Papa did most of the cooking, always making a big mess which everyone else had to clean up. My favorite dish was spaghetti carbonara with eggs, pancetta, and lots of Parmesan. Mama would grate stalagmites of cheese without ever getting her knuckles caught. My task was to set the napkins on a table I barely reached. Andy plucked AB AB on his 3/4 violin and got callouses on his fingers and a red mark on his neck where the chin rest hit.

At night, in my Mcely bedroom, I rehearsed memories of Rome as if they were poems I had to learn by heart. I was prepared to recite them to Mama as soon as she woke up to show her how infinitely wise my Papa was to take us to such a happy place. With daylight I lost courage.

For the next three, four, five days—I don't remember how long—I watched out for the mailman's bicycle; I kept an ear out for the telephone in case Lilli called to say a letter had arrived with the diplomatic pouch; I studied my mother for signs that she knew. She slept a lot, her eyes were red. She had a cold, she said. She blew her nose a lot, but I didn't believe her. Somehow Papa's letter must have arrived without my seeing it. I started following her, looking for clues that she knew. When she opened a door, I braced myself for a slam. When she walked by the ceramic birds on the mantle in the living room, I imagined her arm sweeping out and shattering them to the floor. When she rocked Claire, I stood guard.

"What is the matter with you?" Mama finally asked. "What do you want?" She was sitting at the kitchen table, still in her bathrobe. I backtracked to the door, stood under the transom as we had been taught at school, while a bubble of fear lodged itself in my heart.

"We're going to Rome, not Switzerland. Papa's sending us to Rome." I rushed into Lilli's details—the apartment in Parioli, the school run by the Cabrini Sisters at the edge of Villa Borghese, Andy going to Santa Cecilia. I even told her about the uniform the nuns made you wear, a blue skirt and sweater, a white blouse, and blue knee socks.

"No more scratchy brown stockings that make me look like Pinocchio!" I clenched my stomach, expecting Mama to throw her teacup against the stone floor, accuse me of lying, of being a bad, selfish girl.

Mama finished her tea. The kitchen clock above the fireplace ticktocked loudly and the faucet dripped on the stone sink. She rinsed her cup. "The nuns will turn your soul into a bristle brush. You'll hate them," she said. Then she went to the entrance hall to the telephone.

Andy was in the woods with Rudi's bike. I found Kay instead. "Rome is closer for Papa," I explained, "and I think nuns are nice." Kay's hug didn't reassure me.

When Mama finally came out to the vegetable garden, her hair was combed, her face carefully made up. She had put on the pink linen suit with matching sling-back heels. The jacket was tight around her breasts, which had grown enormous. She'd had to leave the top button undone. A pinned folded lace handkerchief covered her cleavage. Mama stood by the picnic table, straw hat dangling from a gloved hand. "I'm off to the Crusades." She was going to meet with Giorgio, the infidel, and straighten him out. The Rome nonsense was all Giorgio's doing. Papa didn't know anything about it, she was sure of that.

Rudi got in his dilapidated burgundy Skoda to take her to the station. He would have driven her all the way to Prague and back, but his gas allotment didn't allow it. Kay was left in charge of Claire. I slipped into the back seat of the car just as Rudi was taking off.

The train station smelled of manure and goulash. From an open upstairs window, Lale Anderson sang "Tales from the Vienna Woods" on the radio. Standing close to my mother, I recognized the pinned handkerchief as one of three that Lilli had given me for my twelfth birthday. Half an embroidered S jutted from behind one lapel.

When the train came, Mama pointed to the engine with its big white V freshly painted on the front so you could see it coming at night during the blackout. "V for Victory and Switzerland." She wouldn't let me go with her.

I rest my head back in the armchair and close my eyes. How do I remember so well? I don't know, but I do. That day is as clear to me as the movie I saw last week. If Mama were alive, what would she remember? There's so much I don't know.

PRAGUE, THE GERMAN PROTECTORATE OF BOHEMIA AND MORAVIA—JULY 23, 1942

I lower myself onto the chesterfield sofa in Giorgio's office and face him and Mussolini's gigantic mug above his head. I keep my net gloves on, my straw hat on my lap. I want to look composed, in control. "You can't force me to go to Rome," I say in a low, calm voice.

"On your passport, I could stamp TRANSIT TO ITALY ONLY."

"I will use my American passport."

"That could get you arrested as a possible spy." Giorgio's nicotine-stained fingers hook over a cigarette.

"My children will be safe only in Switzerland."

"What can possibly happen in the Eternal City? It houses Il Duce, the Pope, the Colosseum, the Roman Forum, St. Peter's. It's inviolable, protected by God." Giorgio looks at me with a sleepy air. He has a large, drooping nose and no neck to speak of. His chin rests directly on his chest. Andy and Susie have dubbed him "The Pelican." He peers at me as if I were a fish.

"I have an agreement with my husband." I hear my voice tremble.

"You would ruin Marco's career."

"What my husband and I decided is our affair. I will leave with the children for Lugano in two weeks."

"Rome is much closer to Croatia, and after Osijek, Marco is due to be posted back to Rome." Giorgio walks over to his desk.

"Stop interfering, Giorgio."

He hands me a large cream-colored envelope with the blue Royal Seal in one corner. It is addressed to Giorgio. I recognize Marco's narrow, sloping handwriting.

"Go on, read it."

I take out two folded sheets of paper, open them.

. . . I cannot trust her in Switzerland with the children. She will, I fear, find her way to Spain or Portugal and from there sail to America as soon as it is possible. I have foolishly sent back her American passport. I realize now, as you have repeatedly pointed out, that having my family in Switzerland is tantamount to saying I have no faith in the future of Fascism, which is a sentiment that Palazzo Chigi might reward with dismissal or worse. I have three children and a wife to take care of.

I am thankful to Lilli for keeping me informed of Alinka's behavior. The violin incident is frightening, I agree, but I cannot believe the children are in danger. Giorgio—I entreat you and Lilli to treat my wife gently. Her nerves are shattered. In time she will recover.

I stop reading. Cold steeps inside me.

"You wish to leave in two weeks. Good." Giorgio sits behind his desk and lifts the phone to ask his secretary to send someone to buy three tickets—one adult, two children—for Prague-Vienna-Rome, first class. "I'm afraid you'll have to change trains in Vienna, but I'll have someone from the consulate there to meet you."

"To make sure I don't run away."

Giorgio lights another cigarette. "To make sure you have everything you need. You wouldn't get very far even without two children and a baby."

I stand up, walk over to the desk, and lift the telephone receiver. "Call him." We wait half an hour for the call to go through. Giorgio continues to smoke. I stand by the window, my back to him. The glass panes are thick, hand blown, filled with air bubbles. They make the courtyard wobble. Across the cobbled yard, up at a window on the third floor, a workman is scraping the burgundy damask from the wall. A new vice-consul is arriving at the beginning of September. My old bedroom is being redone. My life needs redoing.

Giorgio calls me to the phone.

"You betrayed me, Marco." I'm careful not to touch my lips to the mouthpiece. "Now you betray our children. This time I won't forgive you."

Words spurt back at me. "I know what's best. I have your well-being in mind. The children's safety is uppermost in my mind." A name spills out of the black spigot, a name repeated over and over again. A woman's name that starts wide and ends with a short explosive sound. Similar to mine, but not mine. No, I am not that woman. I will never be that woman again. I hold the receiver away from me and let the sounds spill to the floor.

Giorgio takes the phone, says something to Marco, and hangs up. "I'm sorry, Alinka." I'd like to slap that false look of concern off his face. "What is important is to keep the family together. That is your duty. Italian law stands behind the father. I can't force you to leave Prague, but I'll have to send the children to Rome."

I leave without waiting for the train tickets.

I walk across the river to Wenceslas Square. I need to surround myself with everyday traffic, with people going about their lives. Most of all I need to see the tanks parked on either side of the statue of St. Wenceslas. The tanks are gone, and I can't even find a uniform to hate. It is very hot and the sun is beating on my head. I realize I have left my hat on Giorgio's sofa. I turn to walk toward the train station and see the Alcron Hotel around the corner, on Stepanska.

"I'm glad I found you in," I tell Karl Müller in the dark lobby.

"Frau Alessandrini, my pleasure." He is wearing steel-rimmed glasses that he quickly tucks inside his suit jacket. I didn't know he wore glasses and I've forgotten how tall and big a man he is. Herr Karl Müller, the bear. "How have you been?"

With a hand, Karl Müller indicates an open doorway, just past the heavy mahogany concierge's desk. "Perhaps we could talk a little over tea or a drink." He holds my elbow as he guides me into the tea room. The gentleness of his touch gives me courage. This serious, solid man is a German munitions expert, but he finds me attractive. That's what matters to me now.

The room we sit in is narrow and empty, the only window hidden behind murky beige curtains. The small chandelier sprays a weak, yellow light which gives Karl Müller a softer, younger appearance. Maybe

I too look younger in the dimness. I'm making a fool of myself. I'm desperate. That is my excuse for being here, acceptable or not.

"Not a cheerful place," he says. I feel his eyes on my face, then my neck. They stop at the small, open triangle of my suit jacket. The intensity of his stare makes me smile. He is nearsighted. Karl Müller is almost handsome if one keeps looking at him, the kind of man a woman falls in love with only after repeated meetings, as she starts to depend on his solemnity, his sameness.

"Put your glasses on," I say. He obeys. I slowly unpin the handkerchief and offer it to him. In his large hand, it looks as fragile as a snowflake.

"Alinka, I have a suite on the fourth floor. It has a nice view of the castle."

Afterward, I tell him I want my children in Switzerland. He says he can't help me. I am still Alinka.

CAMBRIDGE, MASSACHUSETTS—APRIL 1956

On a hazy August day, Rudi and Kay used up a month's worth of gas coupons to take us to the Prague Station. On the way, Kay insisted we stop at the gothic Bridge Tower on the eastern side of the Charles Bridge to give Andy and me a last look at the Malá Strana—Little Quarter—where we had lived for two years. Kay took a photo that she sent us in Rome, which we lost.

My eyes followed the bridge with its double row of coal-blackened statues, Kampa Park, the green cupola of Saint Nicholas. Atop the winding steep streets, the spread of Hradčany Castle with the sharp steeple of St. Vitus Cathedral. I waved goodbye to Prague, which in the haze looked like an old print that needed dusting, and turned my mind and heart to Rome and Papa.

It is Sunday afternoon in Rome, and I call the international operator, ask to be put through on the off chance that Claire is home and Andy has gone to a soccer game or a movie or anywhere.

"You're still at it, aren't you?" Andy says as soon as he hears my hello. The words echo, a recurring problem with transatlantic calls. I have to wait to answer him.

"Still happily pregnant, yes."

"That's not what I meant."

"I know it isn't, but I don't understand why my wanting to find out more about Mama gets you so riled up."

"Why?" He starts laughing. "At times you can be incredibly self-absorbed."

It's an accusation I used to level at him when we were younger. "I don't get it," I say.

"If Mama is still alive, and I don't for one second believe she is, but *if* she is, it means she doesn't want to see us. She's wiped us out of her life. We're nothing to her. So leave her alone. Leave me alone. And what about Claire? Think of what it would do to her to discover her mother just walked away and forgot all about her. God, Susie, please! We've licked our wounds and we're doing fine now."

"What if Mama was hurt and suffered from amnesia?"

"What if she's living with someone and has five kids?"

"She's our mother."

"She was our mother. I loved her just as much as you did, Susie, but she's gone. One way or another we've lost her. Make peace with that."

"I can't. Let me talk to Claire."

"*Ciao sorella americana,*" Claire says in a cheerful voice. It's her usual greeting before switching to her accented English. "I received a *dieci* in my Latin exam this week." I congratulate her on getting the highest mark.

"I didn't ask how you feel about my looking into Mama's death," I add. "I was only thinking of myself. I'm sorry." Mama was always a silent presence in our lives, not mentioned. Her picture, a smiling closeup taken before the war, presided over our sleep from each of our night tables.

"*Tu ne quaesieris—scire nefas,*" she quotes, "*quem mihi, quem tibi finem di dederint*. That is Horace in case you have forgotten."

"Latin was too long ago." I wonder if she's stalling in hopes that Andy will leave the room, or if she's willfully ignoring what I've just said.

"Horace is saying, 'Don't ask—it is forbidden to know—what final fate the gods have given to me and you.' Which applies to Mama, too. Maybe Horace is right. Maybe we are not supposed to know, but you will go ahead anyway." She waits for me to contradict her. When I don't, she adds, "I am not sure I want you to tell me what you find out. I try not to think about her a lot, and I do not know how I feel about her dying or her leaving us. Maybe I will think about it and write to you. Maybe not. Look, there is no Elvis here yet, so send me all of his 45s. Please?"

"They're on the way. I love you and I'm very proud of you." I can't stop myself from adding, "I know you can't talk right now, but what you found in Papa's papers, how important is it?"

"Important to me, probably not to you. Do not forget Elvis, please."

I tell her I'll call tomorrow, between nine and ten Rome time.

FIVE

ROME, ITALY—SEPTEMBER 1942

Susie, Claire, and I are taking our early morning walk while Andy sleeps in the *pensione*. My eyes greet a blue sail of sky, warm colors, round shapes. A golden light softens my anger. I'd forgotten the beauty of this city, how majestic is its sprawl. History laid out like an extravagant blanket.

"We've walked into a postcard," I tell Susie. The same one I sent to my parents on my honeymoon, looking at the point where the Tiber curves sharply to the left on its way to the Ghetto, the Tiberina Island, and Trastevere on the other bank. Up in the distance, the umbrella pines of the Janiculum Hill where, years before, I took Andy and Susie to watch puppet shows on Sunday mornings.

The next bridge over, arched low over the river, leads to the dark brick of the Hospital of the Holy Spirit, barely visible behind the sycamores. "A Renaissance pope installed a lazy susan in one of the windows," I tell Susie. "For the children no one wants." Instead of throwing them in the river.

At the end of our bridge, Castel Sant'Angelo—Hadrian's tomb turned into a fortress for the popes—looks like a hazelnut cake, its sword-wielding angel at the top an elaborate decoration.

We cross the Sant'Angelo Bridge, under the gaze of Bernini's sugar-white marble angels, so graceful they look weightless, a far cry from the soot-blackened statues of the Charles Bridge in Prague. The postcard changes. Where I remember shops and houses, I see the beginning of a wide excavated strip of dirt. Mussolini is building a road, Via della Conciliazione, leading straight to Saint Peter's. Against the sky, the main cupola of Saint Peter's is pink with morning sun. A glorious site which prompts me to ask Susie, "Are you happy we're here?"

"When Papa comes," she answers with a scowl. She knows she's hurting me. She also knows I always want the truth.

Marco is already here. He waits for me on street corners. Watches me from windows. I can smell him in the breeze that comes in at night from the sea. Wherever I go, Marco sticks to my skin like dried sweat. Rome belongs to him. "I'm sorry, sweetie, but let's try to make the best of it." She slips away from my embrace and stares down at the Tiber, arms folded over the parapet.

I join her and look down at the brown sluggish water ambling underneath us, in no seeming hurry to get out to the open sea. On the near bank a woman appears from underneath the bridge dragging a branch twice her size. She picks up an ax and starts hacking. I watch the power of her strokes, feel them echo in my chest. The branch is quickly reduced to short logs. I applaud loudly and yell down, "Bravo!" She looks up. A skinny woman with big breasts popping out of a purple sweater and long, shapely legs that end in red socks and wedgies. She waves to us to come down, points at the logs, the empty wheel barrow at the foot of the long flight of stairs.

"She's going to whack us too," Susie says.

"She needs help. Watch Claire." I run to the end of the bridge. Down the many stairs, I don't lose sight of Susie or Claire's pram. I keep watch as I help the woman load the logs into her wheelbarrow. I'm the one Susie blames for everything. How will I ever win her back?

"Your kids?" the woman asks. I nod. "Thanks," she says. Slowly we carry the load up the steps. Susie meets us at the top with Claire. Her scowl has deepened. The woman first takes a peek at Claire, who's fast asleep. "Pretty," she says, then pats Susie's head, which makes matters worse.

"Thanks for lending me your mother. I'm Ersilia, the queen of the black market—eggs, butter, oil, flour made with real wheat—whatever you need." She is somewhere in her forties, with fat cheeks, large, bulging brown eyes curtained by mascara, and long crinkly black hair. "What's your name?" she asks Susie, who doesn't answer.

"First time around I'll give you a discount for helping me out," Ersilia says, looking at me now. "You'll find me just down the street, in Via Tor di Nona, under the Madonna. Ciao, Rossa. Wartime is woman's time, don't you forget it."

CAMBRIDGE, MASSACHUSETTS—APRIL 1956

Sunday night. I pace the floor downstairs, spooning into a pint of coffee ice cream.

One morning in the pensione, after we'd been in Rome only a few weeks, Mama was taking Claire out and not coming back until lunchtime. I wanted to know where she was going.

"To get us out of here."

"Why can't I come too?"

"Keep your brother company. No going out on the street, both of you."

As soon as she left, I woke Andy up. "Mama's gone to find an apartment and we're not supposed to go out."

"No, the police."

"What police? What did she do?"

Andy turned over and curled his back at me. I shook him again. "I don't believe you. How do you know?"

"She asked the Black Spider the address for police headquarters."

"Why does she want the police?"

"To lock you up. I'm going back to sleep."

Andy was playing one of his tricks on me. Mama didn't like the owner of the pensione. She wore the same smelly black dress every day and kept crossing herself whenever she ran into us. Mama wouldn't ask her the time of day. No, Mama was getting us out of this ugly pensione, that's what she was doing.

I let Andy sleep and went looking for the Black Spider for confirmation.

"That's right, she's gone to police headquarters. She's gonna ask them for an exit visa. And good riddance, I say. We're at war with you people. If I didn't need the money . . ."—she crossed herself—"well, never mind, it's not your fault."

I waited in the sitting room, my heart numbed by the thought we were going away again, probably as far from Papa as Mama could manage.

When Mama came home, she treated us to three courses in a nearby trattoria. Andy asked if we were going to Switzerland.

"We're staying right here."

"Then what are we celebrating?"

"You. My beautiful children."

ROME, ITALY—SEPTEMBER 1942

My beautiful children. I can't take them out of the country without Marco's permission. He warned me, even sent me a draft of a letter he was going to send to the Rome Questura. I didn't believe him capable of such cruelty. I was wrong, a kind police sergeant informed me this morning. I threw out Marco's draft, but the words have stayed.

> As I am a diplomat serving our country in Croatia and cannot be on hand to look after my family, I ask for your kind courtesy in making certain that my wife does not take my children out of the country. They are: Andrea, born July 11, 1928, Susanna, born March 21, 1930, and Chiara, born June 10, 1942. It is my right as an Italian father to make this request.

After our restaurant lunch, I walk with the children to the Vatican. We stand in the large square and I let the majesty of the sight douse my anger. Rome is safe, Giorgio said. Inviolable. Protected by God. The Vatican, the Pope, the history of this city will keep Allied bombers away. I will hold that thought tight to my heart.

CAMBRIDGE, MASSACHUSETTS—APRIL 1956

Mama refused to move into the apartment in Parioli that Papa's friends had found for us and, instead, rented a two-bedroom, furnished apartment just behind the café-lined Via Veneto. She liked the name of the street, Via Aurora—Dawn Street—and the place was cheap, but what had convinced her was the grand piano in the landlady's apartment on the floor above us. Signora Cortini loved music. She was only too happy to have a budding violinist practice in her home.

Our apartment was dark, cold, and on two floors. What Signora Cortini called the ground floor was actually a basement with grated windows that could only be reached by standing on a chair. The upstairs was cheerier, with two bedrooms facing the street and overlooking a narrow, gravelly garden filled with stray cats. Mama, Claire, and I slept together in the master bedroom. Lucky Andy had a bedroom to himself.

"The coffin," Andy dubbed the place. Mama told us to think of it as a ship. She wanted us to believe we were on a journey to a wonderful place—Switzerland, then America. She had unpacked only a few of our clothes. The rest stayed in the trunks in our bedroom.

Signora Cortini's grand piano didn't entice Andy to practice, no matter how much Mama pleaded or played for him. "I know my music by heart. Don't worry."

One Monday, at the end of September, Mama and he took the bus to the Conservatory of Santa Cecilia in the heart of Old Rome while Claire and I waited upstairs in Signora Cortini's apartment.

ROME, ITALY—SEPTEMBER 28, 1942

It's lunchtime. Susie and I are eating yesterday's bread, which I've softened with water, a thin layer of precious olive oil, and the last of the tomatoes. Tonight we're going to celebrate with a chicken. It's Andy's big day. This morning I left him at the conservatory, surrounded by a crowd of nervous applicants. Andy said he was calm. Lately he's taken to hiding himself behind a façade I can't penetrate. I wonder if I'm losing the ability to know my children. I am so involved with my own misery.

The first exam was the violin-playing one, followed by a sight-reading exam, then one on his general knowledge of music. I'm to pick him up at four o'clock.

Andy walks in as I'm clearing the kitchen table.

"I flunked the first exam." His expression betrays no emotion.

91

"Oh, honey, I'm so sorry." My arms ache to hold him. "You're so good. What happened? Did they ask for a piece you didn't know?"

"I'm hungry," he says.

I go weak with sadness. Only for a minute or two. Then I fetch my jacket and my hat and grab Andy's arm. I'm taking him straight back to the conservatory to talk to the professors. They have to know about the upheaval in our family—a new baby, a new city, a new home, his father far away. "They have to give you another chance."

"I flunked on purpose."

Everything in me stops, even my heart, I think. "Why? Tell me why."

"I don't want to play anymore."

"I don't believe you. Don't say that!" I want to shake him, slap sense into him, I want to cover him in kisses and tell him how sorry I am for what we've become.

Susie tugs at his arm, big fat tears dropping from her eyes. "Andy, you've got to try again. Please. Do it for me. You're going to be the next Jascha Heifetz, the best ever. Remember? Do it for Papa. He's going to be furious."

"I don't care," Andy says. "Music is useless. If I play or don't play changes nothing. Music changes nothing."

"What do you want changed, Andy? If it's in my power to change it, I will. Just tell me, Andy." Do I mean that? If he asks me to take Marco back, will I? Be the good self-sacrificing mother?

"Nothing. There's nothing to change."

I feel only relief, which fills me with a foul-smelling shame.

ROME, ITALY—NOVEMBER 7, 1942

The Amati has been lying in the darkness of my trunk for over a month. The day of the failed exam I told Andy it was up to him to write to his father and explain. He said he would. A week went by, two weeks and no thunder and lightning came from Croatia. In the children's next weekly letter I added a postscript informing Marco of Andy's decision. They were the only words I have written to him since we arrived in Rome.

Five days ago Marco made a rare phone call to the landlady; we have no telephone. Susie raced up the stairs. Andy took his time. I stayed downstairs.

"Papa is really mad," Susie reported afterward. "I could hear him yelling, then Andy told him, 'You can't make me,' and hung up."

This morning I picked up a letter at Palazzo Chigi, the Foreign Ministry, in which Marco blames himself for not being there to guide Andy, blames the war for having disrupted our lives. He writes that he has reminded Andy that in Rome he is *il capo famiglia*–the head of the family. "Watch out for our women." He adds that he's coming home for Christmas.

A gust of dread strikes my heart.

CAMBRIDGE, MASSACHUSETTS—APRIL, 1956

In October, Mama reluctantly let me go to the Cabrini Sister's school where Papa had enrolled me while we were still with the Vlaseks in Mcely. "Don't let them brainwash you," she whispered on our first visit, after seeing the other students genuflect in front of the statue of the Virgin Mary.

"We'll take good care of her," Madre Giovanna, the headmistress, said under the life-sized crucifix in the hallway.

Mama laid out conditions. "No corporal punishment, I won't stand for it. No telling my daughter that if she looks in the mirror, she'll see the devil. No lies about her hand falling off if she touches herself"—I interrupted with a coughing fit.

"You can walk out any time, Susie," she said while Madre Giovanna fetched a glass of water. "I'll find you another school. You just let me know."

"I want to stay." The school was making me repeat sixth grade because of my weak Italian, but I liked Madre Giovanna's face, as plump and wrinkled as a peeled chestnut, and the garden, hemmed by the boxwood hedges, with its small grotto in one corner from which a gentle Madonna looked over us. I liked all the Cabrini Sisters. Neatly tucked into their long black habits, their faces nesting in ruffled caps tied at the chin with a bow, they padded softly, spoke in low voices, and didn't seem capable of storms of emotion. A school run by the Cabrini Sisters was a bay of calm.

With Claire tied to her chest, Mama took me to school every morning, picked me up at lunchtime. Andy's new school was only a few bus stops away, near Porta Pia, and he was old enough to go by himself. She held my hand during the twenty-minute trip. I would start fidgeting and point to a strangely shaped tree, a pretty hat, a person with a funny walk, any excuse to slip my hand from her grasp. One day I got up my courage and told her I was too old for hand holding. She let my hand go without a word and never tried to hold it again.

It's almost time to call Claire. I'm in the kitchen, sketching the jar of daisies on the table. This morning the quick strokes of the pencil keep me calm, keep the memories coming, keep me awake. The coffee ice cream has long been polished off. My cup of tea is empty. The house is quiet. Too quiet, I realize. The grandfather clock in the hallway isn't releasing its rhythmic tic-toc. David must have forgotten to wind it. Time is standing still, at least in the hallway. My time keeps going backward. Will Claire bring me closer to finding Mama? To knowing what happened?

I look at my wristwatch. Three-thirty in the morning, nine-thirty in Rome. I close the kitchen door and give the international operator Andy's number. Ten minutes later Claire is on the phone. I'm blessed with no echo this time.

"I don't know if this has anything to do with Mama," she says without preamble. "It's just something funny I came across, and I didn't want Andy to find out because you know he's really strict, and going through stuff that's not mine is *verboten*."

I can barely breathe. "What did you find?"

She makes a clucking noise, a sign of annoyance. I'm not supposed to interrupt. I wait, ice-cold water pouring into my veins. She takes a deep breath. "Do you remember that old leather satchel of Papa's? The one that looks like a big doctor's case? It'd be great to use as a school bag, so I took it out of the storage closet when Andy wasn't around, and inside I found Papa's checkbook stubs, years of them. I thumbed through some of them. Boring stuff, but then I noticed he kept giving money to the Sisters of Mary of the Consolation. I didn't know Papa was religious. Did you know? I mean, that tells us something, doesn't it? About Papa. I thought you should know."

"Thank you." I try to keep my deep disappointment out of my voice. "I guess he was religious." Or hedging his bets like the rich of the Renaissance who had chapels frescoed in their name to guarantee their salvation.

"Maybe he sent money in Mama's memory," Claire says. "He loved her so much." She grew up as the light of Papa's eyes, which makes him infallible. She knows nothing of Milena or our forced trip from Prague to Rome.

"Maybe," I say. "Enjoy the satchel. I'm sure Andy will let you keep it. You'll be the envy of your classmates."

"He has to. It's just too neat looking. Please, please, don't forget Elvis. And a Revlon lipstick in frosted pink."

"They'll be in the mail tomorrow. By the way, why aren't you in school today?"

Claire giggles. "I suddenly got this terrible sore throat. How else was I going to talk to you without Big Brother? Tomorrow sore throat will be gone. I'm mailing you the check stubs. They're no help, I know, but they were Papa's, and if Andy or Priscilla finds them, they'll just throw them out. Keep them for me, will you?"

"I will."

"Thanks."

After I say goodbye to my Latin and piano whiz little sister and hang up, I feel hollowed out. I miss her terribly.

Claire, running her fingers across the lace of her blanket, scrunching up her nose when I tickled her feet. I liked to hold her scalp with my hand. She felt like a peach, her fuzz pink in the dappled sunlight. She grew up to have red hair, and I still envy her that link to a mother I still think of as only mine and Andy's.

She was only six when I sailed for the States. When I left her, I was angry, I was unhappy, I was guilty. I never stopped to think what I would lose by leaving. My family. The trivial and grandiose sharing of daily events: gestures of love, frustrations, arguments, joys, sadness, what makes up the fiber of our lives. A loss willed by me. A dumb way to punish myself.

Andy, Claire, and I, we never speak openly of the love we have for each other. Mama took that word away with her. I found it again only when David came into my life. Now, with the baby inside me, I want to shout love across the Atlantic, but I hesitate. I need to find out what happened on that mountain first.

Claire became Mama's still point, her anchor. If she left the apartment, Claire went with her, tied to her chest with a wrap. At home, she carried Claire from room to room in a laundry basket. Sometimes I would wake up and find Mama asleep next to the crib, her head propped on the railing, one hand holding Claire's shoulder or her foot. Andy paid no attention to any of us. He was into boy things—soccer, girls, dirty jokes.

I discovered loneliness. The girls at school came from the best Roman families and, despite the uniforms we wore, they could tell I did not belong in their league. I was too old to be in sixth grade, too gawky, too foreign. Not pretty enough. My nemesis was Luisa. She was always smirking about her daddy, a Fascist Party leader, how he knew Mussolini personally, how Il Duce had once tweaked her cheek and told her she was "*molto bella*."

I boasted back. My father was a friend of Reinhard Heydrich. I had shown Heydrich my drawings, and he had told me I would be a great artist one day.

"Who is Heydrich?" Luisa asked.

Once, when I got out of school late one day, close to Christmas time, I found Mama talking to Luisa at the bottom of the hill. Luisa kissed me on both cheeks and whispered, "You little spy, I didn't know your mother was American."

"You little Judas," I whispered back.

"Why did you talk to her, Mama?" I demanded once we got on the streetcar.

"What's wrong? She introduced herself as your friend."

"I hate Luisa! Never speak to her again!"

"I told her I was happy you had a friend."

"Now she knows you're American!" We rode home in silence.

I never told anyone about Luisa's Christmas present. I found it in my coat pocket the last day of school—an anonymous printed note on which was written a Fascist order that appeared on posters all over Rome. *Taci, il nemico ti ascolta!* Be silent, the enemy is listening.

I dreamt of revenge, but I was too scared to act. Luisa would tell her Fascist Party leader father, so much more important than my own father who wasn't there to protect us anyway. We would all end up in jail.

During those first months, Papa sent old friends, cousins, colleagues from the Foreign Ministry, people Mama knew from her last stay in Rome. "Do you need anything?" "Can we be of help?" "Dinner?" "Lunch?" "A Sunday outing in the country with the children?" She talked to them through the spokes of the garden gate. "No, thank you, we need nothing." How I resented that "we."

Andy won't listen to anything I say. He stays out late after school, smoking on the street corner, playing soccer in the park with boys he refuses to let me meet. Susie blames me for Papa being gone, for being American, for being helpless. My children are helpless too, and as scared as I am. They show their fear with anger. I become frantic, a mouse on a treadmill. Run, run, run. Spin spin spin. For which I am grateful. It stops me from thinking, from despairing.

By seven o'clock on weekday mornings I'm on line at the *latteria* around the corner for milk that isn't always available. If Cesare, the shop owner, feels generous, he slips hard-to-find goat's milk into my shopping bag for Claire. My breasts are as dried up as my heart. Powdered milk is made by Nestlé, a Swiss firm, and is almost impossible to find. Goat's milk is easier on the digestion, according to Signora Cortini and Cesare. More nutritious, ideal for babies.

After the latteria, another long line at the baker for the day's bread, a dark hard bread that tastes like ground-up gravel. Then back home, to feed Claire, make sure Andy and Susie are up and dressed, prepare their breakfast.

Then it's off to school with Susie—Andy goes on his own. When I come back, if it's a Monday or a Wednesday, I line up again, this time to wait for the butcher, a big oaf of a man who tells lewd jokes and hands the best cut of meat to whoever laughs the loudest. When it's my turn, I hand over the list Susie has written out for me so that no one will hear my American accent: a hen for broth, rump meat for stews. Only the cheapest meat because I'm fattening the hem of our bedroom curtains with pink sheets of lira Marco sends me every month. Our getaway, impossible as it is, is never far from my mind.

On the grocer's line I pass the time listening to gossip and household tips. Sauté onions in water when there's no oil; make meat balls with spleen and lots of bread crumbs, cut tripe into very thin strips, bury them in a thick tomato sauce, and pass them off to your children as pasta. If luck is on your side and you have a ham, use the fat to make soap. Your laundry will stink, but at least it's clean.

I listen. My mouth stays shut.

At lunchtime I pick up Susie from school at the streetcar stop, making sure I arrive late, when all the girls have already gone home with their mothers or maids so that Susie won't be ashamed of me.

Cooking gas is rationed and comes only at allotted times—six to eight a.m., noon to three p.m., seven to nine p.m. Sometimes it hiccups on and off. Turning the corner into Via Aurora, often we see women leaning out their windows, consulting with neighbors in other buildings. "You too! Holy Mary, how are we supposed to eat?" No hot lunch that day.

From the three-course, midday *pranzo* that Marco always insisted on, I've switched to sandwiches, American style. Hard sheep's cheese or thin slices of mortadella with great big rounds of fat Susie will carefully pick off. At night I make soup—potato, cabbage, dandelion, bread soup, chicken feet soup. Always soup, garnished with the rounds of fat Susie left on her plate at lunch. Food rations are meager, and I'm a lousy cook.

Gina, the *portiera*, a beak-nosed Neapolitan widow, washes our sheets once a week, a job I gave her after Signora Cortini warned me to keep her on my good side. She might be a spy like so many other portieras eager to denounce any suspicious activity to the Fascist police in exchange for a few lira. Spy or not, I'm glad to hand over our pile of dirty sheets. It's the one job I take no pride in. The rest of the laundry I wash in the kitchen sink. Andy complains about having to dodge the dangling wet wash in the bathroom, but the garden is too public a place for me.

Some afternoons, after Signora Cortini has taken her nap, she lets me play on her piano. I play Andy's music, praying he hears me, praying those familiar notes, despite my awkward playing, will tempt him to pick up his violin again. If nothing else, my efforts keep our landlady happy.

When I lie in bed at night, exhausted, I tell myself I'm filled with fervor. With purpose. I am out to prove how strong I am, how virtuous, an exemplary mother who will fill my children's hearts with love for me. Spin, spin. Run, run. Going nowhere. Staying sane.

Every few weeks I put Claire in her pram and walk all the way to Tor di Nona, by the river, to visit Ersilia. I come back with black-market goodies—once a hunk of Parmesan, another time two eggs or a ream of writing paper. Also some news—a shipment of canned tomatoes arrived at the Fascist Commissary filled with sand; the "campaign for purity" has decreed that women could no longer wear slacks in public; the Americans are sinking the Japanese navy. When I don't want to spend any money, I go just to say hello, to bask in her pluck.

Via Tor di Nona is a narrow, cobblestoned street, sunk twenty-five feet below the Lungotevere road, making it ideal for illicit activities. Ersilia's post is under the canopied fresco of the Madonna.

Susie came along this afternoon. Ersilia was standing in her wedgies, signature red socks and a mangy orange fox coat, rolling a cigarette. The faded ocher walls around her were covered with black scrawls. TERESA—TI AMO DA MORIRE! I love you to death! A MORTE I NEMICI DELLA PATRIA! Death to the enemies of the Fatherland. QUI SI MUORE DI FAME! We're starving here! Flowers that Ersilia said are caper plants grow out of the cracks between the letters.

"They live on nothing, just like me. Ehi!" She fixed her mascara-ringed eyes on Susie as she lit her cigarette. "You look like a mouse fished out of the Tiber." She kissed Susie's cheeks, then rubbed the lipstick marks she'd left with her thumbs. "That's more like it." She dug a compact out of her skirt pocket to show her.

Susie preened. It was the first smile I'd seen on her in a long time.

"You look pretty, sweetie."

"Hey, Rossa,"—Ersilia calls me that because of my red hair— "What's it going to be today? I can sell you two cans of tomatoes that one of my boyfriends swiped from a truck. Delicious San Marzano from Naples, on their way to feed some fat Fascist."

"Not today."

"Always saving, eh? For what? Tomorrow some Fascist pig doesn't like you and it's ciao ciao."

"*Ehi*, Ersì," a man called out from the Lungotevere above. "How much to get you on your back these days?"

"Let's go," I told Susie. Her gaze was aimed at the man, her eyes wide with curiosity. "Come, Susie,"

Ersilia clasped my arm to stop me, at the same time yelling "*Vaffanculo!*" at the man. "*Vaffanculo* you, your father *and* your grandfather!" The man laughed and walked away.

"Don't get the wrong idea, Rossa. Men don't pick me. I pick them, and your kid can use finding out what those nuns aren't telling her. The more she knows, the better prepared she is."

"She's only twelve," I protested.

Ersilia nudged Susie with her elbow, winked at her. To my surprise, Susie winked back. They both laughed, and I felt my cheeks get hot. I should have been angry. Instead I was embarrassed for Susie and envious of Ersilia.

"Where do you get the courage to yell back?" I asked her. "I'm too scared to speak even."

"Listen, Rossa, deaf and dumb keeps you alive. As the Neapolitans say, *Guarde e tace si vuò campá felice e npace.*" If you want to be happy and live in peace, look and shut up. "Nando's a friend, a poor joker. Yeah, we're all angry as hell, and we'd like nothing better than fighting back."

"Yes, that's exactly it. To feel alive again. To feel I count, to feel I have some say in my own life."

"Sure, fight back, but what, who? The whole Italian army, the Nazis?"

My husband, I would have told her if Susie hadn't been standing right there.

"I've got a better idea." Ersilia whistled the first few bars of the royal anthem. A boy, six-or seven-years-old, came sliding from around the corner. "Get me one red shoe. The way to fight is to turn this shit war to your advantage."

The boy came back with the "red shoe"—a half-kilo can of tomatoes wrapped in newspaper. "I'll give you a can for free. In exchange you spread the word around with your chi-chi friends about your friend Ersilia. How I got the best prices." Ersilia wanted telephone numbers. She would call up and mention a little yellow hat. That meant she had butter. A sapphire blue jacket meant sugar; a bunch of daisies—eggs; white wool—lard. She offered me ten percent of what she sold.

I told her I didn't know anyone except Signora Cortini.

"No friends?"

"You."

Ersilia grinned and squeezed her breasts, covered in yellow fuzzy wool that made me think of tennis balls. "I like you too. Take the tomatoes. Your kids will love 'em." She hid the can in Claire's pram and refused payment. "Like I told you, Rossa. Wartime is woman's time."

ROME, ITALY—NOVEMBER 19, 1942

We're going to celebrate Thanksgiving with roast chicken, mashed potatoes, and onions. I've invited Signora Cortini to share the meal with us. She's a large woman with a florid chest, who spends her days seated by a shuttered window in her living room. Under a heavy armor of opinion, she's kind.

It's the first time I've invited her to share a meal with us. She walks through the living room slowly, cane in one hand, pocketbook in the other, straightening the antimacassars on the armchairs, nodding approval at the cleanliness of the apartment. Without being asked, she sits herself down at the head of the table in the tiny dining room just off the kitchen. It's the seat closest to Claire in her pram. Signora Cortini leans over, clasps one of Claire's kicking feet, purses her lips and coos like a love-sick pigeon. I catch Andy and Susie exchanging glances. Signora Cortini has just gotten a new name.

Mrs. Pigeon, unaware of her new identity, plucks English tea and marmalade from her purse. She has saved them from before the war, she says. "In Italy we don't give thanks before a meal, and these days we have nothing to thank anyone for anyway, but we might as well have a civil meal."

We eat the marmalade with the chicken, in lieu of cranberry sauce, and all of us think it's delicious.

The mailman comes while we're sucking on the chicken bones. He rings his bicycle bell to let Gina the portiera know he has mail for the building. A few minutes later our doorbell rings. Susie and Andy jump up and run, trying to get there first.

"Be careful," I call out. I'm sure they're hoping the letter is for Mrs. Pigeon. Every few months she receives an airmail letter with no visible return address that Gina delivers to her door. Because of the mysterious letters, Andy has decided Mrs. Pigeon is a spy.

"It's from Kay," Susie yells. She runs back, smells the letter, then drops it on the table. "Read it now. Out loud. Please."

"Can I have the stamp, Mama?" Andy asks. "Can I have your stamps, Signora Cortini?"

I gaze at the letter and feel an ache in my chest. I miss Kay. I miss Rudi, Peter, the garden, Old Hus. I miss what was.

"Please, Mama."

I put the letter in my pocket. "A letter from Kay is like a maraschino cherry. It should be eaten last, when there's nothing else." In private.

Mrs. Pigeon doesn't budge. She bounces Claire on her knee while we clear the table, gives her her bottle while I wash the dishes and Susie dries. She drinks endless cups of tea. "So much better than that so-called coffee they have the gall to sell us these days," she announces. I don't care. Kay's letter looms. Finally, at five o'clock, Gina rings the bell and announces it's time for Mrs. Pigeon's weekly injection.

I always read Kay's long letters out loud, skipping the bits I don't want the children to hear. During our first two months in Rome, a family of bull frogs made a home under the water faucet by the rose bushes; during one of his wanderings, Old Hus brought home a stray mutt, which they'd adopted; Rudi was building a new picnic table for next summer.

This time the letter is short. I read all of it out loud.

"The Gestapo has confiscated our home. We were allowed to take only our clothes, our pots and pans and Old Hus. We've moved in with the village carpenter and his family while Dr. Paroch's house stays empty. We still have no news of his wife and daughter.

"Don't worry about us. We're hardy folk and will be fine. How are you and the children? Are you any happier? Are your headaches gone? Please note our change of address. Write soon. Love always, Kay."

It isn't that bad, I tell myself. At least they still have somewhere to live.

"Will they get their house back?" Susie asks.

"Sure. After the Allies defeat the Germans." Kay and Rudi and Old Hus, they're alive.

"What if the Allies don't win?" Andy asks.

"Of course they'll win, but be careful not to say that outside these walls."

Susie tugs the sleeve of my sweater. "If they do, what will happen to Papa?"

"He'll be fine," Andy answers. "He's got an American wife."

I manage to laugh. "Ah, I'm finally useful, I see." Marco doesn't need me. He'll always land on his feet.

CAMBRIDGE, MASSACHUSETTS—APRIL 1956

I couldn't stand it that Mama never mentioned Papa. She didn't even have his picture on her night table. One time, when we were in our beds with the light turned out, I got up the courage to ask, "Don't you miss Papa?" She didn't answer me, so I left my bed and got into hers, a double bed where I wanted Papa to be, with all of us.

"Mama?"

"I'm sleepy, what is it?"

"When Papa comes we can move my bed into Andy's room and Claire can sleep with us too. That's what we'll do."

She wrapped her arms tightly across my shoulders. I could feel her breasts squashed on my back, her chin digging into the top of my head. I felt I was in a vise, hating her and yet loving her.

"I see you watching me, Susie. You watch everybody and everything. My little witness, taking in all events, good and bad, not quite knowing what to do with what you see. I'm sorry you see so much, baby. I wish I could erase the soldiers; I wish I could give you a street at night lit up like a birthday cake. So many things to wish for my children. No war, no hate. Safety. A happy family. Roasting marshmallows on the beach. Wasn't that fun, Chipmunk?"

"Let Papa stay. He can sleep in my bed. I'll sleep on the sofa downstairs. Please, Mama."

She let me go and got out of bed. Claire's rattle fell to the floor as she picked her up. I heard the slide of Mama's bare feet across the floor, her nightgown swishing as she danced Claire around the room.

In the morning, while she was heating our *caffellatte*, Mama gave me her answer. "Your father will stay in a hotel."

SIX

ROME, ITALY—DECEMBER 5, 1942

The Allies bombed Naples yesterday," the *dottore* from the second floor tells me as I walk into the palazzo. Before his words sink in, I hear screaming. "*Pieruccio è morto!*" Gina is running up the stairs. "*Pieruccio è morto!*" she yells over and over again. "They hit the center," a woman says. A cluster of tenants is gathered at the foot of the stairs, watching Gina, running commentary. "Pieruccio's her brother." "Poor woman." "Her nephew sent a telegram." "Such a tragedy."

I drop my shopping and start running up the stairs. "It's not your fault, signora," someone yells after me. Gina continues to climb, to scream. "Thousands dead. No one sounded the alarm!" The Allies had come in waves—early in the morning, again in the afternoon. The last time at sunset.

I yell at a pair of women watching from their floor landing to stop Gina.

"There's nothing in the newspapers," one of them says as I run past them.

The engineer on the third floor opens his door, a fat man with long side hair that he combs over his bald pate. "*Dio santo*, what is the commotion?"

I dodge his outstretched arm and run up another flight. "Gina! Wait!"

She stops on the top floor, heaving, head twisting from side to side. Her glasses fall off her nose. I'm only a few steps behind her now. She leans over the railing. I lunge and grab hold of her waist. Gina kicks me, shoves her elbows in my face. I hold on and shout for help.

The engineer finally reaches us. He slaps Gina across both cheeks, then pushes a shoulder under her armpit and lifts her off the floor.

"Skulls squashed open like pumpkins," Gina cries out. "His socks, his shoes gone, stolen!" Holding her between us, we walk her down the four flights of stairs.

On the first floor landing, Mrs. Pigeon makes Gina drink a glass of water. "Come and lie down."

"*A casa. A casa mia.*" Gina wants to go to her small apartment below the guard room of the palazzo.

Her bedroom only has space for a cot and a bedside table. The engineer excuses himself—there isn't room for him. I lower her onto the bed, unbutton her sweater, her skirt, ease the bra straps from her shoulders. When I start to unlace her shoes, Gina shoves her feet, shoes still on, under the covers. "The dead are buried without shoes." She clutches my arm. "Please tell them,"—I have to lean down to hear her—"tell your people to stop killing us."

I stroke her hands clutching the blanket. "I wish I could tell them to stop, Gina. I wish it were in my power to stop the war. I'm sorry for your brother." I'm sorry for all the dead, the maimed, the homeless. At night, in the dark, I feel my heart trying to expand to take them all in, but I always come back to my children, to my anger, my self-absorption. "Is there anything I can get you?" Gina waves me away.

At the door of the guardroom, Signora Calabresi, a handsome, voluptuous woman in her thirties with her war widow's white star always prominent on her chest, hands me my shopping with a shrug. "Americans, Italians, we're all victims here. Thanks for helping Gina." We have passed each other countless times in the entrance, on the street. This is the first time she has spoken to me. "Our opinions are safe with Gina, you know. She keeps her mouth shut."

I want to trust everyone, Gina, this woman, Mrs. Pigeon, but I seem to have lost the ability to distinguish the sun from the shade. I fear whatever move I make, I'll find myself locked in a dark place, unable to get out. "Thank you, signora." I take my shopping and let myself into my strip of garden. Once inside the apartment, my knees give way and I lean against the door. Gina's screams are echoing in my chest now. Naples yesterday? What city today? And tomorrow? And the day after. My people killing civilians.

Behind my closed eyes Andy's severed leg appears. Susie's nail-bitten fingers still holding on to a colored pencil. Claire's head crushed by a piece of wall. I quickly open my eyes wide and stare at Susie's watercolor of lemons on the wall.

How can one human being do this—fly a plane and release death as if it were a bodily function? How does one live after that? Won't they all end up in looney bins?

CAMBRIDGE, MASSACHUSETTS—APRIL 1956

I have barely started on the twentieth century and I have only four classes left to teach before exam time. My course is billed as an overview of the history of art from ancient times to now. An overview from the height of a whizzing plane, in my opinion. I worry that my students will walk away with only small window views of dots of color rushing past them on the earth below. I've done my best, and I'm glad the semester will soon be over. My back hurts, my legs ache. This morning I follow my twenty-five-week-old belly and gladly rest on a chair to one side of the screen.

I start the class with slides of Matisse and Chagall—universally loved. Duchamp leaves them confused, de Chirico indifferent. I don't know if they "get" Picasso or if it's only his genius reputation that leaves them with envious awe. I tell my students, mostly freshmen, to forget for now the history and the theories I've been trying to fill their heads with.

"Put aside your assumptions. Look at the painting with clean eyes. Then let yourself feel."

Then I flash *Guernica* on the screen. I keep the painting before their eyes for a good minute or two, without saying a word. They were just born at the end of the Spanish Civil War, just toddlers during World War II. I want that devastating image of war to become indelible in their brains and their hearts.

On the far right, the figure with gaping mouth and arms outstretched to heaven. That's Gina, our portiera, screaming that the Allies bombed Naples and killed her brother. She built a shrine to him in the cubbyhole where she sat most of the day, keeping guard. His photo, a rosary, fresh flowers once a week.

Tonight in bed I link my legs with David's. "I miss you."

"Me too." He kisses my ear. "Still calling up all those memories?" In the past few weeks he's been too busy writing his paper to listen.

"They've gone on without you."

"I'm sorry I left you alone."

"But I haven't been alone. The more I remember, the closer I get to Mama. I hear her in my head and I'm convinced she hears me too, and our voices are blending together, becoming one voice. I know that doesn't make any sense, but that's what it feels like." I reach for David's hand. "I'm not going crazy, am I?"

"No, my love." David holds me, his cheek against mine. "It only means your mother is inside you."

"Papa said I sound just like her. I don't know if that hurt him or pleased him."

"Both, would be my guess. Have his check stubs arrived?"

"Not yet." We hold each other in silence and I listen to the cadence of David's breaths to lull myself to sleep, but scenes swirl in my head again. Unwanted, this time. Gina trying to throw herself down the stairwell, Mama saving her. Wetting my bed that night. Mama blamed the Manchurian warrior statue guarding the bathroom door and washed the sheet herself, saying Gina needed rest. I thought it was because she too was ashamed of me. She put an empty stew pot under my bed, and Andy wrapped the warrior with a sheet and topped him off with Mama's ugliest hat. I never had to use the stew pot.

A few days later, two hours before dawn, the air raid alarm sounded. It wasn't the first time, but after the Naples bombing, it was a lot scarier. Mama tugged blankets from the bed, we put on socks, shoes, and a coat over our bathrobes, grabbed our gas masks. Andy carried Claire, who cried louder than the alarm. I ran to the kitchen to get her milk and a bottle of water. Mama gathered matches, candles, and what was left of the bread.

For the first time, the stairs to the basement were crammed with the palazzo's tenants. Only Gina and Mrs. Pigeon were missing. *Il dottore* from the second floor tried to keep us calm in a high fluttery voice. "The planes do a lot of growling, then they fly off with their tail between their legs. This is my second great war, I should know." *Il dottore*, in his nineties, liked to remind everyone that he was the oldest person in the palazzo. It gave him authority, like the *Dott.* he had engraved on the bronze plaque on his apartment door, which Mrs. Pigeon claimed he didn't deserve since he wasn't a medical doctor and didn't have a university degree. "Rome has the Pope!" *il dottore* proclaimed. "God protects his own!"

We spread out in the big coal room, now empty of coal and washed clean by Gina. Andy ran to secure a corner—corners were safer—and spread out our blankets. Mama fed Claire to keep her quiet. I sat, leaning against the wall, with my hand in my coat pocket where I kept my rosary. The nuns had convinced me that prayer helped. *Il dottore*'s daughter said her prayers out loud.

"Stop praying," the old man said. "I'm not dead yet."

The war widow, who was childless, turned out the light to "let the children sleep," and lay down next to the fat engineer, who had a steady paycheck working at city hall and was the only bachelor in the palazzo. When many of us lighted candles, the ceiling danced with flickering haloes of light. Would the ceiling hold if a bomb fell? I Hail Mary'd myself into a stupor.

We couldn't hear any planes. The widow told us to sleep, that time passed faster if we slept. *Il dottore*, crouched at my feet, snuffed his candle out with dry fingers. "When you're that old, it doesn't hurt," Andy whispered in my ear.

I lay down on our blanket, leaning against Mama; she was as hot as a stove. I wanted to fall asleep and wake up back in my bed, with Claire babbling in her crib, and the cats meowing in the garden.

Mama blew out the candle and stroked my hip. "The planes are just passing through," she whispered. "The old man is right." A catch in her voice, then, "Don't be scared, Susie." I could barely hear her. "Rome is inviolable."

"What's inviolable?" I asked.

"Shh, shh," someone said. Andy picked up his blanket and moved away. The cold of the wall seeped through my coat. It made me feel alive. "Shouldn't we get Gina, Mrs. Pigeon?"

"They know nothing will happen. Inviolable means we're safe."

"We're like those Christians who hid in catacombs," I said

The fat engineer laughed. "Let's hope we don't end up as skulls in a crypt."

From the door, a boy's voice announced that he had seen the bombers in the sky.

"Topo, you're a snotty-nosed liar!" my brother yelled. Topo—Mouse—was Ernesto, a skinny nine-year-old boy with a squeaky voice and beady eyes.

Topo ran across the room. "American planes. I saw at least twenty! I did!"

The sound of matches. More candles were lit. Murmurings. Invocations. Questions.

"*Santa Maria Vergine*, pray for us!"

"May God protect us."

"How low were they flying?"

"I don't hear any planes. Do you hear any planes?"

"Shh! Can't we at least sleep? I don't want to know what's going to hit me."

Andy stood up, his shadow looming large on the wall. "You couldn't see a thing, cabbage-brain! It's black out there."

Topo jumped up and down. "I saw them, the white crosses on the wings, I saw them! American planes."

"They were not!" Andy threw himself on Topo. They fell to the floor, Andy pounding on his chest.

"He's too small!" Mama cried out as she scrambled to her feet. She started to run, but caught her ankles in our blanket and fell to her knees. The engineer helped her up and she raced across the room. Claire woke up crying.

"It's a circus in here!" *il dottore* called out. The effort made him break out into a string of whacking coughs. Someone snapped on the light. I saw Mama was pushing Andy out of the room.

Mrs. Pigeon appeared at the door, covered in black Persian lamb and silver fox with a matching hat. In her arms, two more fur coats. "Where are you going? The All Clear hasn't sounded." Mama kept on going.

I handed Claire to Mrs. Pigeon and ran out. Mama was sitting on the basement steps, her face yellow from the one caged light bulb hanging at the top of the stairs.

Andy was hunched against the stair wall, jiggling his leg. "They aren't American planes!"

"The planes are coming!" I yelled. "Get back in the shelter."

"Even if you're right," Mama said, "even if those planes aren't American, it's not a reason to beat up a kid half your size."

Andy slapped her arm. "They're not American!" He ran up the stairs. She stumbled after him. "Come back!" A blast of fresh air hit my face.

Andy had opened the basement door. He was out on the street, under the sky and the bombers.

A siren went off and Mama started screaming. I threw myself up the stairs and hugged her. "It's okay, Mama. It's the All Clear. It's okay."

ROME, ITALY—DECEMBER 12, 1942

It's been raining for days. Since the planes. As if, flying across the sky, they've stripped the clouds bare, left them bleeding. We all have colds. Claire has a fever and screams her lungs out unless one of us carries her round and round the apartment. Mrs. Pigeon is playing Florence Nightingale and has practically moved in. I'm grateful and resentful at the same time. We fortify ourselves with the last tin of her precious English tea.

The doctor came to check on all of us this morning. A thick man with a high voice, he told me not to worry. Children always bounce back. He held my hand, stared at me for a long time. I must have looked a fright.

"How are you holding up, signora?"

I told him I was fine except that sometimes . . . I was too ashamed to go on.

"You are tired? You have headaches?"

"Sometimes I worry too much."

Based on that scanty comment, he decided I'm suffering from nervous exhaustion and prescribed a teaspoon of a white powder three times a day. "Your landlady tells me your husband is coming. His presence will make you feel much better."

Right now I have no idea how I'm going to feel.

ROME, ITALY—DECEMBER 15, 1942

I've been waiting more than half an hour at the *macelleria* when an orderly pushes past me to the front of the line. The butcher hands the orderly a neatly tied package. "The best for the colonel," he says.

"While we stand in line for hours and get the dregs," I protest loudly, my American accent be damned. I turn to the other women in line for support. I get silence as the orderly cradles his package as if it were some championship football and shoulders his way through to the door. The guard, who is always stationed at the butcher shop to make sure the ever-shifting laws for food distribution are followed, shouts, "Make way, make way, or I'll fine every last one of you."

When it's my turn, the butcher fills my order quickly and mutters he's only doing his duty. The guard, bulging with self-importance, watches me as I make my way out of the shop. A woman behind me whispers, "*Brava, ci voleva,*" and for a moment I manage to feel proud of myself until I see that the guard, pad in hand, is following me.

"So feeding our valiant army isn't fair, is that what you think?" It's a cold day and his words come out in small puffs of hot air. On his right hand, the long nail of his little finger curves over the fleshy tip, a tool to pick his ears with. "A starving military cannot protect us from the vile enemy, do you not agree?" He drums his pen against his palm and eyes my package of spleen and soup bones. It isn't much of a bribe. I look behind him at the women who have gathered at the window of the shop to watch. He follows my eyes, and straightens up to his full height. He's barely taller than I am. "Move on. I don't want to hear another complaint from you." Mussolini's laws on giving and taking bribes are severe.

Even though I would like nothing better, I'm not so foolish as to wave a thanks to those women witnesses, but I want to celebrate. Claire is safe with Mrs. Pigeon, and so, instead of going home, I take the bus to Tor di Nona. I want to buy cans of tomatoes, some Parmesan if Ersilia has any. Tonight I'll cook a super meal for all of us, invite Mrs. Pigeon, Gina, maybe even Signora Calabresi, the war widow.

Ersilia's spot, underneath the Madonna, is empty. Other women approach me, offering me their wares. "Where's Ersilia," I ask each of them. They shrug their indifference and worry fingers start to clutch my stomach. "She's all right, isn't she? She hasn't been arrested?"

"Who knows?" a woman with a missing front tooth says. "It's been a few days. What is it you need? I got three hundred grams of lard. Pure white gold. My name's Ida and my stuff is better than hers. Cheaper too."

I shake my head and start walking back up to the Lungotevere underneath a low, thick blanket of clouds, which has deadened any bright notes of colors or sound. Something tugs at my skirt. I turn and a round-faced girl looks back at me with large solemn eyes as black and shiny as onyx. She smiles and sways her thin body. No coat or sweater, a too large dress that falls to her sandaled feet. "I know where she is," she says.

"What's your name?"

"Ceci."

"Hi, Ceci. You know where Ersilia is?"

She nods and holds out her hand.

I wonder if this slip of a girl isn't just a clever little liar, but if she is, it doesn't matter. I give her all the coins I have. "Where is she?"

The money disappears into her fist and she grins at me. "Screwing her boyfriend." I watch her scurry down the street like a mouse being chased by a cat and laugh despite myself. I hope it's true.

ROME, ITALY—DECEMBER 16, 1942

"What are you doing?" Mrs. Pigeon is sitting like a dark boulder in her corner armchair by the shuttered window. Next to her a round table overflowing with photographs of a young girl. At her feet a tiger rug complete with a gaping, fanged tiger head that keeps Claire entranced. I have brought Mrs. Pigeon's shopping, a daily chore that rarely brings a thank you. I decide her question is rhetorical.

Mrs. Pigeon tilts her marcelled head my way in disapproval. "First you're frightened to death people will find out you're American and mistreat you. Now you shout insults to the military." News of my protest has spread quickly through the neighborhood. "Your husband is coming and reason has flown out of your head. What will he say about this?"

"I don't care what he thinks."

"You're a naive woman."

I've found confidence, a confidence that I'm sure will carry me through Marco's visit, that will even last me through the war.

CAMBRIDGE, MASSACHUSETTS—MAY, 1956

Two days before Christmas: Papa was waiting for us at Doney's, one of the fancy cafés on Via Veneto, two blocks from our apartment. Mama took forever getting ready, changing suits, lipstick, gloves. I kept saying she looked great, we were late, Papa was going to get angry. Finally I left her in the living room pinning her hat down, and ran, jumping over yesterday's puddles, splashing my legs with icy dirty rain. At the intersection, the *vigile* raised a white gloved arm to stop me. His other arm waved a stream of bicycles and motorbikes through. Directing traffic with a dancer's grace.

I saw his tie first, up the block, on the other side of the street—a cerulean blue. Papa was standing in front of Doney's, his arms full of packages. A beacon, an oak, a Roman column. My Papa.

I called out, jumped up and down, waved my arms. The vigile still held his white hand up. I crossed anyway, swerving past an oncoming motorbike. I locked arms around my father's neck. He dropped his packages, clasped my waist and swung me high. My shoe went flying, my underpants must have been showing, I could feel the cold on the back of my thighs, but I didn't care. "Look, I'm an eagle!" I shouted.

"You've gotten so thin!"

"I've grown another inch."

Papa set me down when Mama approached with Andy. He held out both his hands. Andy shook one. No hugging, they were both men now. Mama stood back, my shoe in her hand. It was a comic touch that broke the look I had seen her practice in front of the mirror all week: a look I saw as bored, which now I think was meant to be impervious, the look of a woman who lives with a moat of indifference protecting her.

She had pressed her rust felt hat so low on her forehead that her eyes were in shadow. "Was the trip from Osijek long?"

"Where is Chiara? Why didn't you bring her?"

"It's much too cold out."

The café was crowded, the windows frosted with body heat, cigarette smoke, and the steam from the hissing espresso machines. We had to wait for a table. I rubbed my face on Papa's tweed jacket, welcoming back my father's smell. Andy boasted about his soccer team at school, how he'd made goalie.

Mama kept taking peeks at Papa from under the brim of her felt hat. I wanted to know what she was thinking. That in the seven months he'd been away, he had lost weight, weight he didn't have to begin with? That his face was stitched together with wrinkles? He had turned forty-three in September and he looked like an old man. Did she wonder, have I done this to him?

"I know a better place," Mama said and led us back to the more modest Via Lombardia, to Cesare's *latteria*. Closer to our apartment and to Claire.

We kept our coats on—the *latteria*, covered in marble, was colder than outside—and sat on worn wooden chairs in front of a table that still had traces of the biscuits Cesare's wife had made there that morning. A crèche made of small, brightly painted terra cotta figures sat in the glass case on the counter, surrounded by the sugarless biscuits.

Andy scraped dots of dough with a fingernail. "Do they put sawdust in the bread in Croatia like here? It's awful."

"They use rocks instead of sawdust," Papa said. "Keeps our stomach full."

While we waited for Cesare to bring coffee and cappuccinos, the three of us played our word game. "Houby"—mushroom in Czech. "Yams." "Speck"—German cured ham. "Koroptev"—partridge in Czech. "Vitello"—veal in Italian. "Orange." "Egg." "Gorgonzola."

When Cesare brought the tray over, Mama asked him to sing. "Please. What you sang the other day from *La Bohème*. It was lovely." She must have wanted distractions.

He eyed her above sacs of skin the color and texture of dried figs. "Sorry, signora, not today."

"I bet he sings only for you," Papa said after Cesare left.

"He's got a horrible voice," I chimed in, and told him how much I loved the nuns, how I didn't mind being put back a grade.

Papa asked questions. Had it been hard to shift from German to Italian at school? Had we made new friends? Did we like where we lived? I said I had lots of friends. Andy rolled up his trousers to show off his soccer scars. No, he didn't miss music. Not one bit.

"I've missed you," Papa said. "All of you."

I waited for Mama to take off her hat—a sign that she was lowering the bridge. She didn't, but she fiddled with her gloves. Immediately I thought, she's going to touch him. She licked the coffee off her lips, she's going to kiss him. She brought her chair closer, she's going to hug him.

She just sat there, thinking what? That he wasn't the man she expected? That he was too contrite, too caring with his children, too obviously in love with her? Had he really changed? Had he lost his arrogance? Is that why he looked so thin? Had he become harmless?

115

"I want to see Chiara," Papa said. "Please let me see her."

"We call her Claire," I said.

"I want to see my daughter."

It took Mama forever to nod her agreement.

Mrs. Pigeon appeared on the doorstep, cane and purse dangling from her arm, Claire half buried in her black Persian lamb. She had put on lipstick and rouged her cheeks. She let go of the baby reluctantly.

Claire looked odd in Papa's arms, a shrunken wriggling toy. "She has your face, Alinka," Papa said. His fingers, long and dark against Claire's skin, began touching her, the way a blind man might, feeling the marsh-mallow soft cheek, the wet pucker of her mouth, the buttonlike bone of her chin, the warm folds of her neck, the translucent curls over her ears.

Mama stood apart.

Mrs. Pigeon kept one fat-heeled foot on the doorstep, never deciding to go. "Have you met Il Duce? He promised the war would be over in less than a year, and here we are the third Christmas and no end in sight. I gave all my jewelry to this war and now I want it back. It's a disgrace, not enough food to go around, and with no coal we're going to freeze. Are they going to bomb Rome? Naples is half destroyed. Imagine, the bombs left a trolley car full of people standing. Dead, all of them."

"Signora, I haven't seen my family in a long time."

"Of course, you must forgive me." Mrs. Pigeon didn't look the least bit contrite. "Send the children up after lunch. I have a chest full of books to keep them quiet."

Mama laughed, a laugh of embarrassment, I think. At least, that's what I felt.

"I brought you food," Papa said as soon as Mrs. Pigeon left. Andy and I carried the packages into the kitchen, opened them quickly. A whole prosciutto, a chicken with its head still on and bits of down sticking out like baby hair, a jug of olive oil the murky color of a grass stain, half a kilo of real coffee, and a bottle of *Slivovice*, Yugoslavian plum brandy.

Papa took up his old role of family cook while Mama fed Claire her bottle and explained that she had lost her milk on the long train ride to Rome. Andy sprawled over the kitchen table with his *Hellenic Stories* and his Greek dictionary, translating out loud, asking about one word after another, Papa protesting that too much time had passed, he didn't remember anything.

My father—the bon vivant, the gourmand, the great cook—looked awkward and incongruous in a kitchen where we had eaten without him for more than three months. He had lost his grace and the smooth, confident movements of authority. He sliced prosciutto and cut himself. He singed the chicken and a feather burned a hole in his sleeve cuff. He spun around, left and right, opening drawers, rummaging through shelves. He wouldn't tell me what he was looking for, and I concentrated hard on anticipating his next need—salt, pepper, a pot holder, a knife, rosemary, why didn't we have rosemary to make him happy? My stomach burned from the tension.

In place of rosemary, I offered Ersilia's can of tomatoes that Mama had been saving. The room got hot, with chicken fat hissing in the pan, splattering over the stove, against the back wall, with the smell of simmering onions and tomatoes, the *Slivovice* bottle popping open, Mama humming to Claire, Andy fighting Greek words. In the garden two cats meowed and left arching trails of dust on the steamed-up window.

Papa poured plum brandy into a glass and held it out to Mama. She accepted, careful that her fingers didn't touch his, and took a sip, held it in her mouth for the longest time. Swallowing made her gasp and spurt brandy down her chin. Papa wiped the drops off with his thumb.

"It burns!" She didn't push him away. My stomach eased.

After lunch, we, the children, were banished upstairs, to Mrs. Pigeon's spooky apartment filled with paintings of saints being martyred in varied, gruesome ways. Papa insisted I take as a gift a glassful of the real coffee beans he'd brought. A bribe to keep us while our parents did what? Fight? Hug? The bottle of *Slivovice* was half empty by the end of lunch. Was that good or bad?

Mrs. Pigeon sat in her armchair, by the closed shutters, looking as if someone had set a ruler to her face and marked what strips of her we were allowed to see. Claire slept in her basket on the tiger rug. Andy peered at all the paintings of the saints and asked where the incense was. Mrs. Pigeon called him an impertinent boy and rewarded him with a stash of Peruvian stamps.

Andy whispered to me. "Ask her if she's a spy."

"You ask her!" How could he think of Mrs. Pigeon when our future was at stake?

The wait was eternal.

I want him. Drunk on *Slivovice*, I want to taste his flesh in my mouth, to suck him dry, to ride him until my body breaks apart. I'm naked and confused by the urge to get up and rinse my mouth, and the desire to float in the too-soft bed with this man who smells strangely of plum brandy, lemony cologne, and chicken fat. I lift myself slowly on one elbow, propping my head up to stop the dizziness. The man is lying naked in front of me, too skinny, but good-looking. His cheek brushes against my hip. I fall back on the mattress and press his head against the rise of my belly. The stubble of his beard scrapes my skin. "I like this." He pushes himself down between my legs. "I like this," I repeat. A stranger is making love to me, I tell myself. It allows me to accept this coupling, gives me license to do and say as I please.

He tries to part my thighs wider and I resist, teasing myself with expectation and giving myself time to sober up. I want to enjoy this love-making with all my senses sharp. I need to remember, nurture this pleasure for the future. I twist away from him, but he pins my hip down with teethlike fingers. "Damn it, don't tease me, Alinka. It's not fair to tease me."

My eyes finally focus. His face is pushing toward me, suddenly familiar. He looks arrogant, overbearing, a blue vein bulging as if it's going to burst any second and split his forehead in two. His lips and chin are still wet. He pulls my hand down on his penis, hard and thick. I close my eyes, my hand in a fist, and picture Marco in his black Fascist uniform with Milena, in her oyster-sheen dress, laughing at me.

I push him away and hunch over myself.

Marco sits up. "What have I done now?"

"You promised Switzerland. That was our pact. Switzerland and safety for our children."

"The children are safe here." He slides closer. I cover myself with a pillow. "But soon you can leave," he says. "I've asked—"

I slap his hand away. "You're a hypocrite. Hypocrite bastard! You didn't keep your promise. You sent us to Ro . . ." Anger and the brandy catch in my throat, tripping the words on my tongue. "You sent us here without even having the courage to tell me yourself. You had Giorgio do it."

"He wasn't supposed to tell you. I wrote you a letter."

"You wrote to him first." I punch the pillow. "You cheated me. Cheated me. Cheated!" I keep punching the pillow, repeating the words, wanting to fling myself at something hard—a wall, a boulder—something that will smash me to stillness.

He grabs my wrists. "Alinka, stop it. Listen to me."

"Don't I count? What is wrong with me? Why, why—" I open and close my hand, looking for the missing words in my fist. "Respect. Love. Normal human things." He lets go of me, and I lean my forehead against the cool of the brass bedstead. I've been here before, in a bedroom, in this state. I lift the bed sheet and press it to my nose, remembering the wet handkerchief smell of that other sheet in Prague. I feel the same gagging pain. Why have I depended so much on this man, let him lead my life so completely? "Why did you treat me that way?"

"I thought you needed looking after. You would have been on your own in Switzerland. Here I have friends."

"Why didn't you ask me what I needed? I'm your wife."

"You were angry, you were hating me. How could I trust you? I was hundreds of miles away. I didn't know what to do. Giorgio and Lilli convinced me it was best for you and the children to come to Rome."

I blow my nose. The outburst has sobered me up, but it doesn't stop me from wishing the impossible. To reel my life back to that birthday party, when I was eighteen, dressed in that blue cotton dress, my breasts wrapped in strips of old sheets that Mother maintained made me look less vulgar. I'd meet Marco, rush to the bathroom to dry my panties, but then I'd walk out the front door, walk onto another track that would not lead me to Via Aurora, in the middle of a world war, with a family I can't hold together. I'm too weak to stomach betrayal, and I can't glean what love there might be in this naked man who sits at the edge of the bed, with only a blanket lying between us. He has deceived me, deceived his children, and by wearing a Fascist uniform only for personal convenience, he has ended up deceiving even those faceless men who died in Russia and Africa.

"Please forgive me," Marco says. He rubs his hand on my knee. His puckered penis stirs.

It makes me sick. I move my knees and wrap the sheet around me until nothing shows of me except my head and hands. "Do you know what I did after Giorgio told me?"

Something in my voice warns him. "Truce, please."

"I want to tell you. You deserve to know about your wife and your friend, Karl Müller."

Marco reaches for his clothes on the armchair.

"I offered myself to him, thinking he could get us a pass across the borders, a pass that didn't require your approval."

"Don't start making up stories." He stands up and slips on his undershirt.

"I'm not making anything up. Karl wanted me." Marco bends down to pick up his underpants, his ass flat, fish-belly white. I inch closer to the edge of the bed, anticipating the moment when he'll turn around with a dumbfounded, hurt look on his face. "Up in his hotel room. Karl said my breasts were the most beautiful he'd ever seen. He was in such a hurry we didn't make it to the bed." I tug at the trousers Marco just stepped into. "Look at me, Marco."

He turns, composure frozen on his face.

"It was good love-making, Marco, long and hot." Karl came too soon and couldn't get it up again.

"I don't believe you."

"I could barely walk afterwards."

"Shut up!" He heads for the door barefoot, fumbling with his shirt buttons. "Shut up!" He spins around, yelling this time, his face red and creased like a child's face about to cry. My expected moment of satisfaction doesn't come. I get off the bed, put on my bathrobe, and fight the urge to run to embrace him, tell him I was lying.

"I wanted you to know the truth," I say.

"That's not the truth. You just want to get your kicks." He's jeering. Not a boy about to cry. Just angry.

I pick up his shoes underneath the armchair. "That too." I hold them out to him. "And to let you know how much I've changed."

He takes the shoes quickly. "You made it all up." He leans against the door and slips on his shoes. "I was trying to tell you. I've asked for a transfer for family reasons. Spain in June, after the children have finished their school year. Spain's as neutral as Switzerland." He tries out a smile, as if showing off new teeth. "You'll be happy there."

120

"What did you tell the Ministry? Your wife can't take care of her children?"

"I said it's not right to separate a family."

"*La famiglia*, the backbone of Fascism. Well, in here"—I point to my head—"there's Communism. Free love. Anarchy. No marriage, Marco."

"That's crazy!"

"I can't stop you from seeing the children, but forget about me. I'm someone else now."

"Do you know what you're doing?"

"Wartime is woman's time. Blame it on the war."

CAMBRIDGE, MASSACHUSETTS—MAY 1956

The garden gate slammed and I ran to the window. Through the slats, I saw a man walking away. Papa? I couldn't tell, it was too dark. Something blue shimmered past the fence. I called out, opened the window, the shutters. He was gone by then.

I found Mama in our narrow bathroom that always smelled of ammonia. Naked, in the bathtub, submerged in cold water up to her chin. "Are you all right, Mama?"

"Wartimeiswoman'stime," she mumbled, stringing the words together. I wondered if she was still drunk. "Doesn't it sound grand, Susie? Full of *Sturm und Drang* and conquest. I've sent your father away for good."

She sank into the cold water of the tub, her hair turning into red seaweed. If she wanted to drown herself, I decided that I was going to let her.

Mama resurfaced and looked straight at me this time. Her face was wet with bath water. "Please, Chipmunk, pray that I'm on the right track this time."

At that moment I hated her too much to pray for anything.

ROME, ITALY—DECEMBER 24, 1942

It's a cold, bright day. The wind has cleaned the sky of clouds and is now slapping at the branches of the sycamores above us, silencing the starlings. Ersilia and I sit huddled on the steps that lead to the Tiber bank where we first met, smoking the pack of cigarettes I've brought her. My lap holds a couple of sweaters and skirts Susie no longer needs. "Is Ceci your daughter?" I ask.

Ersilia flicks ash in the wind. "My kid? Not a chance. Ceci's just a runt that showed up one day, looking for food. Me and the other women take care of her and in exchange she makes herself useful. She can sniff the *carabinieri* coming before they even know they're on their way." A gust of wind splashes her hair across her face. "Nice of you to bring Ceci clothes," she says, "but you see her, you watch out for your pocketbook."

Ersilia takes a sweater from the pile on my lap and ties it around her head. "So, Rossa. I've been up at Magliano Sabina, loading up on goodies. I got a whole prosciutto, two wheels of pecorino, enough eggs and butter to bake a cake bigger than the Colosseum." She buries her chin into the mangy fox jacket she always wears and turns her thick mascaraed eyes on me. "You name it, Rossa. I got it."

I turn to the wind and let it lift my hair, clean my face. I inhale the smell of the sea the wind has brought in—the sea that one day is going to take us home. The minute the war ends. I link my arm in Ersilia's. I need to feel her physically close to give me the courage to ask. "You must know someone in the underground. Get me to them. Please."

"What are you saying?" She looks baffled, but our arms are still linked and that spurs me on.

"The time to sit in a corner and let others decide my life is over. It's time to fight, to stand for something."

"What are you thinking?"

"I could be a messenger, stencil thousands of printed sheets denouncing Mussolini. I don't know. Whatever they need. Please, Ersilia. I'll pay you."

Ersilia unlinks her arm to light another cigarette with the stub of her last one. Lights another one for me and inches closer. "Listen, Rossa." Her voice is low and my heart starts to beat like a moth against a lamp. I was right to trust her. She's going to help me, tell me whom to contact. She holds out my cigarette. I reach for it, but my fingers fumble and the cigarette rolls down the steps. Ersilia runs after it, picks it up, carefully places it between my fingers, sits back down on the step. Still close. Her voice still low. My heart still thumping. The sea air, the wind burning my face. It all thrills me.

"This is what I do for this war," she says. "I sell food, clothes, a few glittery doodads. Necessary stuff. Stuff that can bring back a smile on a woman's face. Nothing that's going to kill you."

The thumping stops. "I don't understand." I don't want to understand.

"You think anyone would use you, *Americana*? If you got lucky you'd last a week and then what? Cigarette burns on those white tits of yours in exchange for information. You've got nothing to tell them, but they don't believe you, and so they take turns pissing on you, and then they fuck you, one by one, over and over again. Just for the fun of it."

I start to gag

"For good measure they stick a little electricity up your vagina or pull your nails out one by one. Look, I'm not making this up. And what about your kids? What are they going to do with you dead?"

I am useless, stupid, stymied at every turn. I can't do anything right.

CAMBRIDGE, MASSACHUSETTS—MAY 1956

Andy and I spent Christmas day with Papa. Lunch in a trattoria, with ugly murals of Venice, the water painted a garish turquoise. The surprise of a heaping plate of rigatoni hiding a forbidden slice of veal. After lunch Papa took me on a carriage ride around Villa Borghese Park, while Andy pedaled next to us on Papa's Christmas present, an almost new black bike. I wore my present, a smelly, stiff Croatian shearling coat with the fur on the outside which I took to bed with me for the rest of that winter.

Under Mussolini's orders, the park had been turned into a vast vegetable garden and grazing field. Papa pointed to my new coat and joked that he should leave me there to graze with the sheep. I reminded him he was the one leaving. Only three days left.

We got off in front of a low building with *Giardino delle Rose*, the Garden of Roses, written in big green letters above the entrance.

"This is where I used to take your mother dancing. There used to be chairs and tables with candles. We were good lindy dancers. People stopped to watch us."

Papa reeled me in and rocked me. "One, two, three, one, two. It's time you learned to dance."

"No! Mussolini's forbidden it." How could he even think of dancing? Papa flung me out, and Andy flew past me on his bike so close I screamed. Andy stopped, and as the three of us stood on that dance floor, Papa told us about being transferred to Barcelona.

"Are we coming too?" Andy and I asked.

"Of course you are."

The three days left with Papa were painfully short. He tried to help us in any way he could. He bought us food staples. He knocked on shop doors for cardboard—there was a tremendous paper shortage—and while Mama sat upstairs with Mrs. Pigeon, we cut the cardboard into rectangles, glued them to the back of my new drawings, and hung them in the living room. He went to a farm in Due Ponti, bought three live chickens and a rooster, and built a wire cage to keep them in. He raked away the gravel from the garden and dug a wide bed along the fence. He made me the custodian of matchboxes filled with pepper, eggplant, and zucchini seeds that he said were easy to grow. I was to wait until March to plant them. Filling my palm with dirt, he showed me how to release the seeds slowly, in an even line. He taught me how to hoe a straight row by sticking a wooden spoon at each end of the row, then tying a string from one to the other.

While Papa shoveled, Andy kept poking a stick into the chicken cage. "What's the point? They'll just get stolen."

Papa kept shoveling. "The point is not to give up."

My way of not giving up was to pray as the nuns had taught me.

I looked up Spain in Mrs. Pigeon's atlas. Barcelona was much farther from Rome than Osijek. Would Mama let us go? With her? Without her?

"I spent my honeymoon on the Costa Brava," Mrs. Pigeon said.

"Did it take you long to get there? How long?"

"Fourteen, sixteen hours maybe. Of course, there was no war then." She sighed and I traced the outline of the country on a sheet of paper, filling it in with an orange pencil, putting in trees and mountains, my father as a matador. I added a chipmunk, a goat, a one-eyed trout, a ginger cat.

The day before he was leaving, while we were putting up the last of my drawings, I asked Papa if I could be a *Giovane Italiana*, a Young Italian. All the girls at school belonged to the Fascist youth organization. They met for Fascist Saturday and special designated days to do exercises, listen to speeches, and sing the glory of Fascism. *"Tu non vedrai nessuna cosa al mondo maggior di Roma, maggior di Roma."* You will never see anything in the world greater than Rome. I coveted the uniform they wore—a black pleated skirt topped by a white blouse and a black silk cap. I was sure that wearing it would make Papa proud.

"That's why I don't have any friends," I told him. "Everyone belongs." The truth was that, thanks to Luisa, the whole school knew I had an American mother. During recess I'd get teased. "Is it true Americans only eat dog meat?" "Mussolini is going to wipe you out!" "USA! USA! *Ultimi stronzi arrivati.*" Last turds in the war.

"Please, Papa."

"One Fascist uniform is enough in this family. Besides, it would kill your mother."

"She doesn't have to know." My father gave me a well-deserved lecture on respecting my mother, above all loving her in this difficult time. "She needs you," he said. I refused to believe him.

"I'm sorry you don't have friends, Chipmunk." He stroked my cheek. His hand was warm and luscious with the smell of tobacco, soap—the smell of safety. He told me to get my coat, he had a surprise for me.

I ran to the bathroom and wiped glue off my fingers. Faith, that's all it took. "Believe in Him," the nuns preached, "and Christ will bless you and comfort you." Papa was taking me to Spain. Now. Without suitcases. Just me. I kneeled in front of the bathtub and thanked Jesus for interceding for me.

A blonde woman stood up from her chair as we walked into Cesare's *latteria*. "Susie, I want you to meet Palma."

I stayed by the door. Palma, Palm, an exotic name, maybe Spanish. A girlfriend with yellow hair, instead of purple.

"Come on, Susie."

"Tell me who she is first."

"She'll help your mother around the apartment."

"Mama will hate her."

"We've already talked about it. Your mother needs to rest."

"When did you two talk? I didn't see you talk."

"You don't know everything, Susie."

How those words terrified me. If I didn't know everything, how could I change things? What would happen to me?

I watched the woman—Palma—take a few steps on high wedged shoes that made her tilt forward. Turquoise ruffles spilled from her coat collar. Bunched on top of her head, dyed yellow ruffles of hair.

"Palma, I'd like you to meet Susie, sometimes known as Chipmunk. She'll give you no trouble."

Palma lifted a hand as if to wave. "Ciao, Susie. You're the wise one, I bet." She had a space between her two front teeth and spoke with the same Neapolitan accent as Gina. "And neat too." She sat down only after Marco sat. Her hands bulged red as if the cuffs of her sleeves were too tight. I stood.

"Palma! What a beautiful name!" Cesare brought over three cappuccini. "Makes me think of Egypt." He started singing from *Aida*, his neck swelling with the strain—". . . *patria e trono, e amor . . . tutto avrai*"—

Maybe Palma was nice. She hadn't chucked my chin or pinched my cheek. She would clean the apartment, cook, do the shopping so Mama could sleep and maybe get happy. Best of all she wasn't Papa's girlfriend.

I slipped my hand into my father's pocket. Despite what the nuns said, I still had nothing to show for my faith.

SEVEN

CAMBRIDGE, MASSACHUSETTS—MAY 1956

On the first of January 1943, a comet crossed the sky. A good sign, everyone said. I decided Palma was the good sign. She didn't cook much better than my mother, but her gappy smile was always available and her cleaning wasn't obsessive and she would heat the water for our baths. She didn't mind that we didn't have a bed for her. "I've slept on hay, kitchen floors, under trees, and in a field of tomatoes. The living room sofa looks like a queen's bed to me." She kept a photograph of Il Duce in her pocket—chest bare, his jaw wide and hard as the spade in his hand. "How I long to feel that jaw right here," she said, holding her cheek, looking like she had a toothache. She made soap in a huge pot with caustic soda, suet, and her own supply of talcum powder that smelled of violets and came from a round purple box. She made apple wine with apple peelings and she made *castagnaccio*—a flat cake made with chestnut flour that made me gag but kept me full for hours.

Palma said she was nearsighted and had broken her glasses, and would I read to her while she washed the dishes or darned our clothes? We agreed that of all the books Mrs. Pigeon had lent me, Manzoni's *The Betrothed* was the best. Each day the story of the star-crossed lovers, Renzo and Lucia, got more complicated, more anguishing. The cruel local lord,

Don Rodrigo, made a bet that Lucia would be his and forced the curate Don Abbondio to call off her marriage to Renzo. And then the plague came and the lovers were separated and Lucia was helpless and Renzo was miserable and Don Rodrigo schemed. Delicious reading for a wartime winter. When Palma's broken glasses never surfaced, Mrs. Pigeon decreed she didn't know how to read.

Stove gas willing, lunch became a hot meal again: eggs if the hens were laying, pasta with lentils or chickpeas and always onions, the leaden castagnaccio to seal the meal. After lunch, Mama went out for long walks with Claire. If she hadn't come home by dinnertime, Palma would send Andy to Cesare's latteria, where he would find her sitting at a corner table, with a cup of untouched milk in front of her, surrounded by marble.

"Why do you go there, Mama?" I kept asking her. "It's freezing cold." Our apartment wasn't much warmer—my toes were covered in chilblains, which I happily burned with a match to trade one pain for another—but I didn't like the idea of Cesare and my mother together. He always got gooey-eyed when he saw her. How could she let him ogle her for hours? He was too old, too ugly. And what if she brought him home? I would die!

Andy was always out. He'd say he was studying at a friend's house, but I knew he was smoking and roving the streets with a pack of older boys. He stole money from Mama's or Palma's purse to go to the movies, the ones that had a variety show with half-naked girls before the feature. I pestered him to take me with him.

"Stick to the nuns, Susie."

"What are they like, the women on the stage? Are they beautiful? Do they dance for you? Do you want to touch them?"

A look of surprise swept across his face. "You should wash your mind with soap."

I started locking myself in the bathroom. Lifting my nightgown in front of the mirror, I watched my hand work between my legs.

ROME, ITALY—JANUARY 28, 1943

Rain leaves slash marks on the windows of the latteria. I tighten my coat around me and sip the coffee Cesare has offered me today because his vigilant wife is busy in the back room. Coming here in the afternoon is turning into a habit. The place is cold, but he welcomes me with a wide smile and, with Claire warm against my chest, I enjoy listening to his singing. Today, he sings in a forced basso register that turns his neck red: "*Ora che I giorni lieti fuggir, ti dico addio, fedele amico mio, addio.*" It's his favorite aria, he tells me at the end. Colline saying goodbye to his coat from *La Bohème.*

"I started singing it when I wasn't allowed to sell sweet biscuits any more. All biscuits now go to the war front. What kind of world is it without sweet biscuits?" He sits down across from me and leans his elbows on the round marble table that lost its sheen a long time ago. "This rain will outlast the war." He's an ugly man, with hungry, drooping eyes that he can't take off me. He has followed my every movement from the first time I walked in here with Claire. He drinks in my lips when I greet him, my arm reaching for the milk bottle, the lift of my breasts with each breath. I cup my hands around the coffee glass for warmth. "I like it when you sing, Cesare."

"Ah, signora, your beauty warms my heart." A laughable line that nonetheless makes me feel vital. He breaks into song again, this time lifting his voice to try Musetta's aria. "*Quando m'en vò, quando m'en vò soletta per la via, la gente sosta e mira; è la bellezza mia . . .*"

"Cesare!" his wife shouts from the back room. "The milk will sour."

CAMBRIDGE, MASSACHUSETTS—MAY 1956

One dinner time in February, Mrs. Pigeon said she saw no reason for us not to join forces. "We might come up with some strengths, some cheer." We moved upstairs for our dinners, Palma happy to cook in Mrs. Pigeon's larger, better furnished kitchen. We had to "dine in a civilized way," which meant sitting up straight, elbows tucked, under a brass chandelier with half the light bulbs unscrewed to save money. The dining table, covered with a lace tablecloth, was always set with silverware, crystal, and fine Ginori china. Mrs. Pigeon presided at the head of the table. Behind her stiff back, a large dark painting showing St. John the Baptist's gruesome head on a pewter platter made sure I lost my appetite.

During one dinner, Andy asked her about the letters from Peru.

"That does not concern you."

Andy lifted his drumstick, waved it as if it were a baton and hummed the first notes of Beethoven's Fifth.

Mrs. Pigeon arched her eyebrows.

We weren't supposed to know that every night at nine o'clock, after they shooed us back downstairs with Palma, the two of them listened to the BBC.

"Andy, sweetheart," Mama said, "you mustn't tell anyone." She and Mrs. Pigeon would end up in jail.

Andy started chewing on the drumstick. "A secret for a secret."

"The secrets aren't all mine, it seems." Mrs. Pigeon's smile was as rigid as a whale bone.

"I snuck back into your kitchen after dinner once to grab an apple." I'd been with him, but Andy was loyal enough to leave me out of it.

"Honesty is appreciated, even if used for barter. And don't talk while eating." A sigh. Four faces turned her way, waiting for Peru.

Mrs. Pigeon took her time finishing her chicken, her potatoes, but when dessert finally came—bread boiled in milk—she let out her secret. The letters came from her husband, who had been on a fur-buying trip in South America when Hitler marched into Poland. He'd been unable to book a passage back. There were too many submarines scouring the ocean. "We wait. One day he'll make it across, and we'll probably find we have nothing to say to each other."

I asked about the girl in the pictures.

"There's an old saying I suggest you children learn by heart: Do not look for answers in others, but only in your shoes."

"What if you don't like what's in your shoes?" Mama asked.

Mrs. Pigeon had no answer.

ROME, ITALY—MARCH 15, 1943

We're alone today. I left Claire with Mrs. Pigeon. His wife has been sick for several days. I take off my coat and walk to the back room. He locks the latteria door and hurries in. The room is tiny, with a narrow desk backed against the wall and a chair. I slip my panties off while he unbuttons his fly and slips a condom over his erection. He sits on the one chair, pulls me to him, hitches up my skirt. My breath catches as I ease myself down over him. I ride him, slowly, ever so slowly. It feels so good. He tries to kiss me, but I turn my face away. He squeezes my breasts, bites my nipples through my sweater and bra. I move my hips, up, down, back and forth, around. I can't get enough of his penis. He grabs my ass and whispers obscenities. I ride him faster and faster. I moan, whimper. I'm shameless in my need.

He grabs my hips and pushes me down harder. A sharp electric current runs through me and I burst, breaking up into a hundred pieces that spin in the air. He gasps and I feel him shudder beneath me. I lean my head on his shoulder and wait for my body to float down, gather back into the mass that is Alice, mother of three children.

Out on the street, I let heavy rain run down my head, fill my shoes, penetrate my coat. My children are waiting, but I'm held motionless by the stream of water rushing past me below the curb. It pulls at me as it hauls the trash of the street—bits of newspapers, cigarette butts, a lost mitten, a dead mouse—toward the narrow black opening of the sewer.

CAMBRIDGE, MASSACHUSETTS—MAY 1956

The cats stopped coming to our garden. Palma said they were probably in stews all around Rome, but I preferred to believe they had left because we stopped feeding them. At night we brought in the chicken coop to keep our two hens—we had eaten the third—and the rooster safe from thieves.

I played with my little sister. She was sweet-tempered, happy to sit on my lap while I sang her love songs. "*Ma l'amore no, l'amore non si può disperdere nel vento con le rose.*" She gurgled along, blowing bubbles of saliva. She had just learned to say *Mama,* and I repeated *Susie* until it made no sense to me, but she stayed loyal to Mama. She didn't crawl around much and refused to stand. Every time I tried to hold her up, she'd wiggle her bottom and push down hard. I called her lazybones, but Mrs. Pigeon said babies had their own timetable.

US planes bombed Naples again, and Gina stopped washing our sheets. Mrs. Pigeon told us we were lucky Gina didn't retaliate by denouncing us for some invented offense. We didn't know that the Italian front on the Don had collapsed and the Russians had freed Leningrad after a seventeen-month siege by the Germans. Up north, the factory workers had just gone on strike for the first time during the Fascist regime. The Axis tide was turning. Mama started asking Mrs. Pigeon how to write certain phrases in Italian. One day it was "To whom it may concern." A week later, "I wish to attest." Days after that, "I give my family permission to transfer."

Bad words, I decided, even though I hadn't yet guessed their purpose.

When she thought Andy and I weren't watching, Mama practiced Papa's signature. The bedroom curtains grew fatter with lira. Something was about to change again in my life. The thought made me sick to my stomach.

ROME, ITALY—MARCH 18, 1943

Andy has chest pains that make him cry. His breathing sounds like a rasp scraping stone. The doctor comes and announces that if we're lucky Andy has pleurisy or pneumonia. "There's a chance he has tuberculosis." A sharp pain knifes my brain. I don't, can't believe him. Andy is angry, rebellious—that's why his chest hurts. A bad cold is taking his breath away. I can make him well again. I know I can. I cover my boy with all the blankets in the apartment, force hot tea down his throat. "He'll sweat it out. He'll come back to being my Andygoat, my sweet violinist." The doctor insists Andy needs to go to the hospital. I can't let him go. He'll never come back to me. There is no cure for tuberculosis.

Mrs. Pigeon comes down and shakes her cane. "You are killing your son!"

"My boy stays here with me."

I send Claire and Susie upstairs to Mrs. Pigeon and sit by Andy, rubbing his chest, catching the mucus he spits out with my handkerchief, singing lullabies he hasn't heard since he was a baby.

Hours later, when Andy has finally fallen asleep, Mrs. Pigeon comes down to sit with me. She has brought me a cup of broth I can't drink.

"I want you to listen to me, Signora Alessandrini, because I am older and wiser than you are. The girl in the photographs upstairs was my only daughter. Four years ago, I lost her. I lost my heart.

"A mother's grief is a dictator. You have no choice but to obey. I know that only too well, but your son is still alive. If the boy is to get well, you have to let him go to the hospital. The power of love is not enough in this case."

In the middle of the night, Andy coughs so hard he spits up blood.

CAMBRIDGE, MASSACHUSETTS—MAY 1956

Two days before my thirteenth birthday, Andy went to the hospital. I was annoyed at first because it meant no one was going to pay any attention to me. The doctor had to carry a blanket-covered Andy to his car. Mama trailed, holding up Andy's Amati, as if the violin were an icon with the power to make my brother well. She wouldn't let me go with them. We stood on the street, Palma sniffing back tears, Gina crossing herself and decreeing that God took as He pleased. Mrs. Pigeon claimed she was going to give prayer another try. I rode after the car on Andy's bike until it reached the arch at Porta Pinciana and sped away too fast for me to keep up.

I wasn't allowed to visit Andy, but Mama stayed with him around the clock. After school each day, I sat on the floor in his room and worked on drawing after drawing. Andy playing soccer, Andy eating a hamburger slathered with sautéed onions the way he liked it, the Vlasek's yellow house with the chocolate bar shutters, a map of Spain, Andy on his bicycle riding along the top of our fence, the rooster on the back seat. With drawing pad on my lap and colored pencil in hand, I felt powerful enough to make my brother well.

Andy stayed delirious, spitting out the fluid accumulating in his lungs, throwing up whatever Mama fed him.

At school I prayed in the chapel to Jesus and the Virgin Mary. Every night, kneeling beside my bed, I asked God to make Andy well. Gina told me to go to Via Veneto, to the church with the skulls in the crypt, and light a candle for each year of Andy's life. I had to borrow money from Palma to pay for them, and as I prayed in front of those fourteen trembling flames, I was sure those skulls were going to roll out of the crypt and hit me. Andy stayed sick.

Palma said I needed to make a vow. "You have to give up something you love very much, and God will see your sacrifice and make Andy well again."

It made God sound greedy, but I was willing to try anything.

ROME, ITALY—MARCH 24, 1943

It's useless trying to shake the terror away. It's in my bones, along with all the other fears. And love that can't cure anything. Love and fear together, so powerful they can burn you to a cinder.

The hospital doctor has decreed pneumonia. A man in his eight-ies. He is still a good doctor, he assures me, and spins Italian words. *"Polmonite, pericolo di tubercolosi, il bacillo di Koch, malnutrizione, poveri ragazzi, pregare, paura, attenzione, affetto, dedizione, cura."* I picture the words as notes on Andy's music sheets, notes held up by bars, as solid as the wrought-iron fence of the garden. I have no choice but to trust that this man will cure my boy.

"Is it true," I ask him, "that the Allies have discovered a medicine that cures everything?"

"Penicillin, yes. Alas, they are keeping it for their soldiers. It will allow them to win the war."

Andy's room is stark, with its off-white walls, the shutters bleached by the sun, the white metal beds, metal bed stands. Six beds, five occupied by boys with lung disease. I stayed the nights too. Palma came with food, a change of clothes. I'm finally grateful Marco imposed her on me.

A few days ago I collapsed, and the nurses sent me home. One was kind enough to walk me to the streetcar stop. They thought I was getting sick, but it was terror that buckled my knees and made me fall. Andy with pneumonia—a first step toward tuberculosis—not getting any better.

They won't let me stay the nights anymore. Here in the apart-ment, scrubbed clean of germs, I watch Claire and Susie from a dis-tance, as I smoke cigarette after cigarette, burning money that should go into the hem of the curtains, weaving dreams of Andy's fever disappearing in the night, of bringing Andy home tomorrow.

The mornings I wait with the other mothers outside the double glass doors of the ward for the doctors to finish their rounds. As soon as the nurses unlock the doors, we rush, a released river of women, eager to feed, empty bedpans, clean, entertain our own and others. We've all brought a bit of home with us. A crocheted blanket to drape over the foot of the bed, a favorite toy, a stuffed animal. I've glued Susie's colored drawings above Andy's bed and propped his Amati by the bedside table to remind him there is still music in the world.

The mother from Frascati, up in the Alban Hills, said that what we leave in the room are votive panels. Italian churches are filled with small painted panels depicting the cured patient and *ex-voto*, silver cutouts of whatever body part had been miraculously cured. They hang on a wall of the church, picking up the light from the candles, each flame another prayer, another flicker of hope.

Yesterday a newcomer came to fill the sixth bed—seven-year-old Paolo with a fever of 105. His mother doesn't look much older than twenty. She kept sponging her naked boy with alcohol, and now can't stop laughing because his fever has gone down three degrees.

I envy her those three dropped degrees. Andy's fever is stuck at 103. His lips are chalk-white, his face a greenish gray under the grease of his sweat. When he coughs, my chest splits in two.

This afternoon the Frascati woman said we need a miracle, but the shrines are so crowded the Virgin can't breathe. "Miracles can only happen up in the hills where the air is good."

"Maybe we should thank God our boys are sick." The knitting woman has heard the German army is taking fifteen-year-olds to replace the dead soldiers.

Andy is going to be fifteen in four months.

I stand in the doorway of Mrs. Pigeon's dining room. "How did you survive? Mothers aren't meant to outlive their children. It's unnatural."

Mrs. Pigeon puts her spoon down and wipes her lips with her napkin. "I was given no warning, no time to bargain with God.

"We were vacationing in the Apennines as we had done since she was five. One July morning she left with her friends in hiking boots and a pair of knee pants she had borrowed from a friend. She fell into a ravine and died instantly. They were ugly pants, totally inappropriate, that's what I told her. My last words to my daughter."

"How do you go on?"

"The body wants to live. It takes over. Feeds itself, goes to sleep, wakes up. The mind worries about dust on the furniture, about the sun bleaching the rugs, about moths in the closet. The heart becomes only a muscle." She sweeps her spoon over the plate to collect whatever is left. "And you, Signora Alessandrini, need to eat and then rest. Hope requires strength."

I have no strength. I am helpless. Prayer, Palma suggests. I've forgotten how.

"You have to make a vow," Susie says. "You ask God for a some-thing and in return you promise to give something up. The hardest thing you can think of."

"Did you make a vow for Andy?

"Yes."

"What did you give up?"

She doesn't tell me.

ROME, ITALY—MARCH 27, 1943

I walk in to the hospital room to find the newcomer's bed empty, sheets removed, the mattress rolled up. Passing the bed, the Frascati woman crosses herself. "Paolo has been sent off to a tuberculosis sanitarium in Abruzzi."

"Easter comes late this year," says the knitting lady. Her needles tick, mark time. "That's a very bad omen."

This afternoon Andy's fever reaches 105. I pray. Desperation justifies my hypocrisy. I am even ready to make a vow, my life for his.

CAMBRIDGE, MASSACHUSETTS—MAY 1956

Preparing exam questions, giving exams, now grading them, have filled my mind these past two weeks. Yesterday the baby entered her twenty-sixth week and she hiccups, sometimes kickboxes inside me, which helps keep me in the moment. We're both healthy, Dr. Page has decreed, although he's not pleased with my excessive weight gain and blames it on my brooding.

Papa's check stubs were in the mailbox with a short note from Claire when I got home from class this afternoon.

Thanks for the Elvis 45s and the lipstick. I'm a cool cat now, pink lips, swinging my hips to Elvis, showing off Papa's satchel. Send pictures of the baby as soon as it pops out. Ciao,

the trout

I'm behind in grading exams, and I have an appointment with my thesis advisor in the morning. I need to get upstairs and work, but I pick up the check stubs—a partial recording of Papa's life from 1948 to

1954—and walk into the kitchen. With a cup of tea and a bowl of cherries at my elbow, I thumb through the first year. I recognize the tailor's name, the dressmaker, doctor, dentist. One check, a generous sum, went to The Sisters of Mary of the Consolation. Most stubs hold names of people I don't know. I stop when I see the exorbitant sum my father sent to my college. August 1948—that's when I put an ocean's distance between me and Papa, Andy, Claire. My family. They went on living their lives, I mine. Separate.

Why did Papa let me go? Because he wanted to keep me happy? Because I had turned against him? Because he blamed me for Mama's death? I don't know. Through the years I've gathered reasons for my leaving: anger, restlessness, the selfishness of an eighteen-year-old. I was shifting blame for Mama's death to Papa, and at the same time hoping desperately that she was still alive in the States.

I had learned the pick-up-and-go routine from Papa. We had moved from Rome to Newport Beach to Prague, back to Rome. He had left us for Prague, for Osijek, and then for Barcelona.

That last one was the cruelest.

Claire's first birthday, June 10, 1943, on a hillside overlooking a sun-glazed Lake Bracciano, thirty kilometers north of Rome: Mama and Papa were inside an abandoned forge with Claire, arguing, dividing, deciding our lives one more time. Papa was on his way to Spain. In four days he was going to leave again. Not alone this time.

A hundred feet below the forge I watched Palma pluck linden flowers as she stood on a half-crumbling aqueduct. I warned her she was going to fall, the rocks were going to shred her skin, make a bloody mess out of her. Mrs. Pigeon interrupted my overwrought imagination.

"An infusion of linden flowers is good for indigestion and calming nerves." She was sitting on a low stone wall below Palma's aqueduct, wiping her face with a handkerchief. It was a hot day.

Andy wanted to go to the castle.

It was far, uphill, Mrs. Pigeon protested. He was still weak, but that hadn't stopped him from hanging out with his friends on the streets, smoking, refusing to come home, driving Mama crazy.

"Renzo and Lucia live by a lake," Palma said. "Susie, how does the beginning of The Betrothed go?"

"I'll go to the castle alone," Andy said.

I wrapped my arm around Andy's hip. He was still thin, his face long, his bones pushing out, with an unfamiliar dark fuzz on his chin which made him look more like Papa. The cough was all gone. Because of my vow, I dared to take a thin slice of the credit.

"I'll go with you," I said. "Just the two of us."

Last night, folding Andy's clothes into a suitcase, Mama said, "Sometimes I feel I'm falling and there's no floor to catch me."

That's how I felt now. The world had shifted and left me hanging.

"I can't stand it, Andygoat." I whispered. I kept rubbing my fingers over his wool vest as if by imprinting the feel of that vest in my skin, I would be able to conjure up my brother any time I chose. "I'll miss you too much." Mama had given him up. I assumed it was her vow to God.

"You'll get my bedroom," Andy said.

"Mama gave it to Palma."

Palma waved her arms. "*Dai*, Susie, recite the beginning of *The Betrothed*."

" 'That branch of Lake Como,' " Mrs. Pigeon quoted, " 'that turns toward the south, between two uninterrupted chains of mountains, all coves and bays.' "

Fifty feet back, we could see our parents standing just inside the stone arch of the forge. Mama lowered Claire to the ground. My little sister wavered back and forth, a sail caught in crosswinds. Papa was talking, his camera on his chest. The breeze carried sound upward, away from me.

I looked at the camera, inert on my father's chest, and imagined myself in its place, listening to his heartbeat, feeling his breath heave and ebb against my cheek.

Yesterday I'd asked Mama, "Why not me, why didn't you give me up?"

She wouldn't answer.

The reason had to do with love, I told myself. Andy was the bigger sacrifice. I'd wished myself sick when I found out. I prayed for tuberculosis, but I didn't even get my usual springtime hay fever.

BRACCIANO, ITALY—JUNE 10, 1943

Celebrating Claire's first birthday with an outing was Marco's idea— our last get-together as a family for I don't know how long. The thought corrodes my insides, but I know this is best. It's a conviction that allows me to face the day. I will not break down, cry, make a fool of myself. To make sure, I invited Palma and Mrs. Pigeon to come along.

Getting off the bus, I stumble. Marco steadies me, holds my elbow until I jerk myself free. "Why not all of us in Spain?" he asks with his low, gauzy voice that in the long-ago past always seduced me. "We'll dance the flamenco and no one will care if you're American or not." I laugh. My heart is shriveling.

In the restaurant we eat *luccio*, a lake fish that tastes of mud, while Mrs. Pigeon, with her ear-piercing voice, lists Claire's accomplishments: her sweetness, her curiosity, how she can play for hours with only a piece of old ribbon. At the table next to us, two men with the Fascist Party button in the holes of their lapels turn to look at us.

Claire's birthday cake is a bowl of rice and sugared milk that she delights in spreading over her face and hair. I start singing "Happy Birthday" in English. Marco, Palma, Susie, Andy, even Mrs. Pigeon with her cane, start bellowing *Tanti Auguri a Te*, their Italian trying to drown out my English. Song ended, Marco goes over to the next table to shake hands with the two party members. I hear "*sono un diplomatico*." They wave him away, their eyes on the heaping plates of rigatoni with cow innards the waiter is serving them.

"Thank God they're hungry," Mrs. Pigeon whispers.

When we reach the aqueduct, I slip into the cool dark forge with Claire. Marco follows.

"I can have you arrested for abandoning the conjugal roof," he says.

"Not the best thing for your career."

"Staying in Rome is not the best thing for the girls."

"He's an angry boy now," I say. "He doesn't listen to me, slips out at night when he thinks I'm asleep. I can't control him anymore. He needs his father." I made no vow to God, only to myself. To have the courage to give him up until the end of the war.

"Come with him. You and the girls. And Palma if you want."

"His lungs are damaged. It's hot in Barcelona. I heard the army is starting to recruit boys."

"Spain is safe. Isn't that what you wanted?"

"Are you sure the Allies are about to land in Sicily?" I ask.

"Last week the island of Pantelleria surrendered to the Brits. They now have control of the Sicilian Channel."

139

"The war will be over soon, then." I look up at the blackened vault, at the rotting wood beams, the cobwebs, the few pigeons sleeping inside the arch. It's only a matter of months. War ended, my boy will come back to me.

"The Germans are still strong." Marco is relentless. "It's going to be a brutal fight and you and the girls are going to be caught in the middle of it. The Allies could bomb Rome to show their might."

"Rome is inviolable. That's what you told me."

"Mussolini and the Grand Council are too stupid to surrender. Believe me, it's going to take at least another year for the Allies to win."

"What will happen to you when they do?"

"You care?"

"You're my children's father."

"I lap at whatever shore I come upon, remember? No one notices small waves."

"Don't take it out on Andy. Whatever you feel about me, leave him out of it. He doesn't like milk anymore, but he has to drink it anyway."

"Stay here if you want, but let me take the girls with me."

"There would be nothing left of me."

"Then you come too."

It would be the simple solution, the best one for the children, but a voice inside me keeps screaming, "Don't go! It's a trap!"

"You're acting crazy. I could, I should take the girls away from you."

I wait for my stomach to unclench before saying, "Each threat punctures another hole in my heart, and whatever good feeling I might one day still find there will have bled out. Leave me be, Marco. The war is about to end. The girls are perfectly safe with me, you know that."

Marco strokes Claire's head, his eyes avoiding mine. Maybe he heard me.

CAMBRIDGE, MASSACHUSETTS—MAY 1956

Andy made me promise to write to him every week and to be good to Mama. I gave him a felt sheath for his pen nibs on which I'd embroidered a goat. I also gave him a copy of *Sandokan's Revolt*, one of a series of exotic adventure books that were popular then. Andy gave me his bike on condition I wouldn't start bawling. I clenched my teeth.

"Meatloaf," I said.

"French fries."

"Salami."

"Ice cream."

"Miss you, Andygoat."

He hugged me. I pinched him to make sure he wouldn't forget me.

The day Andy left, I watched from the jump seat of the waiting taxi while Papa and the taxi driver tied Andy's suitcase on the luggage rack on top of Papa's. Mrs. Pigeon hovered, armed with her cane and pocketbook. "I'll look after them, Signor Console. I'll make sure they're fine."

"Me too," Palma sniffled, her apron a ball in her hands. "I'll take care of them."

"What are you crying for?" I snapped at her.

"You gave up," I accused Papa when he joined me in the cab. He lifted me up and nestled me against him.

"I could take you with me now. The law would be on my side, but I won't do that to your mother. It's precisely because I haven't given up that I've given in to her. Our family still has a future, I promise." He told me to be good. "Help her." He pressed me hard to his chest, twisting my neck. "Show her how much you love her."

Why me alone? If she needed help, why couldn't he stay? Why couldn't we all stay together to show her how much we loved her? I tried to free myself. "What if she takes me to Switzerland? And from there to America? I won't see you and Andy again."

He lifted my face up, held my cheek against his ear. "Never will she take you away, Chipmunk."

What about the forged letter, the lire stuffed in the curtain hems, the belongings Mama was selling to Ersilia one by one? What if I had told him? Would it have changed anything? It's a question without an answer. *Nutzlos*, my German teacher would have said. Useless.

I pick up the check stubs again, look through a few more years. Every January Papa donated the same amount to Le Suore di Maria della Consolazione. Was his generosity an act of penance? For Milena, for sending us to Rome, for losing Mama? Again a useless question. I finish my tea, now cold, and reach for my students' papers on Picasso's shattering of realism.

The day Andy left for Spain, I removed his pictures from their frames to keep him only in my mind, where I can watch his socks start to show underneath his slacks, his wrists stick out of his shirt cuffs, his face darken with the Barcelona sun. Susie wanted the photo of Andy in the consulate garden in Prague, kicking a soccer ball toward the camera. The rest I put in a trunk.

Each day is unbearably hot, too hot for sleep or food. For hours I lie in the bathtub filled with cold water. School is over. Sometimes Susie sits on the toilet seat to keep me company, her head immersed in a book while Claire plays on the bathroom rug. I'm alone now. The smell of tar from the bath soap sweeps under my nose. On the tub's ledge, a glass of sugared water Palma has brought which I won't drink. This reduced world fits me.

Banging at the door. "The brain needs food!" Mrs. Pigeon yells from the other side of the bathroom door.

"Then half the world is brainless," I answer.

More banging. Mrs. Pigeon wearing down her cane. "We've got the war to prove that, but that doesn't mean you have to join them. You can't spend your life in a bathtub."

I get out of the tub, trailing ribbons of water. Wet, naked, my feet and hands puckered like tripe, I open the door and tell her.

"At night the walls thicken, push at me, the bedroom becomes so narrow I can only stand. Then my husband squeezes in. He tells me I'm wrong, everything I do is wrong. Some nights my mother shows up with Marco. She's wearing the navy blue dress she always wore for Sunday services. Winter, summer, always that blue dress. The space is so small, I don't know how they fit in with me. Mother tells me, 'You're wrong, Alice. You've been wrong since the day you were born.'

"In the bathtub I wash the wrong away. I stay clean."

ROME, ITALY—JULY 2, 1943

Mrs. Pigeon has dragged me to the doctor, a *specialista*. "A man who does wonders with nerves," she claims. I imagine a magician pulling nerves out of a hat, limp strings that he waves to the audience while we all applaud.

In his large Parioli office with expensive antique furniture and Persian rugs, the *specialista* has just told me that a certain amount of delusional activity is to be expected during moments of upheaval.

"I sit in cold water because it's too hot. I'm not hungry because it's too hot. I have bad dreams because it's too hot. There's nothing wrong with me."

"She's grieving," Mrs. Pigeon says.

"My husband thinks I'm crazy. He wants to take the children away from me."

The doctor leans over his desk. "Let me explain what crazy is."

I steel myself for a list of symptoms I will recognize: Waking up to Andy's labored breathing when he isn't there, thinking I'm hanging over the earth with nothing to hold on to, looking at my girls and feeling no attachment, followed, seconds later, by a flood of love so overwhelming it clogs my chest. Seeing my children on the street, their bodies in pieces, scattered by a bomb.

"Crazy is an officer"—the *specialista*'s mouth is so dry, his lips smack with each word—"trying to walk, falling, picking himself up, trying again, falling again. Falling so many times his forehead cracks open, and all because he cannot remember he left half his leg under the tread of a tank.

"Crazy is a twenty-year-old soldier who crawls into his mother's wardrobe and sings to himself in Russian all day, '*Italianski suida.*' The Italians are here."

"What about his poor mother?" Mrs. Pigeon asks.

The doctor writes out a quick prescription. "Veronal, one pastille in the morning, one at night. My dear signora, there's nothing wrong with you that the end of this war won't cure."

My thought exactly.

CAMBRIDGE, MASSACHUSETTS—MAY 1956

This morning I sit in the kitchen in front of a bouquet of family photographs that I've plucked from various parts of the house.

Each member of the family is separate, in his own frame:

My sweetly chubby David, in shorts and torn shirt, showing off a newly found pottery shard.

Andy, last year, twenty-eight years old, sweaty after a game of tennis, the stroke of falling dark hair forever gone from his forehead.

Claire, twelve, in the mountains of Cortina D'Ampezzo, wearing my mother's pretty face and red curls, grinning out at the cameraman, Papa.

Papa, in the spring of 1939, posing in front of a plane that is about to fly him from Los Angeles to New York, from which a boat will take him to Europe. Tweed jacket, hat in hand, smiling, relaxed, as though the future were as secure in his hands as the book he clasps to his chest.

My mother, her hair neat, her makeup perfect, is a still life in her tinted studio portrait taken in Newport Beach. After the war, Papa gave each of us a copy of that photo, an heirloom in a silver frame, a tangible legacy I will pass down to my daughter along with the letters that survived.

My family—our memories each shade our mother's story differently. If I could pool our memories into one, it would give a truer picture of Mama and of us. Claire rightfully points out she was only two when Mama died/ walked away. Papa gave me the letters and kept silent. Andy says he's too busy with the present and the future. Remembering her, finding her, is my compulsion.

Every week Mama, Claire, and I took the bus down the Tritone to Via del Corso and Palazzo Chigi, where the Foreign Ministry was located, to pick up Papa's letter.

Their Barcelona apartment had a white grand piano that had once belonged to one of General Franco's girlfriends. Andy was playing the violin again, studying with a maestro who came twice a week and demanded to be fed olives and cheese while Andy played. The maestro's face was as round as a Parmesan wheel, and he spit olive pits at Andy's legs whenever Andy missed a note.

At the bottom of the letter, Andy's pinched, stingy "love you, Mama, ciao Susie."

Mama would tear the strip of Andy's words and tuck it in her pocket. The rest of the letter she let me keep. If we were lucky, Papa would send cans of sardines or tuna, biscuits, and olives in glass jars that miraculously didn't break. The food and the letters only filled me with envy and self-pity.

On July 10, the Allies landed in Sicily. The Italian newspapers reported the supposed conditions of surrender:

Suppression of most of the universities. Prohibition of grain cultivation. Abolition of classical teaching so that the young cannot be inspired by the historical greatness of Rome. The removal of art treasures from both public and private hands. Italians will be forced to buy the sterling at 480 lire. We will be reduced to poverty.

ROME, ITALY—JULY 14, 1943

I write to Marco:

> You accuse me of being selfish and I agree. I left you without thinking of my children. My head was full of arrogance. Since I could not be all for you, I wanted to be everything for them—father, mother, friend. I was nauseated by your betrayal. I in turn betrayed you.
>
> I rejected your political shilly-shallying, "lapping" you call it. But I have not been able to complete one action against this war. Only against you, our marriage, the family.
>
> Susie spies on my every movement with blades of hate in her eyes. I watch Claire stare at corners, at doors, her eyes light with hope. She's waiting for Andy. We all wait for him. Susie also waits for you. I want Andy back. He's my son, he needs his mother. I no longer believe in you, but, if it is any satisfaction to you, I disgust myself.
>
> Everyone here expects the war to be over in a matter of weeks. The newspapers are full of lies. Allied planes fly over Rome almost every night, throwing down propaganda leaflets telling us to overthrow the Fascists. Last night I ran down to the garden and picked up the sheets one by one, thinking, maybe, just maybe one of them was a letter from my son.
>
> There are rumors that the Allies have landed in Sicily. May it be so. How long will it take them to find us?"

I black out the last two lines. They would only be censored.

It's an oppressively hot Monday. Susie and I take the bus to Palazzo Chigi, where the usual cream-colored envelope with the raised Italian Royal Crest on the back is waiting for us. I lean against the tall Roman column at the center of Piazza Colonna, tear the envelope open, pocket the check Marco sends every month, and quickly run my eyes down the length of the letter. "It's from Andy." I hand it to Susie. "The sun is too bright." I wanted Marco telling me he was bringing Andy back.

"'Ciao everyone,'" Susie starts.

"'Yesterday we went to a fishing village on the Costa Brava and ate mariscos as big as Claire's feet! There were rolls and rolls of barbed wire along the beach as if that is going to stop anyone from invading.'"

A drone makes me look up. The sky is a bare blue, but the sound grows louder. I've heard planes before, the RAF, the US air force with its Flying Fortresses, *l'Aeronautica*, heavy with bombs, tearing across the night in packs. "Like dogs looking for a bitch in heat," Andy used to say.

At night. Never in daylight.

The drone breaks into a dull, soft sound, as though a rock hit soft earth somewhere up ahead, too far away to see. The air raid siren starts howling.

"Run!" I tug Susie across the Corso, into the Galleria.

A man shouts, "There's a shelter at Piazza Barberini!" Susie runs ahead of me, pulling me hard, her legs turning into churning windmills, spewing sidewalks. Under the wail of the siren, the drone continues.

At Piazza Barberini Susie stops next to the movie house, behind the mass of bodies pushing each other to get inside the shelter. I wrench her away. "Claire!" She was home with Palma.

We turn up the twisting, steep beginning of Via Veneto. On the steps of Saint Mary of the Conception, a priest is waving people in. "Come! The crypt is safe. Come!"

A crypt filled with the bones and skulls of Capuchin friars, a terrifying sight that will not save Claire. I keep running.

My eyes have to adjust to the darkness of the basement. I am too out of breath to call Palma's name. Gina, perched on a stool by the door, declares that we are turning into sewer rats.

Holding Susie's hand, I pick my way past the spot where the grumpy ninety-year-old *dottore* always sat. He died in May. "I was going to take my sons to Abruzzi last week," his daughter says to her neighbor, Topo's mother. "American planes," Topo says. "They were flying so low I could see the pilot."

His mother swats the back of his head. "Stop making things up."

"I did see them. I did."

"Why are they doing this to us?" his mother asks me. I can't see Palma or Mrs. Pigeon. Palma knows to come down here.

"Palma," I call out. The war widow is asking her dead husband to forgive her sins. Next to her the fat engineer raises his fist at me as I walk by. "You will be damned in hell," he shouts.

"It's not her fault," Palma yells back. I run to her. She's sitting in a far corner with Claire on her lap. The sight of my baby overwhelms me. I sink down to the floor, pick her up, cover her with kisses, take small bites of her neck, tickle her until she squeals.

The engineer keeps shouting. "Bastards! How dare you touch this holy city. Il Duce will make you pay for this."

I'm having trouble breathing. My spine, my stomach, the soles of my feet burn. My head spins. It's a vile thing they've done. We've done. How will destroying Rome win the war?

"I love this city," I tell the room. "I am so sorry." Claire pulls at my nose, sticks her fingers in my mouth. I inhale her sweet smell, but my heart stays clenched. How many dead?

"Mrs. Pigeon wouldn't come down," Palma says. "She said thieves empty whole apartments while people in shelters wait for the All Clear."

Susie is rummaging through her pockets, through my handbag. "Andy's letter is gone," she cries. "I lost it."

"Tonight you can write to him and ask him to repeat his letter."

She likes my suggestion. "I have lots to tell him now," she says. "Barcelona doesn't get bombed, does it?"

"No." I'm a terrible mother.

"I miss him, Mama."

"I miss him too."

"I'm scared."

I pull Susie in, squeeze her and Claire against my chest. "I'll take care of you, my sweeties." I will keep them safe forever. A reason to live.

The All Clear sounds and we stumble out, blinded by the sudden light. "Look, Mama!" Susie cries and runs to our garden gate, which now hangs open. Behind her, Palma claps her hands to her mouth. Our chickens and their cage are gone. Our vegetable garden has been swept clean too. Susie whips her head around and offers me a blanched face with big dark eyes washed in tears. "Don't tell Papa. Promise you won't tell Papa!"

I kiss her forehead. "I promise."

"And when he comes we'll tell him we ate everything up."

"Yes." When he brings Andy back. I tell Susie she cannot retrace her steps back to Piazza Colonna to look for Andy's letter.

The law requires that we stand to listen to the news bulletin. At seven p.m. Gina, Palma, the girls, and I are sitting in Mrs. Pigeon's overstuffed living room, drinking the linden flower tea Palma made, which Mrs. Pigeon insists will "calm our hearts."

We learn the Allies hit the old cemetery of Verano, uprooting trees in the piazza, bursting open sarcophagi, spilling decomposing bodies and skeletons onto the streets.

"At least they're already dead," Gina says. Palma keeps crossing herself.

The roof and portico of the thirteenth-century Basilica of San Lorenzo has been destroyed "by the cowardly forces of the enemy," a pulpit-voiced announcer intones. The "Sacred Father," Papa Pacelli himself, has gone to see the damage.

The Policlinico, Andy's hospital, has also been bombed, while across the street from the hospital, the newsstand where I used to buy the paper remains intact. Palma remembers there was a *tondo* of the Madonna on the wall behind the vendor. "That's what saved him."

"The Madonna was also in the Basilica of San Lorenzo," Mrs. Pigeon points out from her armchair in the corner. "Perhaps she was asleep?"

I listen, but the horror of the news doesn't sink in. I feel numb, emotionally exhausted. Claire starts crying, kicking her feet, twisting to free herself from my arms. I hold her tighter.

The radio warns us of delayed-reaction bombs. All citizens are asked to conserve water and not to turn on the gas as lines throughout the city might be damaged.

Claire screeches. I rock her back and forth.

"Let her go," Susie says.

Mrs. Pigeon folds her hands over the silver handle of her cane, always the sign of an upcoming pronouncement. "Signora Alessandrini, if you keep restraining Claire, she will never learn to walk. My daughter walked by the time she was—"

A blast of anger hits me. "Your daughter has a name! What's her name? Anna? Maria? Claudia? Think of all the dead today. Who would they be without names?" Susie takes Claire from me.

"Sons," Mrs. Pigeon says. "Husbands, wives, daughters, mothers, nieces, nephews."

"No!" Gina protests. "Pieruccio was Pieruccio."

"She was more than your daughter," I say. "She was a human being. Why can't you call her by her name?"

Susie cries out, "Everyone look at Claire." She lifts her sister up on her feet, steps back, holds out her arms. Claire wavers. "Ma, ma, ma," she says with a wet smile. She takes one step, two, three! For a moment, there is no war, no bombs, no guilt or shame. There is only Claire, taking her first step. My heart exults.

We all clap. Claire rewards us with a delighted laugh and flops down on the tiger rug. I start to sob. Gina, who has not spoken to me since the Allies bombed Naples a second time, offers me her handkerchief, which brings more tears, while the radio announcer asks the "valorous citizens of Rome" to leave the city in an orderly and calm fashion. Extra gas will be provided until Sunday, the 25th of July.

"My daughter was stubborn." Mrs. Pigeon's eyes are closed, her face shot through with what can only be pain. "Disobedient. She did all the things I didn't want her to do, but she was, will always be, my beautiful daughter. Donatella Marina Cortini." She opens her eyes to look at me. "You heard the radio. You and the girls should leave. Go to the Questura with your letter and get an exit permit out of this rotting country."

Yes! If only I could. "For where? I haven't saved enough. The Swiss will only let us stay if I can provide for us, and yet they won't give me a work permit."

"Tomorrow we'll go to the post office and take out Donatella's dowry money. You'll pay me back after the war. Your husband won't find out from me."

I rush to her and kiss both her cheeks. "God bless you."

She clasps my arm, leans forward, and whispers, "Your husband asked me to spy on you, offered me money to warn him if you were acting strangely, if you were leaving. I told him nothing." She lets go of my arm and announces loudly, "I'll want that loan paid back in dollars. That will be interest enough."

CAMBRIDGE, MASSACHUSETTS—MAY 1956

Claire took her first step the day the Allies bombed Rome. I like to think she was already bright enough to know it was time to get out of there. Mrs. Pigeon offered Mama money to go to Switzerland. I'll run away, I thought. I'll take Claire and run to Barcelona.

The next morning Mama decided I should go with her to San Lorenzo to search under the rubble for possible survivors. The thought of coming across a mangled body turned my stomach upside down.

Palma was on my side. "Susie is too young! Oh, please, signora, I'll come. Let Susie stay home!"

Implacable Mrs. Pigeon rooted for Mama. "Think of it as a test," she said. "Your entry into the adult world."

She was challenging me. I stared back at her and nodded. I was good at tests and I determined to pass this one. No crying, no throwing up, no emotion at all.

The woman's face was dusty, one arm stiff and upraised. Two firemen bent over her, cleaning her of bricks and rubble. The top blue rectangle of an apron appeared on her chest, crocheted lace around its border. She could have been a statue toppled from its perch in a church alcove, her hand raised in a blessing.

Before my vow, I would have squatted on a pile of bricks and started drawing her, the soldiers, displaced tenants, relatives on their hands and knees, digging into the hills of collapsed buildings, the street crowded with people pushing carts filled with salvaged belongings. I imagined calling my sketchbook *After* and sending it to Andy and Papa to show them what they missed.

A woman with an arm bandaged in a raveled white sweater climbed over the mounds of bricks and called out, "Regina! Regina! Has anyone seen a black cat with white paws?" She wore a man's gray hat that bobbed as she moved. "Regina!"

The thin fireman straightened up and stretched his arms down his thighs. Blond, cute, with a sun-burnt face, he had Andy's same ears, small shells tight against his head. He noticed me and I quickly turned away.

A covey of Dorotee Sisters had set up an emergency canteen on the other side of the street. They offered me *caffellatte* that Mama wouldn't let me accept because I had lost nothing in the bombing. I argued that I'd lost Andy's letter, but she said that didn't count. I sulked and decided she was just plain mean, while all she was trying to do was make amends for the fourteen hundred people the Allied bombing had killed.

A pretty woman with black hair down to her waist stopped to look at the only standing wall of a building. On the fourth floor, a white tiled corner still held a dish towel on its hook next to three shelves stacked with cans. I could make out the bright red of San Marzano tomatoes on the labels.

"How do I get up there?" the black-haired woman asked my fireman. Her housecoat was torn under one armpit, revealing a pink lace slip she kept trying to hide with her arm.

"One gust of wind," my fireman said, "the whole wall goes." He smiled at her. I could wish on all the stars in the sky and never be as pretty as she was or get him to look at me that way.

"I'll wait until it falls down then. I'm not giving up those tomatoes."

A pack of dogs sprung up from behind a crumbled wall. The woman picked up a rock. I yelled and ran between her and the dogs. The dogs bolted. She was left with a rock in her hand and a nasty look on her face.

"Let them be," my fireman said. "They're as hungry as truffle dogs, good for finding bodies."

"They're not getting my food," the woman said.

"Dogs can't open cans," I spit at her. She shrugged and returned her gaze high, to the three stacks of canned tomatoes.

My fireman went back to work freeing the dead woman of debris. When he finally lifted her out, I could see the dark stain of dried blood searing her lap and fresh blood on his hands.

I scrambled over a heap of smashed bricks and held out my clean handkerchief.

"What?" He had blue eyes underneath dust-thick lashes.

"For your hands."

"Thanks." He didn't smile.

I walked away and watched him spit on my handkerchief, lean over, and gently clean the dead woman's face

"Her name is Donatella," I called out.

He stopped wiping to look up. "You know her?"

A lie for a smile, a kiss maybe. "Just her name."

Mama was calling me. "We came here to help, not talk." She was on her knees on top of a mound, picking up bricks, aiming them at the wheel barrow below, usually missing. She looked small in the middle of heaps of rubble, arms lashing out like one of Andy's old wind-up soldiers. Just as helpless too.

An old man with the face of a hawk stood watching her. "Why don't you use a shovel?"

"Someone could still be alive."

I picked up the bricks that missed the wheel barrow and stole peeks at my fireman as he lifted the dead woman onto a cart and pushed her down the street.

"Don't pick up any pens," the old man said. "They'll explode in your face. The same thing with dolls. It's a new English trick, presents from the sky. To think I fought with those murderers in the Great War." He took a sip from his tin cup, twisted his hawk's face. "Nuns make lousy coffee."

We worked all day, clearing bricks, chunks of plaster, tiles, shoes, kitchenware, jackets still on hangers, a set of embroidered white linen towels that the old man claimed, saying they belonged to the dowry of his next-door neighbor. The only dead we found was a calico cat. I was glad it wasn't Regina.

We went back to the San Lorenzo quarter the next day with Palma. On Thursday, July 22nd, our third day of digging for survivors, English and American troops entered Palermo, Sicily. In Rome it was hot and windless, and the stench at San Lorenzo was so bad that we tied kerchiefs over our noses and mouths. We'd worn out our gloves and had no skin left on our fingertips. I looked for my fireman, but didn't find him.

While we waited in a knot of people for the bus home, Mama announced it would be our last day of paying our dues. "Tomorrow I'm buying our train tickets."

"I won't go." I would stay in Via Aurora and live with Palma until Papa came to get us.

Mama lowered her kerchief. Her face was two-toned, the top half black with dirt, the bottom part white with anger. "What is the matter with you?"

"I won't go. You can't make me!" If this was a test to the adult world, I didn't want to pass it. "I'm staying here!"

"What are you upset about?" the woman behind me wanted to know. "You're alive, aren't you?"

Palma shushed me, rubbed my shoulders. "We'll see the world. You'll read me new stories."

In my head I wrote a telegram. "Mama is kidnapping me Stop I'll never see you again Stop Stop her." I'd send the telegram and then go to the Foreign Ministry and tell whoever would listen.

Mama raised her hand. I offered my cheek, ready to be struck. She stroked that cheek, her blisters spongy against my skin. "I'm not bad, Chipmunk. I'm not."

I stepped back from her hand. Good and Evil, the nuns had branded the two concepts in my brain. Black and white. One or the other. No in-between, no gray area, no ambiguity, no confusion. Good or Evil. It was my choice, and I had chosen sides a long time ago. How secure, how strong I felt knowing what was what. Mama didn't stand a chance.

The bus stopped in front of us, swung its doors open. The knot of people plowed through us. Mama waited for me to climb on first. Maybe she was afraid I was going to make a run for it. I felt empty of bones, dizzy. My stomach heaved and I bent over the curb, retching up my lunch sandwich and an endless stream of bile. The bus left without us.

Mama held my head as she always did when I threw up, but that one time, I want to think that her hand on my forehead was also a gesture of forgiveness.

The next day, Friday, Mama slipped into her purse the letter she had forged with my father's signature, giving his wife and children permission to leave the country, and walked to the *Questura Centrale* for an exit permit. The line snaked down two flights of stairs. By the time police headquarters closed at two p.m., she was ten people away from the permit room. The usher told her to come back on Monday.

I didn't send Papa a telegram and I didn't go to the Foreign Ministry to tell them my mother was taking me out of the country without my father's permission. I kept thinking of the dead woman in San Lorenzo, her stiff arm upraised to fend off the wall that had buried her.

EIGHT

ROME, ITALY—JULY 26, 1943

Music wakes me up. I get out of bed and open the shutters to light the color of ashes. On the street people are dancing between pools of quivering water. Old women in housecoats waltz with the tips of their slippers catching on the cobblestones. A woman, dressed in flame red, breaks away from her partner. "We're rid of him!" Her arm lashes out at me like a tongue of fire.

"*Venga, Signora Alessandrini, venga,*" the partner says. "The next dance is mine."

A bathrobed blonde, head covered with curling ribbons, turns into a yellow chrysanthemum as she twirls with her chenille belt following her. The crooner gets stuck. "Today, today, today . . ."

With furry eyes I make out a gramophone propped up on the windowsill of the building across the street, hear a long scratch of sound as a hand nudges the needle. "Today we are wed," the crooner sings. Rabagliati, Palma's favorite. With that recognition comes the sensation of hot air settling on my face, the smell of last night's fried onions, the buzz of bees. I recognize Cesare dancing with the war widow all in red. The bathrobed blonde with the curling ribbons lives on the third floor. The angry engineer is waltzing Gina. The pools of water turn into blankets of shattered glass. Rugs hang out of windows as in holy days.

"Fascism is dead!" Cesare shouts. Whoops of joy from the dancers, from the surrounding windows.

I'm in a dream. The shutters next to mine open. I can see the tip of Susie's shoulder, pink with fading blue flowers. She's real. "Is it true?" I ask her. "Is it over?"

"The radio announced it last night."

"Why didn't you wake me? Why didn't anybody tell me?"

Her flowered shoulder shrugs.

"The war is over then?" I shout down, still afraid to believe. Is it over that easily? During the span of one night, the sun dipping into the ocean and coming out clean?

Cesare runs up to the gate. I have not stepped into his latteria since that sordid afternoon in his back room. "The king has accepted Benito Mussolini's resignation. Field Marshal Badoglio is the new head of state. Badoglio says he's going to keep Italy's word to the Germans," Cesare's voice dips and peaks, "but no one believes him. The Americans are bringing sugar with them, and I'll be selling sweet pastries again. *Gloria all'Italia.* Come dance with me, *bella signora.* The war will be over in a matter of days."

Happiness flashes through me as red as the war widow's dress. "Today," I sing out with Rabagliati, a wonderful today. The exit visa will be easy to get. The train tickets too. No one will want to leave the country now.

"Oh, *signora mia.*" Palma looks up from the garden, tears streaming, probably the only person on the street who still loves Mussolini. "What will happen to him?"

"*Gloria all' Egitto,*" Cesare sings from *Aida*, drowning out Rabagliati.

I get dressed and quickly set out toward Via Veneto. Susie joins me without asking questions as we arrow through the throngs on the street. Every Roman is shouting. Every church bell is ringing. All the car horns of the city are honking. Susie and I run up Via Nazionale, slapping the sides of trucks and buses full of people waving the Italian flag, singing *Risorgimento* songs of freedom and rebirth. Along the flank of one bus, someone has painted *FINALMENTE!* I yell,

"*Evviva!*" and from the roof of the bus a woman throws down a white carnation which I slip in the button hole of my blouse.

When we reach the *Questura*, a squat man in civilian clothes is standing fascist straight, with spread legs, in front of a clutch of people. "Come back tomorrow. Police headquarters is closed."

I'm too keyed-up to feel disappointment. A boy, curly haired, fifteen, sixteen years old, strides up to the squat guard. "Not sure whose ass to lick this time? Is that why you're out of uniform?"

More boys surround us, seven or eight in all. Bare-chested, showing off tanned muscles, they hit their thighs with fists hungry for a fight. I wrap an arm around Susie's shoulder and start to inch backward. The first boy shoves the front page of *Il Messaggero* against the guard's chest. *Viva L'Italia Libera!* the headline reads. Hurray for a Free Italy!

"Show me a black shirt," the guard says. Fear is pulling his face out of shape. "Show me a black shirt and he's with the fish in the Tiber."

The boys laugh and the tension dissipates.

I ask the guard, "The *Questura* will be open tomorrow for sure?"

He fills his chest with air. "What's for sure anymore?"

"I am," I say.

Ersilia sweeps into our living room on high heels she's tied to her ankles with packing string to keep them from sliding off. "I am the torch of freedom!" she announces. She is dressed like a Hollywood star, in a low-cut, yellow silk ball gown. The train draped over one arm, black lace gloves to her elbows. Behind her, Ceci, her hair curled up in multicolored ribbons, nestles into an armchair, instantly at home.

"Who are you?" Susie asks her. "You're wearing my clothes." Ceci sticks out her tongue.

"Don't be rude, Ceci," Ersilia says. "We're in a fancy home here. Ehi, Rossa, can you believe it? Il Duce behind bars and us dancing in the street." She turns back to the front door, which she's left open. "Coast is clear, Nando. They've put down their guns." She laughs. "He's an idiot."

She loops her train around me, pulls me in, kisses me on the lips. "Time to celebrate, Bella!"

Susie slips under the train, letting the silk shudder across her arm. Nando trudges in, loaded down with two suitcases. I recognize him as the man who asked Ersilia how much it cost to get her on her back. A heavy square face, with the thin mustache of a cartoon villain.

"Why is she wearing my clothes?" Susie asks. Ceci has fallen asleep.

"I've brought you stuff," Ersilia says. Her crinkly hair is piled on top of her head like Palma's, spikes instead of curls. "It's free, too." She orders Nando to open the suitcases. "Put everything on the sofa. Let their eyes fill up first."

Nando unpacks bottles of wine, half a wheel of cheese. "Certain families have left their residences in such a hurry they forgot their food!" She runs her hands down her hips. "And their clothes." She picks up a package wrapped in a wool scarf and hands Susie one end. "Pull!"

Susie tugs; the scarf unravels to show a shiny mass of meat.

Palma gasps. "A pork loin!"

Ersilia heaves the loin in the air, lets it fall in the crook of her arms. "Pink and fat as Mussolini's ass!"

"And we're going to eat it!" Susie shouts.

Ersilia wakes up Ceci and they take over the kitchen. I send Susie to invite Mrs. Pigeon and Gina while Ersilia cuts holes in the meat, stuffs it with the garlic and rosemary Ceci has chopped. Palma digs into the Parmesan wheel with a screwdriver and offers jagged pieces of cheese after Mrs. Pigeon and Gina join us. "It's woman's time," Ersilia tells Nando, and with a curt bow, he leaves. I've had no wine, but my head spins anyway. My skin hums. I feel every muscle, every sinew of my body. The heat of my blood rushing through me. This day has turned my life, the girls' lives, around. Instead of a wall, we face only possibility. The golden ring is only inches away. It's up to me.

Instead of eating in the dining room, we crowd around the kitchen table, not wanting to abandon the glorious smell of roasting meat. Claire sleeps through most of dinner. Susie and Ceci wipe their plates clean and snitch sips of wine from Palma's glass. She pretends not to notice, and I'm too happy to protest. Mrs. Pigeon chews her food slowly and tries to avert her eyes from Ersilia's flamboyance and

Ceci's dirty face and hands. It's a battle she loses every other minute. Gina eats three helpings. I get high.

Ersilia has also snitched a record—Benny Goodman. Susie reads off the titles of the songs, Ceci trying to mouth the words after her. "Sugar Foot Stomp." "Moonglow." "The Sheik of Araby." "I'm a Ding Dong Daddy from Dumas."

Ersilia shakes her head. "Can you believe those bastards?"

Mrs. Pigeon heaves her mighty chest up and speaks for the first time. "Signorina, there are children in this room!"

"Can you believe those Fascists?" Ersilia flutters her mascaraed eyelashes at Mrs. Pigeon. "Same word isn't it, signora? What I'm trying to say, and the children have to hear this, is that they, those Fascists, those b-a-s-"—

—"t-a-r-d-s," I join in. Ceci laughs and nudges Susie. They both repeat the spelling.

—"forbid us to play American music. If we did, we'd go to jail. And those Fascists, behind closed doors, swung their Ding Dong Daddies to the King of Swing. And now they're going to swing at the end of a rope."

"It's not over yet, signorina," Mrs. Pigeon portends. The oracle of Delphi has spoken and I don't believe a word.

"We don't have a record player," I announce. I want to dance. Mrs. Pigeon and Gina don't have one either. We debate asking the other tenants.

Mrs. Pigeon thinks it's dangerous. "It's not over."

"Suit yourself, signora." Ersilia knots her train out of the way around one arm. "I'm dancing." I start la-la-la-ing the only song I know from the record: "Nice Work If You Can Get It." Ersilia unties her heels, kicks them off, and swings Susie around the kitchen table. Palma dances alone. I spin Ceci until she gets too heavy. Then we gyrate solo. Mrs. Pigeon bobs her head, but stops if anyone looks at her. Claire manages to sleep through the din.

At the end of the evening—wine bottles empty, the roast polished off, the cheese wheel looking like a bombed-out crater, the table cleared, the dishes washed and put away—we flop down on our chairs around the table and sing a chorus of thanks to Ersilia to the tune of "Happy Birthday." Black tears run down her cheeks.

Ceci laughs. "You got cracks in your face."

"It's all right," Ersilia says. "Everything is finally all right."

We believe her. Thanks to a full stomach, now Mrs. Pigeon does too.

ROME, ITALY—AUGUST 3, 1943

Lethargy took over after our celebration. I could use the excuse that I was simply hung over, except what hangover lasts a week? Something was holding me back. "Exhaustion," is Mrs. Pigeon's opinion. "Too much, too quickly." It's a plausible reason, which exonerates me.

I'm filled with the need to know everything that is happening and have spent these past days with the girls devouring the newspapers in Mrs. Pigeon's cool, dark living room with the rugs beaten clean and rolled up for the summer. I've learned that the Council of Ministers has officially dissolved the Fascist Party. A senator committed suicide. Taxi cabs, lugging gas tanks on their roofs as part of an experiment of the old government, are now mandated to park in front of police stations in case of need. The papers warn us against "false news." A curfew was declared from 9:30 p.m. until dawn. The military has taken over police duties. Public and private meetings have been forbidden. Political prisoners are now free. All public portraits of Mussolini have vanished. Shop windows display photos of Badoglio and the king as if they too were on sale.

"No one is a Fascist anymore," Mrs. Pigeon noted yesterday. "And isn't it ironic that the Eliseo is playing the musical *Goodbye to All This*."

"Will they hurt him?" Palma kept asking after we heard that Mussolini was arrested. Now that the papers have revealed that for years Il Duce had a mistress, Palma worries about her too.

In the bombed quarter of San Lorenzo, the soup kitchens set up by the nuns feed three thousand people a day. The schools are full of evacuees. When the Princess of Piedmont visited some of them, she got her hand kissed.

"Oh, she's so elegant," Palma said, looking at the picture over my shoulder. "What I wouldn't give to have a large white hat like that."

Claire keeps tearing off corners of the paper and throws them up in the air in a celebration of her own. Susie sulks or reads to Palma in a corner.

Every day I read the "Has anyone seen" requests, my heart gripped by all the children, wives, husbands, parents that are missing. "Looking for a son," I want to write in. "Anyone with information, please write." But my son is safe. With his father. I have no right to complain, but I seek him anyway.

Air raid alarms keep going off at lunchtime and in the middle of the night. We drag ourselves in and out of the basement. Susie finally finishes reading *The Betrothed* to Palma, who cries at the happy ending.

Like all the other government employees, Marco is no longer a Fascist. The king and Badoglio are his bosses now. Mrs. Pigeon's telephone stays silent. Instead he sent a telegram. "All is well now Stop we wait for you."

I could answer, "My heart is not well." Instead, last night, while Susie and Claire slept next to me, I wrote a letter.

Marco—I need to do this one thing—take the girls to Switzerland. On my own. I know they would be safe in Spain with you. They will be safe with me. I don't know if you want me or just the girls. I don't know if I want only Andy. I don't know if we can still glue our marriage back into a solid whole. Too many things I don't know. My act of defiance—that's what you called it, remember?—this getting away from you (because Rome is full of you, Marco, you know that. It may even be one of the reasons you forced me here), going into clean territory, clean not only of war, but mainly of you, will clear my head. Allow me this time. Understand me.

As soon as we settle in Lugano, I will let you know our address. I've thought that you might visit us there, that we would talk, but then I remembered that occupied France will stand between us. The war will have to end before I can look at your face again.

Alice

This morning I walked to the *Questura* and waited three hours for our exit permit. No one bothered to check the file of persons not allowed to leave the country, the file with my name on it. The letter with Marco's forged signature stayed inside my handbag. Fascist rules no longer apply. I'll get the Swiss permits at the border. The letter I will mail at the train station the morning I leave.

CAMBRIDGE, MASSACHUSETTS—MAY 1956

A few nights before Mama bought our train tickets, I woke up to her weight on my bed. When I opened my eyes, the light was on and she was grazing her hand over my shoulder, my head.

"What is it, Mama?"

"A nightmare. I just wanted to make sure you're okay. Go back to sleep, Susie."

I moved over, opened the sheet to let her in as she did with me when I had nightmares.

"What was it?"

She snuggled against me. "I dreamed we were climbing the Matter-horn, the three of us roped together. On the other side of the mountain, your father was waiting for us. We kept going, leaping over ravine after ravine like mountain goats. It was easy. Almost like flying. In front of the last ravine, I could see Papa. He was waving at us, urging us on. I leaped, but this time I didn't reach the other side. I spiraled down the ravine, it was thousands of feet deep, I couldn't see the bottom. I was pulling you and Claire down with me." She was crying. "I'm doing my best, sweetie. My best for you and Claire."

"Mrs. Pigeon's daughter fell down a ravine," I reminded her. "That's why you had the dream." I prayed for God to change her mind about what was "best."

ROME, ITALY—AUGUST 6, 1943

At the train station, I wait only forty-five minutes to buy two second-class tickets. Claire rides free. Palma is staying with Mrs. Pigeon. We leave in two weeks.

"Maybe you don't have to leave now," Mrs. Pigeon says when I come back. Her face is stern, chest expanding at the sight of our train tickets, arming herself against another loss. "We finally have our beautiful Italy back."

"It's not my country," I tell her.

"It's mine," Susie protests. Back downstairs I sit her down at the kitchen table and make her write out "I am an American" a hundred times.

CAMBRIDGE, MASSACHUSETTS—MAY 1956

We were leaving and I hated Mama for it. I felt as though she had imbedded a hook in the roof of my mouth and was pulling with all her weight.

After picking up the tickets, we went to say goodbye to Ersilia. The picture that is in my head is of her standing in the splotchy shade of the sycamore trees on the Lungotevere. Behind her, the terra cotta roofs, the church spires, the Janiculum Hill with its hat of pines. Castel Sant'Angelo looks blanched in the heat. The cupolas of Saint Peter's waver as if in boiling water. The air smells of tar.

Ersilia was wearing my mother's pink silk dress with peach blossoms. She'd belted the dress, which was too big for her, with a *carabiniere's* black belt, resting the heavy silver flame buckle on one hip bone. "I've got to sell your stuff in a hurry, before the Americans get here with theirs."

What Mama had kept of our belongings could fit into two suitcases. "They're bringing weapons, not clothes," Mama said. She knew from the BBC that the Allies were still stuck in Sicily. "Maybe they're not coming at all."

"Sure they are, and we'll get lots of meat and silk and mink and chewing gum." Ersilia clapped my face between her hands. I pulled away. Another goodbye. I was getting good at it. Act fast. One, two, three, yank! Like getting rid of a milk tooth. Something else will grow in its place.

Her mustache glinted gold in the sun. Her eyelashes were crusts of mascara. "Keep dancing." She wiggled her hips and sang, "I'm a Ding Dong Daddy from Dumas."

"Mama is taking the record with us. It's only going to break in a million pieces."

Mama stroked my hair. "It might not break. We can hope for that. Try, Chipmunk."

Ersilia pressed her lips against both my cheeks, rubbed the lipstick over my cheekbones. "Remember me, keep Rome in your heart, and never cry. It's murder on your face."

ROME, ITALY—AUGUST 13, 1943

Badoglio keeps assuring the Germans that the war will continue, and in a deadly tit for tat, the Allies are pelting all of Italy with bombs, especially the northern industrial cities. Naples, because of its port, got hit again twice within a few days. Twenty bombs dropped on the Royal Palace and the BBC announcer boasted about a job well done. I keep apologizing to Gina and Palma, which is of no help at all. We all feel so utterly helpless under this onslaught.

Bombs have destroyed railway tracks to prevent supplies going through, and I worry it will prevent us from leaving. In Genoa— apartment buildings, theaters, schools have collapsed. Livorno is almost completely destroyed. The Allies want unconditional surrender.

There are rumors that the Vatican is urging the government to move its military facilities out of the city and make Rome an open city, which means it wouldn't be bombed anymore.

I've hidden our train tickets in the hem of the bedroom curtains along with the money and mostly stay in bed, with the excuse that I'm coming down with a cold. Anxiety is paralyzing me. Claire takes more and more steps on her own. Outside it's blistering hot. It storms, it hails, the humidity coddles my feeling of imprisonment. Palma claims God is showing his anger at the country for staying in the war.

The air raid alarm starts howling.

CAMBRIDGE, MASSACHUSETTS—MAY 1956

On August 13, Allied planes bombed Rome for an hour and a half. While I took Claire down to the basement, Mama leaned out of the window and yelled *"Basta!"* until Palma dragged her away. Later, Mama realized she had yelled in Italian. "They couldn't understand," she told me.

That evening Palma and Gina took me to Saint Peter's Square. The Pope was making a special appearance. It would be the last time I would see Papa Pacelli for who knew how long. We were leaving in a week.

The Bernini colonnade had turned into a dormitory. We had to step over a runner of mattresses to get to the open square, where every inch was filled with human bodies. The crowd cried, crossed itself, shouted, *"Che Dio ci salvi!"* I fingered the train tickets I had snitched from the curtain hem before leaving. Maybe a prayer in the Pope's presence would keep us in Rome.

The Pope appeared and raised his fingers. The crowd surged forward. I pressed back not to lose my balance. I couldn't see Gina or Palma. The Pope made the sign of the cross. A wave of wails washed over the square. Someone behind me pushed and I fell against the person in front, who elbowed me back. Suddenly I couldn't stand it, being pushed, being at the mercy of others. No one was going to help. Not God, not the Pope, not anyone. It was up to me. I reached in my pocket, took out the train tickets, tore them up in as many pieces as I could, and scattered them like confetti in the air above me.

It was an act of rebellion for which I will always be ashamed. Remembering, I steep my guilt in the rosy tones of nostalgia, but the core remains sharp, hurtful. I can't go back and change the story. I can only retell it to myself a thousand times, a rosary of penance.

My disloyalty would have terrible consequences, but I was too selfish, maybe too young, to think of consequences. Like the Allies, I wanted my mother's unconditional surrender.

"Don't lie! You stole them!"

I denied again.

"I want them back!" Mama was on the bedroom floor, the hem of the bedroom curtain sagging open behind her. "Did your father ask you to do this? This is his doing, isn't it?" She was shouting. "He made you do this."

I shook my head.

"Answer me, Susie!"

I swore to myself I would always stay calm, never, ever be like her. "You always blame everything on Papa. It was my idea."

She howled my name.

"Don't scream at me."

"Why do you hate me so much?" Her voice swung low. "Why do you hate me?" A roll of money unfurled in her lap.

I straightened my spine, chin up, head erect. "I don't hate you." I was St. Joan, saving France from the enemy, saving the family.

"Then give me the tickets!" She started crawling. Why hadn't I torn up the money too?

"Give them back!"

"What about me?" I backed away, feeling my chest jabbed by a hundred elbows. "What about the things you sold to Ersilia? My books, my watercolors, my bike. Andy gave me that bike. It was mine!"

"I'll buy more tickets!" Her voice heaved. "I'll buy them again and again and again until I have no more money left and we'll starve to death." A swath of light from the bedside lamp lay across the lower half of her face. For an instant I remembered waiting for that chin to dip into my lamplight, her lips, only an edge of deep red lipstick still on them, pursing to kiss me goodnight. "God, Susie! Why?"

"Why couldn't we go with Papa and Andy?" I cried. "Why are you so mean?"

She plucked her lap clean of money and lay it at her feet. We looked at each other from opposite shores of the room. The silence expanded, swelled until the walls of the room seemed to thin to the breaking point. I clenched my ears shut against the upcoming explosion.

Mama lifted her arms, opened them, her hands inches from my face, her fingers stained from her chain smoking.

"I'm sorry, Susie."

She touched my cheek. She smelled burnt.

"I want to come with you to the station," I said the next day as Mama lifted her hat from the clothes tree in the entranceway. "Please."

She turned to look at me. Doubt, distrust clawed at her face.

"It's okay now, Mama."

"What's okay, dear?" Her voice was light, uncaring.

"Switzerland." It was a lie, but it was the best I could do. My tongue would not form the words *I'm sorry*.

"Let me come with you, Mama."

"You won't like the station. It's crowded and smelly. You'll hate Switzerland too. No use pretending any different." She put on her hat, picked up her gloves, and shrugged on a smile. "Do as you please."

"Tearing up the tickets, fighting her, it's here that my guilt begins," I tell David at the kitchen table, our dinner plates now empty. "If we had left Rome in August, Mama might still be with us." I had never told anyone what I did, my guilt at first only a pebble that I could shift aside at will, which through the years, thickened into a sharp-edged rock. I'm supposed to feel lighter now that my secret sits on the table in plain sight. David lifts me from my chair and holds me, and I'm engulfed by sadness.

ROME, ITALY—AUGUST 20, 1943

Susie throwing the tickets away, I feel betrayed, isolated, inconsequential. I bleed with fury. My thoughts are confined to a narrow corridor—get out of here, to safety, to Switzerland, out of the Alinka life. I allow Susie no voice, but allow her to come to the station to buy new tickets. Not out of any kindness. I'm numb to her.

Rome has been declared an open city. Refugees pack the train station. Children, parents, grandparents, with hungry, sun-parched faces, sit, stand, eat, sleep in hives of bundles and cardboard suitcases tied with string. The smell of sweat and rancid grease hammers at my nose and throat.

A boy with a shaved head covered in scabs clutches a crucifix against his stomach and asks, "Where's the Vatican?" I give him a lira. Susie gives him directions.

As we move up the line to the barred ticket window, a woman shrouded in black clasps her hands together and falls on her knees on the station floor. "God is here," she announces to the five children surrounding her. They all cross themselves.

This time, I buy third-class tickets while the ticket seller chants a litany of bad news. Rail service is at a minimum. A train full of repatriates from East Africa has been hit as it pulled into the station; the government needs trains to get the military out of Rome; what trains there are have been oversold many times over.

I watch as hope limps across Susie's face.

The ticket seller flashes dentures at us. "The trip may take days. When do you want to leave?"

"As soon as possible." Susie makes a mewling sound and my heart softens. "Why don't you pick the date, Susie?" It's my offer of friendship, of renewed trust, a small momentary clearing in my head that she probably interprets as an act of spite against her willfulness, a knife digging deep.

"The tenth of September," she says. My wedding anniversary.

I buy the tickets with a silent face.

CAMBRIDGE, MASSACHUSETTS—MAY 1956

On September 8, 1943, Field Marshall Badoglio announced on the radio that the Italian government had requested an armistice of General Eisenhower, commander-in-chief of the Allied troops. The day before the Allies had almost destroyed the town of Frascati, in the Alban Hills just south of Rome, home to good wine and German army headquarters.

Mama waltzed Claire around the living room. "No more flashlights, blackout curtains. Tonight all the lights of Rome will turn on and we'll have a Milky Way we can almost touch." She pointed Claire's hand to the ceiling. "Up, up, that's the happy place. We'll see lights all the way to the Swiss Alps."

Not even the armistice was going to stop her. God was taking a long vacation. I picked up a pencil and slashed lines across the newspaper. A drawing of sorts, a vow only partially broken. Nothing recognizable. I didn't have that kind of defiance yet.

When I went with Palma to the latteria the next morning, Cesare leaned over his worn marble counter with his face fat with rumors. Hadn't we heard the rumble of cannons all through the night? The Germans were shooting just north of Rome. Mussolini was dead, killed during a military operation in his prison on the Gran Sasso. The Americans were about to land in Civitavecchia, only 72 kilometers north of Rome.

"They'll reach Rome by tomorrow."

The beaded curtain behind Cesare swept open and a sparrow of a woman came out. "Go back to singing opera," his wife said. "The lyrics make more sense."

At noon Cesare closed the latteria. Other shops had never opened, except for the bakery from which Palma brought back bread and one more rumor. Badoglio and the king had fled the city.

"Are we in danger? Are we not in danger?" Palma wanted to know.

Mrs. Pigeon told us the war continued, we had simply changed enemies.

I stood at the garden gate most of the afternoon, watching the street. Church bells tolled. The war widow clattered past, announcing that the government had declared an emergency. Gina said the bells were only tolling for vespers. I watched them argue and felt only the numbness of defeat and a pair of eyes watching me from the bedroom window.

"Don't worry," I called up to Mama. "I won't run away." Behind me, ready on the doorstep, our two suitcases, plus a knapsack filled with Claire's things, and two pairs of hiking boots that had belonged to Mrs. Pigeon's daughter to "protect you from the gelid Swiss winter." We were leaving the next day.

That night, just as we were going to bed, Mrs. Pigeon came down with the BBC news. The Allied Fifth Army had finally landed in Salerno, just south of Naples, on the Italian mainland. "They won't come tomorrow, but they'll come soon," she said. "Are you sure you won't stay?"

The air raid siren went off. We could hear bombs in the distance. "I have to get the children out," Mama said. "It's our first step home."

The bombing didn't last long. I went upstairs and with Mama's nail scissors cut my hair into a crown of stubs.

Mama said I should have learned from her. "It doesn't do a bit of good."

September 10, our D-Day. The sky was gray. It rained. The latteria stayed closed, but Cesare rang our gate holding daisies for Mama and more rumors. Mussolini was alive after all, but the English had arrived at Cisterna, south of Rome, and the streets were rumbling with German trucks retreating. A meeting of all the workers had been called in Piazza Colonna, in front of the Foreign Ministry. "An important day, signora. Who will take Rome? The English, the Germans?"

I didn't care. I wanted to be on the train, the leave-taking over with, on our way to whatever was waiting. Palma had used her curling iron to turn my hair into tight, nasty stubs. I looked hideous, I felt worse. "If we're going to go, let's go, Mama!"

"It's way too early."

Cesare fussed over my mother, apologizing because he had failed in his attempts to borrow a car to drive us to the station. No one had gas. He kissed her hand and, with slow deliberation, as a man about to divulge important information, he sang, *Addio, dolce amica mia, addio,* then whispered, "You are a glowing light in a dark cellar of coward faces."

"One day," Mama said, "you'll sing at La Scala."

"First they have to rebuild it." I turned away from the sight of my mother kissing him.

While we were eating our last lunch in Mrs. Pigeon's dining room, the air raid alarm went off. We ignored it. After lunch Palma and I exchanged presents. I gave her her own copy of *The Betrothed.* She offered me a turquoise taffeta blouse she had made out of her dress, ruffled to match my hair. Mrs. Pigeon followed us down to our apartment with her cane and pocketbook, her face brittle with emotion. She held Claire in her lap until it was time to leave. The air raid alarm didn't stop until 3:30. Before the taxi came, Mrs. Pigeon embraced Mama and slipped a fat envelope into her pocket, which I later discovered held her daughter's dowry money. Mrs. Pigeon hugged me to her chest so tightly I could count the stays in her corset. It was the first and last time she touched me.

"Take care of her," she said. I didn't ask if she meant my mother or Claire.

During the endless wait before we left for the train station, I sat at the kitchen table and picked up a pencil. I ran my fingers up and down the wood, wet the graphite with the tip of my tongue. I reached for the butcher paper that had wrapped our lunch tripe, spread it flat with the palm of my hand, and sketched Claire's sleeping face. In exchange for Andy's health, I had vowed never to draw or paint again. I left the drawing on the table for Mrs. Pigeon to find. God was nowhere.

The taxi driver said the Germans were fighting at Saint Paul's Gate on the Aventine. At the Spanish Steps, German soldiers had thrown hand grenades at passersby. German tanks were parked just beyond the railroad station, at Santa Maria Maggiore. Rome was being invaded.

"They aren't wearing uniforms," he said, "but you can always tell a Kraut by his slaked lime skin." He stopped at a corner of Piazza dei Cinquecento. The station was a thousand feet away. "I'm not risking my life for a fare. I've got a family too."

He unloaded us four hundred feet from the station. Mama hurried on, Claire tied to her chest, the knapsack on her back, carrying one suitcase. I dragged the other one. Mama reached into the pocket of her jacket and waved an envelope at me. "I have to mail this letter to Papa when we get inside the station."

Before I could start wondering what that letter said, shots rang out. They were coming from the other side of a row of umbrella pines in the middle of the piazza. A small group of men were huddled behind the trees and oleander bushes, their rifles aimed at the Hotel Continentale on the far side of the piazza. The gunfire sounded no more dangerous than branches cracking. I worried I'd never get the suitcase to the station.

A van stopped in front of us. Boys with bandoliers of ammunition crisscrossed over their chests jumped out. The tallest boy was bare-chested and carried a machine gun. They walked in a tight group, ten boys with dirt smeared on their faces, the whites of their eyes shining. It's a movie, I thought. Wallace Beery and his boys fighting the Mexican revolution.

Mama dropped the suitcase and ran up to the bare-chested boy. "Get out of here!" She grasped his machine gun. "Don't die!" He jerked the gun away from her, and she fell. Claire, still tied to her chest, started to cry. I kicked the suitcases to where Mama sat, one leg folded under her, the other sticking out at an angle.

"The train is going to leave."

Mama shouted after the boys, who were bounding across the piazza, "Go home to your mothers. Don't get killed!"

I didn't stop to think that this was my chance. Let her sit on the ground worrying about those boys and the train would leave without us. With my free hand I tried to get her up. She was hushing Claire. "The train is leaving, Mama. We have to go."

She clutched my ankle. "Run. Grab his gun."

I squatted down. "Don't you want to go to Switzerland?"

"He'll die if you don't stop him." Her voice shredded. "You broke your vow. Why did you break your vow? Now Andy is going to die! You have to get his gun!"

"Andy's in Spain!"

I called out for help. A woman came over. "Shock," she declared without asking any questions. She lifted a bottle and poured water over Mama's head. Claire started laughing, holding out her hands to catch the water, splashing it on herself.

Mama stood up on her own. She looked exhausted, confused; her face dripped water as though she were crying her heart out. I thought of taking her back to Mrs. Pigeon and Palma, but what if she didn't remember what had happened? Then missing the train, going back to Via Aurora would be another of Susie's dirty tricks.

With the woman's help, we made the train by four minutes.

ITALY—SEPTEMBER 10, 1943

The train smells. Sweat, cheese, something else, something that burns in the back of my throat. We're late and all seats are taken. The boy. He made my heart race. He looked so much like Andy I got muddled. I wanted to save him. Save all the boys. We sit on our suitcases in

171

the third-class corridor, Claire on my lap, standing passengers' knees in my face, knocking against my shoulders. My head is wet. I touch it to see if it's blood.

"It's just water, Mama."

I examine my hand. Just water. Why does my head feel broken? I unclasp my purse. Instead of a handkerchief, I find the letter I meant to mail to Marco at the station. I show it to Susie. "I forgot."

"You'll mail it in Lugano."

"Yes, in Lugano." Always logical, my Susie. She didn't get it from me. I put the letter back in my purse.

We stop outside Bologna and someone cranks down the window. The tracks are under repair from a recent bombing. Prisoners are filing past the windows to work on the tracks. A woman sitting in front of me claims they're English. She can tell by the small red rectangle sewn on their shorts. It matches their skin, blistered red from the sun. An Ogden Nash verse pops in my head—"Mad dogs and Englishmen go out in the midday sun"—and I laugh. One of the prisoners hears me and turns to stare at me. He's only a foot or so from the open window. I stand up to hand him my uneaten sandwich, but a man behind me grabs my arm. "*Signora, é vietato.*" It's forbidden. I free my arm and fling the sandwich out the window. I can't see where it lands, but the prisoner doesn't pick it up.

The prisoners are marched away. We sit and wait. Four, five hours go by. The train suddenly belches and groans, then starts rolling again. Shouts, clapping. I want to join in. The train is finally moving, and I'm finally getting us out of Italy, out of the war, but I can't get rid of the weight sitting on my head.

The conductor, a fat man with gold buttons curving high over his stomach, takes our tickets. Our destination is clearly written out: Bellinzona, where foreigners are registered before being allowed to go elsewhere. "Switzerland is out. The Germans have closed the border today. This train's last stop is Milan. If you want to go anywhere else, you'll have to change trains."

I stare at the heave of his stomach.

"We've got a diplomatic passport," Susie says. "We can cross any border anytime."

"Italians and Germans are enemies now, little one. Unless you're in the German army, no one gets in, no one gets out. Milan is the last stop on this train."

Susie shakes me. "Mama! We can't go to Switzerland."

Claire wakes up and starts crying.

"We can't go, Mama!" Susie must be happy.

There is nothing to add. Too late. We'd missed the golden ring by one day. I rock Claire. She always helps keep my head straight. "Shh, baby, shh. We'll be fine. Just fine."

After the conductor announces we are about to arrive in Milan, I take out my letter to Marco and tear it up. There's no point to it anymore. My escape to Switzerland was just a dream.

CAMBRIDGE, MASSACHUSETTS—MAY 1956

German soldiers flowed between the tracks at the Milan station. Mama stared at them wide-eyed. "We've gone backwards!" She banged her fists against her forehead. "What is wrong with me? I got it wrong. I got it wrong again. Why am I in Prague?"

"You're in Milan, Mama." I lifted the suitcases and told her to follow me. The station bar was clearly Italian, with its huge shiny coffeemaker and cups roosting on top to keep warm. Out loud I read the printed list of offerings: *Espresso, cappuccino, caffellatte, chinotto, sambuca, panino con prosciutto, panino con formaggio.*

"That list is from before the war," the barwoman said. "Now I can give you chicory and milk. In the morning a fresh bun."

"Hear that, Mama? She's speaking Italian. We're in Milan."

We spent the rest of the night on half a bench in the third-class waiting room thick with cigarette smoke, snores, and body odor. I didn't dare sleep, afraid Mama would wander off.

I was filled with guilt. Had we left at the end of August, as Mama had wanted, the border would have still been open. Worst of all, I had broken my vow with God. The nuns were right. God was all powerful. And Mama was right. It was all my fault.

I wondered what it would be like to simply walk away. To walk until I was older and I could forget I ever had parents. I drifted off to sleep, woke up in a panic that disappeared when I saw Mama curled on the floor at my feet, Claire nestled inside her lap, both of them still fast asleep. I slipped one of Claire's clean diapers from the knapsack, tied it around my mother's ankle and my own, and closed my eyes again.

I woke up to Mama trying to put Mrs. Pigeon's boots on my feet. She was already wearing hers. Claire, sitting on the floor, played with the diaper still tied to my ankle.

"We're going to walk across."

"We're in Milan, Mama. Miles and miles away from the border. We'll never make it."

"We'll take a train to the border. There's a big map downstairs. I've already picked the place. Come on, I'll show you."

"How can we walk across? They'll shoot us."

"We'll find a way."

I picked up our suitcases and shuffled—the boots were too big for me—behind my mother and sister to the map downstairs. Mama pointed to where the Swiss border crossed the Alps and swooped into Italy, almost touching the edge of Lake Como.

"Cernobbio, on the border side of the lake, that's where we're going."

I wanted to believe the sweet set of her mouth. "That's the lake where *The Betrothed* takes place. 'That branch of Lake Como that turns towards—' " My voice slipped. Mama was looking at me, with a sweep of freckles covering her face, her eyes bloodshot but smiling, her hair combed, lipstick put on. She was all right again.

"Why does it make you cry, Chipmunk? Do you miss Palma?"

I nodded.

We went to the ladies room to wash up. Mama said she stank of coal, we all did, that the Prague station had also smelled of coal. That's what had confused her. Smell was the sense most hooked into memory, she said.

"The smell of lemons! Remember, Mama, how you used to squirt lemon juice in my hair to make it shine?" That sudden recollection made me want to hug her.

"Lelelele," Claire started to sing.

Mama lifted her up and propped her against the back wall of the sink, turned on the faucet. There was no soap.

"We haven't seen a lemon in how long, Mama? Maybe we'll find them in Cernobbio."

She took her hairbrush from her purse and started scrubbing Claire's hands. "Your papa abandoned us in the Prague station. What I remember

174

most is the smell of coal." She moved the hairbrush up and down Claire's arms. Claire was gasping, her face turning as red as her arms.

I tried to grab the brush away from Mama. She pushed me away. Claire howled. I tried to grab my sister. Mama slapped me, a blow that sent my head reeling to one side. She slapped my other cheek, evening me up.

"Shut up!" she screamed. "I don't want to listen to a little girl's whiny voice. All I want is to get out of this smelly station and this life!"

We were hungry and the train to Como wasn't leaving for another hour. While Mama ordered caffellattes and buns, I tried to stop Claire from crying. I skipped, an imaginary rope in my hands. "Mabel, Mabel, set the table . . ." Saucers rattled behind me, milk gurgled under the steam spigot, a rag swished at the end of a broom as a girl cleaned the floor. Claire bobbed her head with each jump, forgotten tears rolling down her cheeks, sucking her hand.

"Mabel, Mabel, set the table, don't forget the salt, vinegar, mustard, pepper! Wheee!" I spun around, felt my skirt whip my thighs. Claire stuck both her hands in her mouth and let a smile gather behind them. I spun again, aiming for a laugh. I stopped in midspin when the barwoman yelled, "*Signora, no!*"

Mama was leaning sideways, her back to me, in front of the espresso machine. Walking into the room, she had admired its crouching hump, said the metal was "gleaming with heat." Now the barwoman was pulling at her arm, with a look on her face that I now know to be of horror.

"Mama?"

She twisted around to my voice—her right arm didn't move—and offered me a smile as reassurance. I came closer and saw that she was holding her right hand flat against the espresso machine. She had picked the hottest spot, next to the steam spigot. She smiled and leaned into the hand, forcing it to stay flat against the scorching metal.

The barwoman pulled Mama's hand away slowly, afraid the skin of her palm would stay stuck. "I have no butter or oil," she said. Mama's palm had turned bone white. "Butter is what you need."

Mama thanked the woman, told her not to worry about the butter. The pain in her hand had to keep for a while, she said. "It gives me clarity, it demands complete attention, it keeps me sane, you understand?"

I didn't understand.

Mama let me wrap her hand in a diaper. "Why did you burn yourself?"

She rubbed her chin against my forehead. "I slapped you with that hand."

A hand to nudge me out of bed on a school morning, to tug my braids loose, two firm hands on my shoulders to straighten my posture, a cool palm on my forehead when I had fever. Fingers laced with mine to cross the street, buttoning dresses, grazing my cheek before a goodnight kiss. A hand to brush the sand off my legs. A hand squeezing my chin to tell me how much she loves me. My mother's hand, never, ever hitting me.

A hand that hasn't touched me since that night on the mountain.

Mama lost it at the Milan station. I didn't help with that either, fighting her every chance I got, but she came back. In Cernobbio she was fine. She said it was the smell of freedom coming over the mountain that did it. Burning her hand was, after all, an act of love.

NINE

CERNOBBIO, ITALY—SEPTEMBER 11, 1943

No smell of coal here—only a throbbing hand, a frightened Susie, a hungry Claire. The sun is still high as we cross the lake from Como, the air hot with cool edges, as if it has dipped into the green lake. Claire's curls shine pink, Susie's face shines with perspiration. She won't take off the shearling coat her father gave her for Christmas.

I squint at the mountain behind us. The perimeter of my vision is blurred, but the center is true. In that center of vision, I see a clear bead, like a drop of water for parched lips. I saw this lick of light at the Milan station after the burning. My hand throbs and how-do-you-know-how-do-you-know chugs in my ear, but I see it as clear as I see Susie and Claire. A plan.

I point my good hand to the lighthouse on the mountain rising east of Como. "Do they use it as a searchlight?" I ask one of the ferry men. He has the skin of a turtle and the hump to match.

"The lighthouse has been dark since the beginning of the war." The ferryman uncoils a line; we're about to land. "The light used to swing past my house. My wife complained it was like being whipped. I miss it."

I'm not going to be dark like that lighthouse. I'm going to function. I have to. For my girls.

Behind the boat terminal, Piazza Risorgimento, the main square. In the center the welcoming sight of a fountain with a bowl as blue as a California pool. Men huddle in small groups under trees, shifting caps in their hands, eyes aimed at their feet. Old men, no women. No one young. Sitting in the outdoor cafes of the two hotels facing the square, German officers sun themselves like slimy gray lizards. I tie Claire to my chest again, lift one suitcase with my good hand. I want us to run away from that sight, but my new-found clarity helps me. "Cross the square slowly," I tell Susie.

We walk along side streets, looking for a place to stay, avoiding those with views on the lake. "Cheap," I keep repeating. "Cheap. Cheap." I sound like a farmer calling hens. At a *Vino e Olio* shop, I ask the owner about a place to stay, my eyes fixed on the mirror behind him, pockmarked with age. "Not expensive." I concentrate on the large brown stain on the seat of his pants, feeling like a beggar. Hungry too.

He reaches for a bottle. His reflection moves with him. The stain is still there in the mirror. For posterity. "You have any sons?" he asks. I look at him. He's an ancient man, with a long, pleated face that ends in a lantern jaw and a gray beret that hugs his head like the cloth caps on Jitka's homemade jams. Someone safe, I think.

"Just us."

"In two days they've rounded up twenty boys." He pours red wine into two shot glasses, offers me one. "Gratis." I thank him and drink. He downs his glass in one gulp. My hunger gets worse.

"Some too young to be anywhere but with their mothers. Shook 'em right out of bed." He taps the bottle, swings it back up on the shelf. "Here, at Bellagio, Varenna, Tremezzo, all around the lake. Ferried the boys to Como with machine guns at their backs. Deutschland or the firing squad. You can report me if you want. Luigi Scolino, Gigi to my friends. There's only me left. If you've got a boy or a husband, send them over the Bisbino quick, that's my advice. If not, enjoy your good luck."

"We need a place to stay."

"You've already told me. The nearest pensione is two streets up. *Miralago*, but you can only see the lake in your dreams." He lets us leave our suitcases and knapsack in the corner, behind a crate of empty wine bottles. Susie finally dumps her coat.

178

Miralago—in a narrow, climbing street—has the right price, breakfast and dinner included. The owner shows us a large second-floor room with two windows facing a printing shop. I don't speak, not wanting to reveal my nationality right away. Susie tells her we'll take it. Back downstairs she asks for my passport. Fascist law requires her to register the names and personal information of all the guests with the local police. I hand her my Italian diplomatic passport, which lists Susie and Claire. Which tells her where I was born. She opens it, reads, snaps it shut. "No foreigners."

"My passport is Italian," I protest.

"You're not."

We try three more pensiones. One is full. Another has lake views, which makes it too expensive. The last one doesn't want small children. Before closing the door, the pensione maid slips Susie an apple.

CAMBRIDGE, MASSACHUSETTS—MAY 1956

Cernobbio—small, peach-colored, flanked on each side by imposing villas and trees, with an Art Nouveau wrought-iron boat terminal waiting to welcome visitors—a pretty resort town, the guidebook might say. It was filled with German soldiers, which must have frightened Mama, but it was still a perfect place for her to rest. After a few tries we found a pensione on the same street as the town cemetery. Lady Eva—that's what her English lodgers had called her before the war—was only too happy to learn that we spoke English and offered us a second room free if Mama would give her English lessons. I was ecstatic. Finally a room of my own again.

The day after we arrived, a Sunday, a German glider made a daring landing on the Appenine ski resort of Gran Sasso and freed Mussolini. Mama stayed in her room for the next few days and let me take care of Claire. Every morning Lady Eva, smelling of vinegar, removed the bandage from Mama's hand, spread ointment on the burn, rewrapped the hand in clean strips from old sheets. I sat at end of the bed, following the tangle of dark veins that now crossed Mama's forehead and temples. I think I was trying to parse her face, to understand the secret map of her mind, one that would reveal the future. When she fell asleep, her face smoothed. I would leave none the wiser.

Lady Eva asked no questions, and by the end of the first week I had taken over her English lessons while Mama rested. We would sit under

179

the chestnut tree in the front yard every afternoon while Claire played with Sixpence, Lady Eva's little white and black dog.

"The sun is warm today," I might start.

"The weather, it is about to change."

"Sixpence is a funny name for a dog."

A startled look. "Laugh name?"

"Strange."

A sigh of relief. "*Ah, sì.* He is the light of my days. I find him by the lake. Mud all over, thin as my little finger. My Manchester boarder say he is so ugly nobody pay a sixpence for him." Lady Eva offered chamomile tea. "The cemetery is filled with savage plants of chamomile."

"Wild plants," I corrected and shivered at the thought of drinking tea leached from the bones of the dead.

We had separate pots, hers larger than mine. When she closed her eyes, halfway through the conversation, my tea watered the weeds. The conversation would peter out by the end of her pot, as her eyes stayed shut and her mouth gaped open, the acrid smell stronger than ever. Not vinegar, cheap wine, I discovered after sticking my nose in her cup. Two bottles a day, which I would soon start filling for her at Gigi's *Vino e Olio.*

I wrote to Papa, gave him our new address, in case Mama hadn't, described Lady Eva, Sixpence, the pensione, asked him to send money, added "we are all well." In a postscript for Andy, I added that I missed him.

One morning during our second week in Cernobbio, Mama came into the kitchen fully dressed. She wore her heavy green tweed suit, her travel suit, and Ersilia's linen cloche. She had tied her hair back with one of my ribbons and put on a dark-red lipstick. The sight of her made my knees buckle. We were leaving again, crossing over the mountain, disappearing into Switzerland.

I leaned against the stone sink where I was drying the breakfast dishes. "Claire likes it here. She loves Lady Eva and Sixpence and the lake is pretty and—"

Lady Eva spilled her cup. "You're not departing, are you?"

"Susie has to go to school," Alinka said. "Where is the nearest one?"

"Oh yes!" I shouted. "I can't wait to go to school."

"We can't afford nuns, Susie."

"Any school. Here."

In the principal's office, under a picture of the king (Mussolini's photo, which usually appeared in tandem with the king's, had been replaced by a bleached-white square of wall), Mama held her bandaged hand to her jaw and pretended she had a toothache and couldn't speak. I showed off my report card from the Cabrini School. Good grades and a character assessment from Madre Giovanna. "Studious and obedient in class, but does not seek out friends. She has to work on her haughtiness and a tendency to think she is the only one to have the right answer."

"I wish very much to come to your school," I said.

The principal, Professor Casciano, readjusted the papers on his desk. The heel of his hand pressed what hair he had left back on his scalp. "School starts in two weeks. *La signora* has to register as a new resident at town hall, pay the school taxes. Then we will be happy to take you."

In two weeks, school for five hours a day, surrounded only by strangers. I pumped Professor Casciano's hand. "*Grazie. Grazie tante. Molto gentile.*" He looked startled by my enthusiasm.

"Thank you, Mama," I said as we walked out. Mama let go of her jaw, but said nothing. We went to the town hall, behind the main square. I filled in the papers, paid what was required, bought notebooks, a wooden pen box, pen, pen tips, ink, pencils, a bright pink eraser. Before the saleslady closed the wrapping, Mama shook the ink bottle one more time to make sure it didn't leak. It was a gesture I recognized from Newport Beach, from Prague, a normal mother gesture.

On our way to the lakefront, Mama asked me to follow her into a dark, narrow *merceria*, a notions shop walled by dust and boxes of buttons, threads, underwear, aprons, sweaters. She pointed to a sweater in the window, white wool with cables down the front. When I tried it on, the wool had the musty odor of the lake. Mama tilted her head back. The only light bulb picked up the tears she was trying to stop from rolling down her cheeks. "You look pretty, Susie." She bought the sweater and told me to wear it in good health. "Now one more errand."

At the lakefront we turned left, walking along the water's edge until we reached a wide gravel path. At the end of the path, an open gate led to a park. A nurse walked a man under the spreading tent of a towering tree. His head was a turban of bandages. With the long white cloth covering her head, the nurse looked like a novice waiting to take her vows. The sign on one of the pillars flanking the gate read: *Villa d'Este. Militarische Krankenhaus. Ospedale Militare.*

As we walked through the gate, a hand dropped on Mama's shoulder. "You cannot go in," a sun-burned guard said in German-accented Italian.

"*Ich bin sehr—*" she started to say. I am very—

Very what?

Very angry?

Very tired?

Very crazy?

I am very relieved to give my daughter away?

"*Ich bin sehr—*" my mother repeated. I didn't let her finish.

"We came to see the tree." I pointed to the towering tree with its looping branches.

"Yes, it is astounding." The guard smiled, his teeth startling white. "A cedar of Lebanon that even our Black Forest does not boast."

CERNOBBIO, ITALY—SEPTEMBER 27, 1943

In the main piazza with its blue bowled fountain, I've seen men in bandages, nurses pushing wheelchairs. I've seen the direction the wheelchairs are going. There's a hospital somewhere in town. I've finished the drops the Roman doctor gave me. I need more, or something else to keep me alert, yet calm me down. Mussolini freed, the area packed with Germans. Boys being taken away from their homes, sent to Germany. Will girls be next? Forced into slave labor, locked up in some factory to help the war effort? The Germans are desperate. I can see it in the officers hanging out at the hotel cafés. They laugh too loud, drink too much. Their faces are taut and their eyes flicker.

I need a doctor, a *specialista*.

"At Villa d'Este the German doctors put together bodies," Lady Eva tells me while she washes the dishes and I dry. A generous woman. She has cooked us supper from the first night even though it wasn't part of our agreement. "Only officers. They cut the skin from the behind and use it for patches, like mending an old shirt."

"Where do I find a doctor for nerves?"

"I show you." Lady Eva unties her apron, unhooks her scarf from the hat stand in the entrance. "A good place," she says without emotion, as though I've asked her directions to the nearest food shop.

We walk to the lakefront, Claire tied to a pillow and a wheelbarrow, Sixpence spurting ahead and back, urging us on with yelps, Susie scuffling behind. On land, the lights are already submerged under blackout curtains. The lake mirrors the darkening sky.

Lady Eva, her scarf securely knotted on top of her head, points to the lighthouse across the lake, its light shut off, its white body turning blue. "You not see, but the cure house is to one side of *il faro*. In the town of Brunate." Villa Faro, a clinic for nervous disorders. "My cousin go there for a month before the war. She now is fine."

"How do you get up there?"

"A small train climbs the mountain. It is pulled by chains, one train goes up, the other down, like a scale. On top a view that cuts the breath."

CAMBRIDGE, MASSACHUSETTS—MAY 1956

The night after Mama tried to go to the German military hospital, I woke up to Mama clutching me. I leaned away from her. "What's wrong?" In the dark I couldn't see her face.

"I dreamed I was locked up in the lighthouse with a view of the world, but my head wouldn't turn on. I'd rather die, Susie."

I felt helpless, lost, not able to distinguish love from pity. I let my mother fold me back into her body.

"I'll take care of you, Mama."

No word from Papa. The weather stayed warm. Mama sat with us during Lady Eva's English lessons, joining in the small talk, leaving corrections to me even though my English was rusty. Since California I had spoken it only with her. Claire walked, tumbled, crawled on the grass with Sixpence. Mama watched me study. She touched me a lot, hugs, kisses. I returned them, happy that she hadn't gone up to the Villa Faro, that she was well again. Her hand was now free of bandages, the palm the color of ripe plums.

In the entrance of our school, Mussolini's photograph replaced the king's after Hitler allowed Il Duce back into Italy. Salò, a town on Lake Garda, seventy miles away, became the headquarters of the new Fascist Republic. On October 13th, the Italian government, headed by Badoglio, declared war on Germany. All over Italy, the army, the police, the carabinieri threw off their uniforms by the thousands and headed for home or *la macchia*—the woods hiding the resistance fighters.

On the same day, in Moltrasio, the next town over, the Fascist militia shot a man for wearing army-issue boots, claiming he was a deserter. He was sixty-three years old. Lady Eva didn't wait for English conversation to start drinking her wine.

At school I earned the nickname *puzzetta*—little smell, short for *puzza sotto il naso*—smell under the nose. My classmates thought I considered myself better than anyone else. I was flunking algebra.

One Sunday afternoon, a clearing in the clouds. I was standing on the outside terrace of the Olga Regina Hotel on the main square, with Claire and Sixpence. Inside Lady Eva was helping to serve the officers of the new Fascist militia and their girlfriends—chamomile tea, herb tea, tree bark tea for the women, chicory coffee for the officers, cakes and pastries for both. Every Sunday I waited outside for Lady Eva to sneak me the leftovers she scraped off the plates: buttered pieces of half-eaten toast, pound cake crumbs, spoonfuls of baked apple, once a whole éclair with a few traces of crème anglaise left. My mouth was already tasting the sweets to come, when a tall string bean of a boy walked by me and through the French doors. I watched him stroll down the length of the dining room with a hand plunged into his gray flannel pockets and a Fred Astaire gait that instantly made me want to learn to dance. One hunger replaced another.

When Lady Eva got home, I shut all the windows, cranked up the record player in the sitting room and put on Ersilia's Benny Goodman record. I asked Lady Eva to dance with me. She fell back on the sofa.

"My feet are full with stones."

I lifted Sixpence in my arms and did a lousy imitation of a fox trot. Claire was too heavy.

I saw him again, a few days later, behind the glass door of Gigi's shop. He had on the same flannel slacks showing two inches of argyle socks, a blue sweater, and a white French-cuffed shirt. Watching the cuffs wing out as he glided a glass of wine to his mouth, I judged him terribly sophisticated not to have bothered with cufflinks.

I opened the door. The bell jingled. Gigi paid no attention. He was slamming his hand on the marble countertop. "What are you? Dumb? Arrogant? You're seventeen years old and you parade yourself in front of the militia as if you were Mussolini's best friend. Keep that up, Claudio, and you deserve to be stuffed in a uniform and sent off to kill your own!"

I silently filled my mouth with his name. Claudio. A mouth-widening name.

Claudio offered Gigi a cigarette, lit one himself, and twisted himself around to grace me with a first glance. I swung my two empty wine bottles and stared back. Curly blond hair tight on his scalp, small blue eyes, a narrow nose, tanned skin the color of hazelnuts. What I liked most was his long body, as smooth and pliable as lake water.

He dragged on his cigarette, didn't bother to smile. "Ciao."

Inside me the tide rose. "Ciao," I sent back and offered Gigi the bottles to refill. Claudio gave Gigi a smoky wave of the hand and loped past me. Behind me the bell chimed notes I hadn't heard before. Do-mi-fa-re.

"Be careful, Claudio," Gigi called out. The door clicked shut.

For nights I heard do-mi-fa-re, imagined the smile I hadn't seen, saw us dancing under the green air of the astounding cedar of Lebanon that even the Black Forest couldn't boast, felt us swaying side by side in the bottom of a row boat. I threw off my nightgown, pressed the pillow against my torso and quietly masturbated.

"Let's go for an outing," Mama said one Sunday at the end of October, "before the weather turns. To the lighthouse, like in the book. The view must be splendid." I didn't know what book she was talking about and I didn't want to go up to Brunate. That's where the Villa Faro was.

"Let's go to Como instead. I'm scared of going up in that funicular." Mama's nerves didn't need fixing.

"Don't be silly, Chipmunk. Nothing will happen." Mama went inside to get Claire and her hat. I started raking leaves. Lady Eva had gone to church. Sixpence hurtled to the garden gate. The spokes were high and thick, and all I could see was a slice of skirt, a leg. I dropped the rake and walked over.

"Susanna, cara!" The drowning r was unmistakable. I picked up Six-pence and opened the gate. There was Lilli Scarditti, immaculately dressed, gloved, and hatted, holding up a small ribboned package of pastries she got who knew where. She stepped inside the garden, leaned over to kiss me but changed her mind when I raised Sixpence to my chest. Her sudden appearance scared me. Why was she here? What did she want?

Instead of saying hello, I asked her, "How did you find us?"

"Your father told me. He wants to know how you are. You look well, and your mother, how is she? Is she all right?"

"Couldn't be better," Mama said from the doorway, her bad hand hidden behind her. "So you're stuck in Italy too. I thought you'd still be in Prague."

"Momentarily inconvenienced, never stuck. It's too beautiful a country." Lilli plastered a plastic smile on her face and waved the package at Mama. "I brought pastries with real cream."

"How nice of you," Mama said, without inviting her in. "I'm sorry, we're just leaving."

"I also have a letter and money from Marco for you. Cash, instead of a check. He wasn't sure if you had a bank account here, which is the reason he sent the letter to me. Besides, in the current chaotic situation,"—she shrugged—"mail service hiccups." That explained why Papa's letters hadn't arrived. "Thank God for the diplomatic pouch."

Lilli handed me the pastries, walked over to a garden chair, wiped it with her handkerchief, sat down, and snapped open her handbag. She put a fat envelope on the table next to her. "Now, Alinka, tell me everything. How is Giorgio's godchild?"

"Claire is growing," Mama said. "Happy. She just fell asleep again." A lie, as I could hear her gurgling behind Mama. As Lilli could.

"What brought you to Cernobbio?" Lilli asked. "The border is closed. There's no way of getting to Switzerland now."

Something happened to Mama's face when Lilli said that. It sort of faded, as if someone had run an eraser over it. For a moment I thought she was going to faint. She walked over to the far side of the table and sat down. "The weather is far better here than in Rome."

Lilli nodded, but she didn't look as though she believed Mama. She went on to tell us about her predicament. Her mother, who lived in Milan, had been sick and Lilli had left Prague in July to be with her. Her mother was better now, but she felt she couldn't leave her. "Besides, I can't go back. My diplomatic passport is of no use. The Germans are our enemies now. Ridiculous, but there it is. Thankfully Giorgio left Prague in time. Someone higher up was kind enough to give him a tip about the government surrendering to the Allies. He's living at the consulate in Lugano. Along with hundreds of other Italian refugees. Of course, he could stay in the best hotel, but he feels the refugees need him there. You know what a big heart Giorgio has."

Mama said nothing.

"I heard that there are ways of getting to Switzerland," Lilli said. "Have you heard that too?"

"No." Color came back to Mama's face. Unnatural color. She did know.

"It's best to wait it out here." Lilli stood up and walked around the table to kiss Mama's cheeks. "You're much too thin. You need to rest. For your children's sake if not your own. Promise me you won't do anything foolish."

"I don't know what you're talking about."

"Yes, you do. Take care, Alinka. Do be wise." Lilli came over to me and linked her arm into mine. Sixpence jumped out of my arms. "Your father misses you very much."

As she spoke, she pushed me toward the gate. Was she going to share another secret as she had done at Claire's christening?

"Don't let your mother take you away," she said once we reached the gate. "Your father asked me to tell you he wants you to stay right here. The minute he can, he will join you."

Magical words that I wanted to believe.

Mama went to her room after Lilli left, saying she had a bad headache. No more outing to Brunate. I couldn't have been happier.

CERNOBBIO—OCTOBER 30, 1943

Alinka—I was confident that you and I could make peace, if for no other reason, to keep the family together, but your stubbornness, your total disregard for my wishes as a father for what is best for the girls, has shown me you are of a different mind. I am not to be forgiven. So be it.

I only ask that you now stay where you are. I will keep sending you money with Lilli's kind help.

I entreat you, do not try to cross the border with the girls. The border guards will shoot you and the girls on sight or, perhaps worse, throw you in jail. What these men are capable of doing to women and even little girls is stomach-turning.

Your anger has gotten the better of you. Your strongest desire is to disappear in the miasma of refugees in Switzerland where I won't be able to find you. As soon as you can, you will take the girls to America and never let me see them again. I won't allow it.

Hateful words. I tear up the letter, light a match, and watch the words curl, blacken, thin into nothing. Anger has gotten the better of him. Understanding nothing, he has sent Lilli to spy on me, to shine a searchlight in my head. I have no time to lose.

Gigi at the wine shop tells me that the sisters who run Villa Faro know people who can help. I laugh at the thought that Marco's money will pay for our crossing.

I need to go up there, but I'm assailed by terror. I need help, help for the passer, help for my head. I feel like a negative, helpless to make a single move just when I need to be at my most keen. I stay coiled under the covers of the bed, looking up at the ladder pattern the closed shutters leave on the ceiling. It's a double ladder. One for me, one for Susie and Claire. It's a way out. I only have to learn how to climb it.

CAMBRIDGE, MASSACHUSETTS—MAY 1956

"It's just for a week," Mama said. "At the most two." The doctors at Villa Faro would give her medicine to make her strong again. She worried about Claire. Lady Eva and I reassured her. Claire was going to be fine, I'd make sure of that. Lady Eva got drunk only in the afternoon, by then I was home from school. But Mama, I couldn't help her. What if she didn't get better? I threw that thought away, went to bed with Lilli's words as my blanket—"The minute he can, your father will come get you."

I went with Mama down to the boat terminal, pushing Claire and Sixpence in the wheelbarrow. Mama wore her travel suit even though the day was hot. A man's fedora a pensione guest had forgotten years before kept the sun off her face.

At the terminal, she stepped onto the boat quickly, without hugs or kisses. She wanted to make the trip alone.

I watched her settle down at the prow of the ferry with Mrs. Pigeon's knapsack in her lap. Above her, in the distance, the lighthouse, a stroke of white against the sky. "I'll be as good as new," she said. The ferryman turned on the motor. "The old Mama," she shouted.

The boat glided forward. I waved. She waved back with the burnt hand, the palm still dark. I took Claire's hand and waved it. Claire started crying. Sixpence licked her face.

I'm ashamed to admit that what I felt standing on that dock was relief rather than sadness. Mama at Villa Faro meant we weren't leaving. At least not yet. And maybe up there she would change her mind, and we would wait here until the war was over and Papa came to get us. I had no way of knowing that I was already losing her.

The first days after Mama left, Claire would sleep only in Mama's bed, Sixpence curled next to her, Mama's pillow under her nose. During the day, she stumbled on her short legs through the house, checking every room, as if Mama were playing hide-and-seek with her. She went out in the yard, looked in the woodshed, under the chestnut tree, up at its branches where the sparrows gathered. Mama's pillow came with her, dragged behind her as if it were another dog, gathering dust and leaves. She called it Ino, not able to pronounce the full word: *cuscino*. At the gate she pushed her face against the wooden fence, imitating Sixpence, a corner of Ino in her mouth. She would wait for hours, Sixpence beside her.

After a week my sister shifted her allegiance and tottered after me. She had tantrums when I left in the morning, screaming so loud that after a few days, a sleepy, hastily dressed Lady Eva walked me to school, pushing the wheelbarrow loaded with Claire, Sixpence, and Mama's pillow. When I came back at lunchtime and tried to hug Claire, she bucked and beat her fists against my chest, payback for leaving her. An hour later she would climb into my lap, the best of friends again. Off we'd go—homework flung aside, Sixpence trotting ahead, Claire swaying in the wheelbarrow as it clunked over the cobblestones—down the tight back streets, safe from soldiers. I ended our walks at Gigi's shop to fill Lady Eva's bottles with wine, hoping Claudio would show up.

After English conversation, while Lady Eva slept, I took Claire out one more time, getting bolder as the light got weaker. I stretched my legs along the lakefront, walking from the gate at Villa d'Este, down past the main piazza to the boat terminal, then south to the Visconti villa where Mussolini had once stayed with his mistress. I imagined my future dependent only on the length and strength of my legs. I never looked up across the lake, to Brunate and the lighthouse rising on the mountain like a white cypress.

As we walked, women's comments whisked past us.

"What are the two of you doing on the street alone at your age?"

"It's dangerous out here. There are soldiers about."

"Hurry home. Curfew is in an hour."

"Does your mother know?"

I lengthened my stride.

My sister was a good reason not to study, a perfect cover for my restlessness. Later, when I had reason to want to be alone, I said she was a boulder on my chest. I didn't permit myself to think that I enjoyed taking care of her, that I craved her dependence on me, that she had folded herself into my heart. If I did, I might lose her.

After two weeks, with Mama still not back, and no letter from Papa, I locked myself in Lady Eva's only bathroom, sat on the floor, and used the closed toilet seat as a writing table.

Dear Papa, Mama is in a mental clinic because she burned her hand.

Because she hit me.

Mama thinks she's crazy. It's been two weeks. The doctors must think she's crazy, too.

I ended up writing that Mama had fallen from the ferry and broken her arm, her right arm, her writing arm, but she was doing well. I thanked him for the money he'd sent with Lilli, but asked him not to have her visit anymore because it upset Mama. I filled the letter with details about Claire stringing words together, about Sixpence barking and wheeling around in a circle at the sound of a motorcycle. How I was learning to cook. Sautéed chestnuts, boiled chestnuts, spaghetti and chestnuts, potato and chestnut puree, dandelion leaves and chestnuts. I wanted to set fire to the tree, but then what would we eat? Fried mortadella only appeared once a week.

I wrote about *il prete*, the priest, that Lady Eva put in my bed to warm the sheets and dry the lake dampness—a curved wooden contraption inside of which rested a copper pot filled with embers. The first time I walked into the room and saw my humped bed I thought of Mama in her Prague bedroom, asleep, her belly big with Claire.

To Andy I wrote that every night we listened to classical music on the radio, which always made me think of him.

The four-page letter cost extra at the post office. "Don't you know there's a paper shortage?" the post mistress complained.

A letter filled with one lie and many details to cover it.

I wrote to Mrs. Pigeon and Palma, used the same excuse to explain Mama's silence.

Mrs. Pigeon's answer, addressed to Mama, managed to reach me in just ten days. "Rome is a disaster," she wrote.

Ever since a cyclist had thrown a bomb at some German officers on Via Veneto, the neighborhood was being guarded by armed platoons. She included a long list of *Verboten* actions: riding bicycles, the use of certain sidewalks, communicating outside the city by telegraph or telephone, spending the night in someone else's home.

"To be seen wearing sunglasses (in this weather an absurd idea, but then everything is) or carrying a package can get you a bullet between your shoulder blades. An eight-year-old boy cannot ride a bus for fear he will be plucked and sent to build roads or dig trenches. Jews are in hiding. In one day over a thousand of them were rounded up in the ghetto and shipped God knows where.

"Our ex-allies are also requisitioning empty apartments. I have convinced Gina, our portiera, to move in with Palma in your old apartment. They send their regards.

"Please do not let the girls go on any hikes. I would enjoy a photograph of them. Claire must be flowering in the lake air. Get well soon. Cordially, Ivana Cortini."

With Lady Eva's camera I took a picture of Claire and Sixpence and sent it to her. The mail worked again in this case. After the war, I went to visit her. The photograph was on her piano, next to her daughter's photos. Papa had repaid her the dowry money she had lent us. She had no news of Mama.

After lunch each day, I rouged my cheeks with Mama's lipstick, swore at the hair I had chopped off, and using Claire as my cover, looked for him. Gigi's shop, the back streets, the waterfront, in the hotels of the main square. One day I stopped to read the Call-to-Arms posters now plastered on the walls of every street and thought, he didn't listen to Gigi, they've stolen him away, I've lost him. Suddenly stunted, my legs began to ache. I stopped my walks, but kept pulling at my hair to make it grow.

Lady Eva went to see Mama at Villa Faro, to bring her more money to pay for the extra time Mama was staying there. She started dipping into her tea pot as soon as she got back.

"What are they doing to her?"

She drank three cups before she answered. "I do not know."

"Can I go see her?"

"She wishes you see her only when she is well, but she say to you she loves you and misses you, the baby and your brother. She appreciate your watercolor greatly and she send you this." Lady Eva unlatched her purse and brought out a pear. "To share with Claire. *La tua Mamma* will return soon."

I took the pear. It was mushy, bruised, delicious looking. "When is soon?" I wondered if there was a way I could save it until she came back.

"Poor little one!" Lady Eva poured wine into my cup. "You miss her much."

"I'm not little." I sipped, felt my throat tighten against the acidity and the thought of my mother coming back into my life, a new cleaned-out mother. Maybe someone who wouldn't recognize me, or if she did, had forgotten that she used to sing to me, comb my hair, do all the things every other mother did.

I bit into the pear and spurted juice onto my white sweater. "I'm in love," I declared, and told Lady Eva all about Claudio. She let me cry into her scarf.

TEN

CERNOBBIO, ITALY—DECEMBER 2, 1943

I sleep a lot, take pills and short walks in the garden. My plan is still in my head, as clear and daunting as before. I asked to see the Mother Superior, a small muffin of a woman with hard eyes. "I need a passer to cross the border with my two girls," I told her. "You're not strong enough," she claimed. The trip is dangerous. I will need to have all my wits about me. The doctor asked me to make a list of who I thought I was before, who I was now. "Whatever pops up in your head. It will help you."

I wrote words. Hair, teeth, bones, lost, photo in an album, abandoned, flesh, fury, misplaced, captive, home, coward, fixated, adulteress, mother, sane, pliant, hope, forgotten, vagina, hunger, mad, mountain, electricity, seedling, stubborn, breasts, caress, love, ghost, American, house of cards, wife, baby, heartbreak, pail in a courtyard leaking rain.

I threw the list down the toilet and told the doctor I couldn't be found in the dictionary.

CAMBRIDGE, MASSACHUSETTS—MAY 1956

During the weeks Mama was at Villa Faro, Lilli came back to Cernobbio, without pastries or money this time. She had no news of Papa. I told her

193

Mama had gone to Como for the day, but before she left, I caught Lady Eva muttering to her at the gate. She swore afterward that she only told Lilli how she and Sixpence enjoyed our company, but I didn't believe her. That Papa would know made me sad, because he'd worry even though he might be happy we were not going to Switzerland, because he'd be upset I hadn't told him, because maybe he wouldn't take Mama back, because he might ask Lilli to take care of us. I was relieved too. Someone else would worry about Mama. I could fill my head with Claudio and thoughts of love.

CERNOBBIO, ITALY—DECEMBER 4, 1943

Lilli showed up in my bedroom this morning. Not imagined. Flesh and bones and too much perfume. That's what woke me up, the clogging smell of bruised violets and that other smell that makes my head spin.

What was I doing in this crazy house? She wanted to know.

How could I leave my children in care of that drunken Eva?

I didn't answer her. No matter what I say, she's going to take my children where I will never find them. I have to get out. The Mother Superior just told me I was free to leave, but she couldn't help me with a passer. "Rest for another week," she said.

My room still smells of violets. And the smell of coal. Lilli brought that too.

CAMBRIDGE, MASSACHUSETTS—MAY 1956

A few days after Lilli's visit, I was coming back from the bread store. Just as I opened the gate, it started raining, fat drops that pocked the dirt road, and Claudio stepped out of the cemetery, not two hundred yards from me, a ghost made flesh. My heart skittered with joy as he walked toward me with his long Fred Astaire gait. Two other boys came with him, heads thrown back, the three of them blowing smoke circles in the air.

"Ciao again," he said. No smile. I pretended I didn't recognize him. He wore button cuffs this time, unbuttoned and his fingers were the longest I had ever seen on a boy. He kept on walking, and I watched him go, all of me seeming to sink in the softening ground. When he reached the corner, where the dirt road turned into cobblestones, I called out, "Hey." He turned around, his face like a flash of a lantern in the gray-filled street.

His friends kept going. He plunged his hands in his pockets and walked back to me. I stooped down, pretended to pick a pebble between my fingers and offered him the button I had just snapped off my blouse. "Did you lose this? Your cuffs are loose." The rain was coming down hard now.

"Maybe." He took the button and looked at Lady Eva's house. "You live here?" I nodded. He asked if he could visit tomorrow. "It's getting too cold for the cemetery."

I crossed my arms over my heart, afraid he could hear it. "Are you hiding?"

He stroked my wet cheek with his long fingers. "Five o'clock," he said.

Claudio came the next day, without his friends. And the next. Every day except Sunday. To keep warm, we all sat in the kitchen in front of the wood-burning stove, with chamomile tea on the table and Claire on his lap. Halfway through tea, when Lady Eva sank down in her rocking chair, snoring lightly, I offered him wine, hard-to-find matches for his cigarettes, food I had saved from lunch by saying I wasn't hungry. I listened. He was from Milan, and when the Germans had closed the border, his parents had sent him to hide out in his uncle's villa in Torno, across the lake. He'd been coming to Lake Como every summer since he was born. He would show me around, take me to his uncle's house, where we would raid the kitchen. The man who owned the *Vino e Olio* shop had been his uncle's gardener for ten years, that's why Gigi thought he could order him around. Claudio was eighteen, would have been in his last year of *liceo* if the Germans hadn't taken over Italy. He planned to go to the university to become a lawyer like his father. His eyes were blue, his lips full and dark. He kept licking them.

"You're not from here," he said.

"No." I didn't elaborate, wasn't going to tell him about my parents. I wanted him to ask me questions. I wanted not to tell him anything.

When questions didn't come, I swept Claire off his lap, put her down on the floor. She howled. Claudio picked her up, blew smoke circles in her face and gave her his widest smile. "You're beautiful." He was in love with my sister. I picked up Sixpence. We played cool.

On the next visit I dragged the record player into the kitchen and showed off my forbidden American music. He listened to Ersilia's record, sang the words to "Nagasaki," his favorite—"where the men all chew tobacky and the women wicky-wacky-woo"–and didn't ask me to dance.

Claudio did try to help me with algebra, but his head came so close I ended up not understanding a word. Sometimes he was tired or moody and would stretch out his body over two chairs, smoking, watching Claire rock on my knees, listening to the music. For an hour or two I let myself travel to a happy point in the future. With a family of my own.

I tried my first cigarette in that kitchen and coughed it out of my system. When I least expected it, I got my first kiss, which I still cherish like a crumbling four-leaf clover pressed between the pages of a book. After the kiss, Claudio said I was too young for love.

"Fifteen," I lied.

"I might just wait," he said and kissed me again. This time I pressed my chest against his and told him I loved him.

The next day he didn't come back. The day after that was Sunday, his off day. I blamed my unladylike boldness, my flat chest, my plain face, my horrible hair, my age. On Monday I lighted the stove, made tea, and waited.

"The mention of love grows wings on men's feet," Lady Eva said, my red eyes telling her all she needed. Waiting, we drank directly from the bottle, all pretense gone. She fell asleep; I threw up.

The next day I took the empty bottles to Gigi. "He's gone," he said before I could ask. The militia had caught him and his two friends in a bar in Torno and ordered them to report for military service the next day on penalty of being shipped to a labor camp in Germany.

"When did the militia find him?" I asked, needing to reapportion blame, to know if he would have come back to Lady Eva's kitchen. "What day exactly?"

"Those bastards didn't get him. He slipped away during the night. We'll have to wait out the war to see him again."

I dropped one of the bottles. A sliver stuck in my ankle.

Gigi handed me the broom.

I swept up the broken glass, picked the sliver from my ankle, watched the blood bloom in the gray of my sock. Gigi filled a new bottle, asked me to pay only for the wine, then walked me out of the shop, to the end of the street where we could see a wedge of the mountain above Cernob-bio. Gigi pointed. "That's the Bisbino. Switzerland is on the other side. *La Betulla* is the crossing point."

La Betulla—the birch. I tried to find the tree at the top. The tip of the mountain was bare, covered in snow, a flash of silver in the sunlight, like a bird's wing. Below the snow line, a green spray of pines and chestnut trees.

"After the war, he'll be back," Gigi said. "He's safe, that's what counts." His smile was another crease on his face.

I walked back to Lady Eva's, telling myself how happy I was for Claudio, but when I got to the kitchen I turned on the record player, took Sixpence in my arms, and danced to "Nagasaki" with tears jiggling out of my eyes. Gigi's words kept coming back, a refrain louder than the music. "After the war, he'll be back." I would wait. I was good at waiting.

I skipped school one morning and took the ferry across to Como. On the funicular up to Brunate, I watched the sun scrambling over the mountain behind the lighthouse. The northern wind had cleaned the sky into a sharp blue. Below, the lake was black with a low ribbon of cloud running across it. On the far side, an ocher patch of the *Militarische Krankenhaus* peeked through the trees.

I wondered if Mama could see this view. As the funicular climbed closer to Villa Faro, I imagined the cable snapping, the car plunging back down into the lake. Would she see me drown?

A few streets down from the funicular stop, two girls in blue uniforms and white caps came out of a tall iron gate. They walked toward me.

"I'm tired of cleaning up after her," one of the girls whined. VILLA FARO was stitched in dark blue on the chest pocket of her uniform. "Every time that woman gets the jolt, she dumps on the table."

"That's your fault," the other girl said. "Take her to the bathroom first."

"I dooo, Luisa! She's just being spiteful."

I stepped in front of them. "What's the jolt?" They were talking about Mama, I was sure of it. Mama shitting on the table the way I had peed in my bed in Rome. Scared to death. "Is it a medicine?"

The whiny girl said, "Why should I tell you?"

I held out a fifty-cent piece. "What's the jolt?"

She slipped the coin in her pocket. "Electricity, what else? We tie the patient to a table and the doctor sends lightning through her."

"Doesn't it kill her?" In Newport Beach I had seen a dead puppy once, his mouth still gripped around the light plug.

The other one, a pouty girl with frizzy hair, said, "Burns their brains clean. Epileptics never go crazy, that's why they do it. It doesn't hurt."

The whiny girl giggled. "But if they're really bad, then the nuns hold them down and a doctor cuts a hole in their brain and they become zombies."

197

I stepped back, let her smirking face pass me, resisted kicking her. I walked to the tall iron gate topped by a cross and peered at Villa Faro, a crumbling gray stone house ringed by a gravel drive and patches of desiccated geraniums and weeds. Iron bars covered the windows. Behind a second-story window, I thought I saw a woman. Mama, I decided, needing certainties. I pictured her leaning into the glass pane in her green tweed suit, like a plant reaching for light. Mama with her hair singed, skin blistered and dark, shiny with ointment smelling of mint and grease. Mama, who would rather die than not have her mind turn on.

I walked away. On the far side of the villa, another gate, another building, smaller, more modest, behind a row of fruit trees and a large vegetable garden. A nun was on her knees, weeding. I walked around the corner of the fence to the other entryway, wondering if the pear Mama had sent me came from one of those trees, hoping the nun would give me another one, one I'd share with Claire this time. At this gate, a small bronze plaque.

Now, with dawn peeping under the window shade and David warming my forehead with his breath, I close my eyes to see it better. It's stained, badly in need of polish. I can barely make out the words, and then they pop right into my head. My heart starts to hammer. The coincidence is too great. The truth must be there, on that plaque. I scramble myself out of bed and hurry to the kitchen, where I left Papa's check stubs. I thumb through them. In my excitement I see nothing but scribbles. Slow down, Susie. I turn on more lights, sit down and try again. There it is, the first payment. *Le Suore di Maria della Consolazione* Papa wrote in his tight, oblique handwriting. The same words were on that plaque.

I debate waking David to tell him, but I can hear his caution, his need to cushion what might be a terrible disappointment:

Could be a coincidence. There must be many branches of the Sisters of Mary of the Consolation. Or:

Didn't you tell your father she had spent time there? Maybe that's why he gave to them and not some other institution. Or:

She died across the lake from there. He's commemorating her death. Or:

Honey, we're happy. We have a good life. Can't you let it go?

I close the door to the kitchen and call the international operator. In Italy it is 11:45 a.m.

"I am sorry, we cannot give you the name of our residents in the past or the present." An old voice, a nervous one. Maybe she has never received a call from the States.

"I'm her daughter. I need to know. It's extremely important."

"That you are this signora's daughter is what you tell me over the telephone and I wish to believe you, but the rules require that we see with our eyes who you are, and even then it is not our policy to give you the information you wish."

"My father sent you money for years. Marco Alessandrini. You can look it up. Why would he send you money if she's not there? He was a terrible Catholic."

She says nothing. I get angry. "I need to know if she's alive, that's all. Is she alive? Can't you tell me that?"

"I understand your anguish."

No, you don't! You're a nun, you know nothing about giving birth, about wanting to have a clean story to tell your baby, one without the lead weight of guilt. "I'm coming to Italy. I'll get a lawyer. I'll bring all the documents you want. You'll have to tell me."

"If you come, your birth certificate will be enough to show us who you are, and then it will be up to the Mother Superior. I cannot help you over the phone. Goodbye, signora."

"That means she's there," I say to the dial tone. David's arms embrace me from behind. His chin rests on the top of my head.

"They wouldn't make me go all the way to Italy if she's not there, would they?" I ask David.

"I wish I knew, my love. I wish I knew." He sounds so sad that I cover his hands with kisses. We go back to bed and console each other with gentle, sweet love-making.

Over breakfast, David suggests that Andy should be the one to go up to Villa Faro to face the nuns. "A man's request always carries more weight. Sad, but true, as you well know." I read the subtext. With the baby coming we can't afford to throw money away on what might be a wild goose chase. "The plane trip," he adds. "You're six months pregnant."

"Seven in two weeks. I'll ask Doctor Page. I'm sure it's fine." It has to be. Every fiber of my being is already there, at Villa Faro. Hope is blinding me, but I don't care. "Andy wants nothing to do with this and Claire's too young to go." I'm not going to tell her or Andy. It would be cruel if nothing comes of it. Besides, I want to be the one to find her.

CERNOBBIO, ITALY—DECEMBER 18, 1943

I am sitting in the Mother Superior's office, under her stare, steeling myself against her verbal assault. I've just told her I'm leaving.

Her flinty eyes leave my face and rest at a spot beyond my shoulder. "Your confidence is admirable. Today is Saturday and unfortunately Doctor Petrini won't be in until Monday. I'm sure he would want to see you before you go." She looks back at me and smiles for the first time since I've met her. "It will give you a chance to rest two more days."

"I won't change my mind."

She leans forward, hands folded. Her expression is almost kind. "In most cases electroshock treatments wipe away the patient's destructive fixations, but I see that is not the case with you. You will undoubtedly keep trying to find a passer and attempt to cross into Switzerland. I wish you luck, but I need to run this clinic in an orderly fashion, and I ask you to stay until Monday so that Dr. Petrini can talk to you and then sign the release papers. Will you do that for me?"

I owe her no favors, but I say yes anyway. Two more days will only strengthen my resolve.

CAMBRIDGE, MASSACHUSETTS—MAY 1956

This morning, a clear warm day, Mrs. Stein, my favorite art pupil, and I waited for her daughter-in-law on a bench in front of the Senior Center. After a few minutes she rummaged in her bag and handed me a wrapped package. "Ziporah, that's my daughter-in-law, she said I shouldn't give before the baby comes. It is bad luck. But you're a Christian, bad luck is not for you. Open, I want to see if you like."

I unwrapped the package and unfolded a yellow baby sweater with buttons in the shape of daisies. "I love it!" I hugged her. "You're the best."

"Ziporah made it, but I teach her. It is my pattern. She is a good woman, like a real daughter. I wish you a daughter like Ziporah."

Suddenly I was telling Mrs. Stein all about Mama's disappearance, about Villa Faro and my father's payments to the nuns.

"Your head is full of do I, do I not, yes?"

I nodded.

"You are thinking, what if I open the package and there is nothing. How will I live after that?"

I kept nodding.

"At Passover, during Seder we hide the *afikomen*, a matzoh we have broken in two. We hide it and it is lost to the children, who must find it. Every child is only thinking of finding it because finding it brings a prize. Your mother, she is your *afikomen*, the half that was broken away. Maybe she is hiding in the villa, maybe she is not, but you, my child, to get your prize, must look."

I'm lying on the sofa in the living room, listening to Perry Como croon on television. David is out to dinner with friends for their monthly boys-only get-together. I'm luxuriating in Dr. Page's green light, in Mrs. Stein's words. I'm full of love and hope tonight. I wait for David to walk through the front door, the old glass pane which needs new putty shaking its own sweet notes. It's his walk I noticed first, as he made his way to the podium at the Student Center to deliver his talk on Egypt. His is a reluctant amble, pigeon-toed, as if he is in no hurry to reach a destination, as if he has no reason to leave.

I tell our baby about her father, how he dismantled my diffidence stone by stone, how he has lifted me and placed me on a higher shore. How he will keep her or him safe.

Tonight I will take David to bed. I will trace the curve of his shoulder as he falls asleep and wait to hear his corrugated voice tell me in the morning that he loves me, that he would come to Italy with me if we could afford it. That he understands. I will watch his Adam's apple tread his throat and think of holding it in my mouth as if it were a cool fruit. I will wait for the writing callous of his middle finger to skate down my nose before he kisses me.

I am happy. We have a great life, but I am going. My heart still trembles at the thought of it. I'm full of questions and doubts, but I must go. I won't find if I don't look. I have the ticket in my hand. On June 18th, I am flying to Milan. A train will take me to Como, the funicular up to Brunate and Villa Faro.

CERNOBBIO, ITALY—DECEMBER 20, 1943

It's early morning, still dark out. Luisa, one of the nurses, slips into my room with a man in tow. Aldo, her older brother. She won't let me turn on the light. I can't see his face, but I smell earth on him.

His hand is rough against my own. A big man. A farmer by day, a passer by night, he says.

"You can trust Aldo," Luisa whispers. "And you'll be fine in Switzerland. They're not sending anyone back now that we've been invaded. Jews or Christians, rich or poor, anyone who makes it across the border, they take in."

I get out of bed, reach for my bathrobe. "How much?" I ask. Is he real? Is Switzerland finally possible? My head and heart are jumping hurdles at breakneck speed. I can't think clearly, don't dare believe.

Aldo takes off his cap and sits down on the bed. Luisa slides out of the room.

"A mile in, the Swiss guards will pick you up. Sixty days of quarantine." He sounds like a dog growling a warning, but the words are good. "You'll get food, clothes. They'll put you up in schools, camps, wherever there's room. You'll have to work to pay them back. The Swiss, they have money and clocks for brains, but you and the kids will be safe. You've got kids, right?"

He wants details: How old? Are they obedient? Do they scare easily? Are they crybabies?

"They'll be little angels, I promise."

He pulls me onto the bed and pushes his hand under my nightgown, threads thick fingers through my pubic hair. I let him, assuming it's part of the payment. One man raping my vagina is no different from another man raping my brain. Maybe it's all part of the treatment. After he is through, he stands up with his pants gathered at his ankles and states his price. It's high. I have no idea how much money I have left, but I would say yes to a million dollars.

"Take us over Christmas Eve. It'll be dark." I point to the gouged-out moon sitting in a corner of the cross bars. "The border guards will be eating, drinking too much."

He laughs at me. "You *are* nuts if you think drink stops a German." I laugh too, safe in the thought that I've never been saner.

He fucks me again. This time the thought of crossing over makes me come.

CAMBRIDGE, MASSACHUSETTS—JUNE 1956

Christmas Eve: I was in the kitchen with Claire on the floor and Benny Goodman on the record player. Lady Eva was helping to serve dinner at the *Olga Regina* and scraping leftovers into a pail for our Christmas meal the next day.

I hummed to the music and cut slits across the backs of a pile of chestnuts, dropping them into boiling water. With the hotel leftovers, a mealy chestnut puree. "To keep us warm," Lady Eva said. Outside, the temperature had dropped to freezing, an unusual event for the area.

Our Christmas presents were in a basket by the crèche on the window sill. Lady Eva had shown me how to make a doll for Claire out of one of my knee socks. Brown buttons for eyes, a pen point for a nose, a barrette for the mouth. For hair, she had dug up a torn red leather glove. Lady Eva's present was a picture I'd taken of Sixpence and Claire lying on the flowered settee. Mama's present was a photograph of Claire and me by the lake. I was going to bring it to her in the morning, my first visit, a surprise. I was scared. Was she still Mama? Would seeing her again be horrible or wonderful?

Sixpence barked, scratched at the kitchen door. I turned off the record player and heard angry knocking. I instantly thought someone had heard the American music, and now the police were at the front door. I slid the record between the dish towels under the sink, a new fear now sour in my mouth. As I left the kitchen, Sixpence shot out between my legs, his yapping a siren wave of alarm.

I opened the front door to cold air and Mama, a black outline against the night. Her appearance was so unexpected I went numb. I don't think I even said hello. She smelled of rubbing alcohol when she hugged me. "Where's the baby?"

"Claire?" Had she forgotten her name?

Sixpence kept barking. I picked him up, filled my arms with him. "She's in the kitchen."

Mama ran past me, lifted Claire from the floor, almost dropped her as if unprepared for her new weight. Claire thought it was a game and grinned, showing off her two new teeth. I watched my mother rub her nose against Claire's cheek, sniff her scent. Every caress she gave my sister had the force of a tide pulling me away, isolating me. I tried to read the signs on her face. It was thinner, tighter, as if stitched back against her skull. Her hair was long, matted down. Her green tweed suit was covered in wrinkles. I looked at her forehead. No hole.

"We're leaving." She tightened her grip on Claire, who started to cry. "Shh, no crying. No crying all night or we're dead."

"Where are we going?" A dark ring circled her wrist. A two-inch strap, the same purple her palm had been after the burn. "Where are we going?"

The other wrist was ringed too. Had she done this to herself again, placed her wrists on a burning stove, turned them around slowly until the skin seared into a perfect bracelet? I shrank away from her and felt my stomach begin to heave.

"Go upstairs and pack, sweetie."

"My name is Susie."

"Put on all the sweaters you've got. Get a blanket for the baby. Dress warmly. Slip on Mrs. Pigeon's boots."

"They're too big."

"Wear them anyway." She jiggled Claire on one hip and opened kitchen cabinets, rummaging in drawers. Her body quivered. I remembered the chestnuts and turned off the boiling water. Sixpence jumped high against her thighs, trying to reclaim Claire, who was still crying.

"Are we going over the Bisbino?"

"Yes. Where does she keep the food?" She whirled around the kitchen. "Hurry, Susie. Please! Go pack."

"The border guards will shoot us." There were new signs up all over Cernobbio. *Ordine di fucilare chiunque . . .* Too many people were crossing over, Gigi had told me. "They'll kill us."

"The guards only shoot men. Women and babies are useless to them. We'll be safe."

Claudio was safe. He hadn't been among the dead bodies displayed outside the barracks for anyone to see.

Upstairs Mama packed one suitcase with Claire on the bed, Sixpence already whining beside her. I stayed by the door, my ears stretched to the sound of Lady Eva returning. She would talk sense into my mother. It had snowed on the Bisbino. It was cold. It was Christmas Eve. Papa wanted me to stay right here.

"You'll have to take your pillow," I said. "And Sixpence. Claire won't go anywhere without them."

"I'm here now. And the dog's not ours."

"The food you stuffed into your knapsack isn't yours either."

She found the money I had hidden in Mrs. Pigeon's boots. "There's a sickle moon tonight. Not much light."

I pleaded my case. Told her about the posters with orders to kill anyone trying to cross over on sight, about how Lady Eva stole food for us, found us clothes, how she stopped asking for the rent money. I picked up Sixpence from the bed, shut him out of the room. "Look at Claire!"

Claire was wailing while Sixpence howled behind the door.

"She'll cry all the way up the mountain. They'll hear us and shoot us dead!"

The suitcase wouldn't close. She asked me to sit on it. I did as she asked, but kept my feet on the floor and leaned my weight forward instead of down. "Please let us stay."

She pushed her knee against the corners of the suitcase, pressed down on the latches, clicked them shut.

"We have to wait for Lady Eva. We have to say goodbye."

Mama held up boots. "Put on another pair of socks and they'll fit you."

LOGAN AIRPORT, BOSTON—JUNE 18, 1956

Pan Am has called my flight. Passengers push forward to the gate. I hold back, unwilling to let go of David's hand. He covers my face with kisses. "Send a telegram the minute you have news," he says, "and take care. For both of you." He holds my head and looks at me with his gentle eyes. "If she's not there, you still have me. I'll never leave you." I believe him and, for as long as we hold on to each other, I feel loved, innocent, fulfilled. Then the stewardess at the gate calls my name. I'm the last passenger to board the plane.

ELEVEN

IN FLIGHT—JUNE 18, 1956

My last Christmas Eve with Mama we waited in the northern outskirts of town in the chapel of the Madonna of the Graces.

"We need grace." Mama kept looking at her watch. "We'll give Aldo one more hour. If he doesn't come, we'll go without him. A birch is all we have to find. *La Betulla* in the snow."

I dipped my hand in the font, surprised that the holy water wasn't frozen. I walked up to the altar and lit two candles, for light and reassurance. Two plaster saints held up a painting of a red-robed Madonna. *Virgini Immaculatae* read the frame. How many more Madonnas were there? I paced the short nave in my shearling coat, my feet fat with socks. The boots were still too big. Saint Mary of the Graces, Saint Mary of the Dead, *Ordine di fucilare chiunque*, Saint Mary of the Conception, Saint Mary of the Angels—

"I told Aldo it had to be tonight," Mama whispered. "Tonight with the sickle moon."

Saint Mary of the Soul, Saint Mary of the Consolation—

"It's the right night. *Heilige Nacht*. The guards will be drinking." She told me about the sixty days of quarantine to make sure we weren't sick, how we'd sleep wherever there was room, how we'd have to work. I'd go to school, work after school and on weekends.

"What happens if you're sick?" I asked. "When we're in quarantine, what happens if you get sick? Do they send us back?"

"Physical sickness, that's what they're interested in."

A blast of cold air and Mama's face lighted up. In the glare of Aldo's flashlight, she looked made of plaster too. "Where's the money?" Aldo said. He reeked of manure.

I stopped pacing. Saint Mary of the Peace, Saint Mary of the Miracles—I couldn't think of anymore Marys. Mama stood up, took out the neatly folded bills she had found and handed them over. Aldo counted the money and stuffed it in a pants pocket. "You've got too much luggage. Dump one. It'll make things easier."

"I've stripped myself down to two daughters, a knapsack and one suitcase," Mama said. "That's where I stop."

Aldo took Claire from her and shook his heavy head. "No one listens." A lion's head, I thought as I watched Claire disappear in his bulk. He only wants to steal the suitcase. Maybe Claire too.

We walked up the dirt road, past the high walls of villas. The road twisted into a forest. I stopped. I couldn't see the moon. Or the lighthouse. The lake had become a lighter patch in that blackness, a thumb's imprint in a pool of ink. Lady Eva would be back by now, with pastries maybe. "Come, come girls. Yumyum to eat!" She'd find my note.

Mama tugged at my arm. Above her, Aldo held Claire and waited, as still and sturdy as the pines surrounding us. "No stopping," he said.

The climb got steeper. Aldo took the suitcase, Mama took the knapsack from me. The exchanges were made only to the sound of our heaving breaths. We left the dirt road and made our way up a slope thick with trees and brambles. It was so cold I was sure my lungs were going to crack.

Lady Eva would get new boarders and forget most of her English. I wondered how long Claire would remember Sixpence.

After almost two hours, around eleven o'clock, church bells started ringing. Aldo held out an arm to stop us. I dropped down to the ground. We were still in the woods, on the outskirts of Rovenna, a small town one third of the way to the Bisbino summit.

"We'll take a break," Aldo said. The rest of him made no sound.

"I have no patience left." Mama kept on walking. Aldo pulled her back.

"Rest! If you have food, eat it now." He shined a flashlight at a wide tree, one hand cupped over the beam. "Sit there." Then it was dark again. The bells kept ringing.

Mama's feet cracked twigs. Her breath came in short rasps. "I won't wait."

I crawled to the tree. My lungs were splintered, my feet blistered. "I'm not moving." I also knew those bells shouldn't be ringing. With the war, churches had stopped ringing the hours after dark. The last bells were for evening service. At six. At six, I had been warm in Lady Eva's kitchen, slitting chestnuts, listening to Benny Goodman and the deep bells of the Church of the Savior from the center of town. I was never going to get up again.

Aldo pushed Mama down next to me. He lay the suitcase in front of us and lifted the lid. Clothes spilled out onto my legs. They felt warm. He nestled Claire inside the suitcase. "If she wakes up, give her more of this." He handed me a flask. "Wait for me. I have to make contact in town. Don't talk."

I heard the swish of a branch whipping back. The manure smell went with him and it became quiet again. The bells had stopped. I opened the flask, sniffed. Whatever was in it smelled vile. I took a sip anyway. The liquid flared inside me. It felt good.

"*Fuorusciti*, that's what they call people like us," Mama said. I shushed her.

"Gone out. Exited. To me that word is as joyous as the sound of those bells. Out of here. Out of the war. Last week they shot an eight-year-old boy because he wouldn't let go of his father's hand in front of the firing squad. Out of my life."

"You said children were safe."

"Girl children. Girls don't make war." She clasped my hand and leaned into the tree. Our breaths slowed, became inaudible as we waited for Aldo to come back. My stomach hurt. I blamed the liquid I had drunk.

Aldo came back, crouched in front of us, his smell and heat intact. "The Germans caught two deserters at *La Betulla*."

Mama let out a meek hoot, the cry of a baby owl.

"Shhh!" Aldo shook her. I felt my rib cage closing, shutting out air. *Ordine di fucilare chiunque.* The words were real now. "They're dead," I said.

Mama let go of my hand, stood up. "Find another route! I won't go back."

"We climb to the sanctuary." Aldo's voice scraped my ear. "Right under their noses. It's windy up there and they won't expect anyone coming tonight. Not after those bells warning everyone."

I pulled myself up. "We should go back."

"We'll be fine," Mama said. "The worst that can happen is they'll send us back."

I felt Aldo bend down, heard the two snaps of the suitcase closing. He had Claire now. I could see her pale face against his darkness. At the top of the mountain he was going to let us go. Mama, Claire, and Susie walking into another country. If the border guards didn't shoot us first. Papa would never find us again. I would never find Claudio.

I ran, stumbling downhill, making too much noise. Thumping, swishing, scratching sounds that clawed at my heart. I heard the snap of branches behind me, imagined them rifle shots. I ran faster, dodging trees, jumping over brambles, tripping over them.

"Susiiiie!"

I had a sudden flash of my mother strapped to a table, scared out of her mind, yelling.

"Susiiiie!"

My legs stopped as if caught in a trap. I stumbled forward, fell on my knees.

"Susie, where are you?" Her voice was close, calmer. She had heard me fall. My hands groped the ground, looking for what had tripped me. No rocks, no protruding roots. I had fallen on the desperation in my mother's voice, a desperation that scared me more than the possibility of rifle shots.

"I'm here, Mama."

I shut the book on the past and close my eyes. I have to get some sleep. In a few hours the plane will land in Milan, then Como. Then what?

What if I find her at Villa Faro and she doesn't recognize me? What if I don't recognize her or she's not the mother I remember, the one I need now?

What will I do if she's too sick, faraway? So faraway I won't even be able to touch her?

What if I look at her and all I feel is shame? What if on seeing me, she turns her head away? What will I do then?

The plane is about to land. I'm almost there, but I can't do it. Andy is right. Leave well enough alone. Once I know the truth—whatever it is—no coddling flight of imagination will change it. It's better this way. If she's still alive, she'll have learned to live her days without us, maybe even enjoyed our absence. I have no right to crash into her life, upset whatever balance she may have created for herself.

I'll wait in the airport for the next plane back. I'll tell David I didn't find her. She probably isn't at Villa Faro. She's probably buried in some unmarked grave I will never find, no matter how hard I look.

The baby is restless inside me. She doesn't like flying; she doesn't like my thoughts. I've scared her.

MONTE BISBINO, ITALY—DECEMBER 24, 1943

I crouch down beside Susie. She's crouching and her breaths are shallow from her run. "I can't bear to lose you, too. I can't."

"I just needed to pee."

"We'll go back if you want."

She stands, pulls up her underpants. "I didn't want to pee in front of that man."

I want to make her understand so that she can forgive me. "All the time I was in that place, I nailed pictures in my head. The one I saw best was of you, sitting next to me at the window, planning our lives. It was real to me. They never shocked that picture out of me. I had nightmares sometimes. That they bored a hole in my head, gave me a lobotomy. I could see them remove the drill from my brain with you and Claire stuck to the tip. What was left of my family, that's what they were taking out in my dreams. I'd wake up thinking there was nothing left of me. But I always came back to us at the window, looking out on our future lives, and I was fine."

I hear the rustle of dry leaves, smell Aldo. "Are you going over or not?"

I take Susie's hand. "Do you want to go back? Do you?"

"Let's go," Aldo says. "We've got a long climb ahead of us."

Susie stays silent, saying everything. I let go of her hand, stand up. "We're going back down. It's too dangerous." How else can I show her how much I love her?

"Sixty-three people have gone over thanks to me and not one of them got hurt."

"We're going back down."

Susie tugs at my arm. "We're going over. They'll never get us."

211

"Are you sure, sweetie? We can wait until the war ends."

"I just wanted to pee."

Aldo moves ahead. "Let's go then."

We climb back to where Aldo has left the suitcase. It takes only a few minutes. Susie didn't run far.

LINATE AIRPORT, MILAN—JUNE 19, 1956

Waiting for my luggage, I change my mind again. I can't accept the thought of giving birth to my baby and Mama not being there. That she'll grow up and Mama won't be there. That Mama will never be proud of me. That she won't see my mistakes. That she won't console me. That I'll be a mother without a mother. I need to find her, to know, no matter how heavy that rock of truth may turn out to be. I need her to recognize me, to hold me, to forgive me. To love the baby. Maybe we've lost too much time. Maybe we won't be able to console each other, but we can try. Touching my feet on Italian ground, on my old homeland, has filled me with optimism.

I feel you close, Mama. Wait for me.

MONTE BISBINO, ITALY—DECEMBER 24, 1943

The sanctuary is six thousand feet high, and the trees thin out as we climb in a line, our breaths following the rhythm of our feet. Every few minutes I sneak a look back to see if Susie is still with me. Claire, drunk, sleeps on Aldo's shoulder. The sickle moon climbs with us. We meet snow, a thin crunchy layer that deepens into pillowy mounds. The silhouette of the sanctuary comes up on our left. We can rest here for a few minutes, I think as my heart pounds against my ribs, but Aldo cuts away to our right and dips away from sight. I grab Susie's arm and break into a run to keep up with him.

MILAN, ITALY—JUNE 19, 1956

I take a bus to the Milan train station. Beggars huddle against the wall of the long marble stairway up to the tracks. The Italian postwar boom eludes them, and I'm again reminded of how lucky I am, how grateful I should be for the life I have. I give money to a little girl who sings a little ditty to thank me. I feel worse in the bar, with its abundant display of

cornetti, pizzette, and *tramezzini.* I don't know if it's because of the beggars or the sudden jolt of memory of Mama burning her hand against the
espresso machine in this very room. The heat doesn't help, or the thick
fog of cigarette smoke choking me. I leave without the cappuccino I crave
and walk down to Information. Como is only a forty-five-minute ride from
Milan, and there's a train every hour. Just east of the town, on top of a
mountain, sit Brunate and Villa Faro.

My body shakes with the movement of the train. My heart beats to a
much faster rhythm. I stroke my belly to calm myself, to calm the baby,
who answers me by sticking her foot hard against one of my ribs. Maybe
her way of saying, '*You* keep cool, I'm doing fine.' I look out the window
at the snow-covered Alps streaming past, and a memory slips in front of
my eyes.

We're running. One of my legs plunges into a hole hidden in the
snow, and I fall on my face. I lie there, listening to the heave of my chest,
each breath a sharp sting. Let them go without me. I'm too exhausted to
move.

Aldo lifts me up, swings me on his back, locks my legs in his arms.
I lean forward, my hands tucked in, and bounce with him, piggy-back,
warming one cheek, then the other against the leather of his shoulders.
Mama carries Claire. As time passes, Aldo's manure smell turns into the
hot waves of Lady Eva's kitchen stove. The crunch of his footsteps becomes
the repeated clinks of Lady Eva's wine cup meeting its saucer. Aldo's hair
on my forehead is Sixpence's fur. I fall asleep to the thought that we're
going back after all.

I wake up to the wind on my face and a tinkling sound. Aldo is lowering me to ground that looks as soft and white as a freshly made bed. The
cold wet of the snow against my cheek pries my eyes open. The tinkling
sound persists, sounding like the bells the altar boys ring during Mass,
except farther away. I take it for the tail end of a dream and start to stand
up, then feel Aldo push me back down. I squat next to Mama, who is on
her knees. Aldo, the tallest of us, crouches. We're hiding, I realize, seeing the boulder in front of us. Where the boulder dips, then ends, I see
treeless dunes of white. We are at the top of the mountain. At the edge
of the horizon to my left, a spattering of lights.

We have reached the border. The sickle moon is just above us, weakly
showing three rungs of barbed wire fence along the swing of the crest,
backlit by the white cover of a neighboring crag. The fence is eight, ten

feet of glaring snow away, with the rest of the rungs buried under a snow drift. Fifty feet beyond the fence, the mountain drops out of sight.

The barbed wire is ringing at the cusp between Italy and Switzerland. Bells, hundreds of small Christmas bells, running up and down as far as I can see. Thousands I can't see. One thimble-sized bell will set off all the others. "They'll hear us," I whisper.

Aldo's lips are cold against my ear. "Past midnight, the wind is always up. They will think it's the wind. You'll be fine." A wave of heat hits my face as Aldo opens his coat. In his hand, cutting shears. I feel myself crumble and lie down, resting my head against the suitcase.

"Watch out for stumps when you run to the fence." Aldo's voice grazes above me, no louder than my breath. "The bastards cut all the trees down."

Mama shakes me. I sit up. On the side of the boulder, Aldo is on his stomach like a shot-down bear. "We're going," Mama whispers. Aldo snakes his way around the boulder, out of sight. The wind is louder. So are the bells. "Lie on your stomach and follow him. When he cuts the wire, you and Claire slide under. I'll be behind you with the suitcase."

I elbow my way along the groove Aldo's body has left. When I reach him, the fence is only two feet from my face. Aldo puts a zonked out Claire in my arms, and starts digging into the snow drift with his hands. The lower rungs of the fence appear.

Mama crawls up to us on all fours and kisses Claire's head, then mine. "Hold her tight. Remember you only have a foot of headroom. I'll be right behind you."

I tuck Claire under my coat and slide into the trench Aldo has dug. My nose can almost touch the lowest rung of barbed wire. I watch Aldo fit his open shears between two bells. A new gust of wind sweeps snow in my face. Aldo snaps the wire. The bells jingle violently for the length of a never-ending heartbeat, then settle back to the wind's slower rhythm.

"Go," Mama whispers.

I push Claire forward in the opening, push my body through, wrap her tight to my chest, and I'm off, racing Andy in our California pool, swallowing water, snow, my shoulders and arms pulling me forward, my stomach tight for endurance, my head low for least resistance. The bells goad me on. I'm trying to set a record. I will beat them all in this race to a new life. I will win.

We are a rolled blanket tumbling down the gentle slope of the mountain, gathering snow like an avalanche lurching toward the black bed of pine trees. I don't stop to look back, to make sure Mama is following me. As the white space between the fence and us widens, the weight of that avalanche lifts off me. I forget about racing Andy, forget the border guards who might shoot me, forget what it's like to be scared, forget I'm holding Claire. Like the fence bells, I swing in the wind. I am motherless. Fatherless. Without a brother or a sister or a boyfriend. No one to leave me, forget me, not love me. No one to stop me from going forward. Going back. Just me, choosing my own way.

A pair of legs stops our descent. "Don't be afraid," a man says in Italian. "You're in Switzerland now." He lifts me up, slaps the snow from my back. Mama said nothing about a man meeting us. I won't let him have Claire. "My mother is coming."

"She stayed back. It was too dangerous for you to come together. In a few days she'll come. Don't worry. She'll be fine. So will you."

I don't believe him. "She said she was going to be right behind us."

"She didn't want you to be scared."

"Will she know where we are? Will she find us?"

"Of course. It's part of the plan."

I believed that man. He had a kind voice and fed us beloved chocolate. "She'll come in a few days," he kept repeating. I needed to believe him. The alternative was inconceivable.

We raced to Lugano on his motorbike, Claire tied to his chest with rope, me hugging his waist for dear life. Our new home became the Italian consulate. I waited for Mama to appear, then waited for a letter. No one had news of her, not Papa, not Giorgio, who also lived at the consulate, not Lilli stuck in Milan. Not even Mrs. Pigeon. Mama simply disappeared.

June, 1945, the war had ended, and it was time for another train ride, this one with Giorgio and Lilli. A crowded, smelly, dangerous ride according to Lilli, who was convinced she would be robbed. In Florence, the train broke down. Everyone had to get out with the luggage. American soldiers patrolled the station, and when I saw one look me over, I answered with a giggle and "Hi, I come from California. Where are you from?" Up close he smelled of food.

"Hampton, Virginia. What's your name?"

I told him, then added, "We haven't eaten in days." Which was almost true. The sandwiches Lilli had brought with her tasted awful. He took pity on us, took all of us to his mess hall in a jeep, and fed us powdered eggs and real bacon before putting us on the train again. I thought I deserved thanks from Lilli and Giorgio, which I didn't get.

When Claire and I stepped off the train in Rome, Stazione Termini was jam-packed with people rushing, running, wandering, searching. Wives, husbands, parents, children, relatives, friends, were hugging, laughing, crying, sharing their joy, their relief that it was all over, that they were alive.

Papa stood at the end of the platform, his face appearing and disappearing behind other heads. I ran to him, dragging Claire. He looked fatter, but he was still my handsome Papa. Claire cried when Papa picked her up. She didn't know who he was. When he hugged me, his arms felt shorter, as if they had lost their reach, and the smell of him was faint. Memory enriches.

Andy looked thicker, solid, too strong to tease anymore, the hank of hair that always fell across his forehead cut short. He shook my hand and told me I'd gotten very tall for a girl. Our mutual awkwardness went away after a while, but the distance between us was great now. We were framed by different memories.

Our new home in Parioli was a palace to me. We had our own bedrooms, two bathrooms, each of us had our own set of towels. Mine smelled of talcum powder. On my bed, clean soft sheets the color of cream. Dinner was delicious. US army-issue split-pea soup, fried SPAM with cheddar cheese on top that came in big khaki-colored cans. An Italian tomato for dessert.

Papa waited until I took a long, very hot bath and got ready for bed to come to tell me about Mama, how the border guards had shot her the night we escaped.

"Terrible news can only be told in person," he said.

I didn't feel anything right away, maybe because Mama dead didn't make sense, or maybe because after a year and a half without her, the idea of Mama had become faint.

"Can we go to her grave?" I asked, after slipping into bed.

Papa looked down at his hands resting on the bedcover. As his silence expanded, I thought he must be too sad to talk, so sad he might start sobbing if he opened his mouth. It's so much easier to transfer the unbearable to someone else.

"I don't know where she's buried," Papa said without looking at me, and the only thought that came to me was—how was I going to say goodbye?

During the night I absorbed Papa's news with bad dreams, and in the morning I woke up with another, deadlier thought. Mama was dead because of me. I had torn up the train tickets. I had picked the date for the second set of tickets. It was all my fault. No one knew except Mama, and she was dead. I could confess to a priest, because priests are sworn to secrecy, but God didn't fit into my landscape anymore, and so I told no one.

It was weeks later that I asked, "How do you know she was shot?"

"Your passer told Lilli. Giorgio asked her to find out what had happened to your mother."

"The Swiss man who picked us up said Mama was coming later."

"He didn't want you to be upset."

"No one fired a shot."

"You mean you didn't hear it. Isn't that what you mean, Susie? By then you were too far away to hear it."

"I guess." He asked me never to question her death again. I couldn't disobey my grieving father. By putting the questions in a safe corner, I managed to put her death away. And my guilt. The war was over and I was fifteen and starved for a new, fun life.

MONTE BISBINO, ITALY—DECEMBER 24, 1943

I tell Susie to go first with Claire. Those are Aldo's orders. Susie first with Claire for safety's sake. I'm the bigger target. If the guards start shooting, they'll go for me first. I'm taking the suitcase.

I kiss them both, tell Susie never to look up or back. "Just keep going. I'll be right behind you."

Aldo snaps the wire. The bells jingle wildly, slow down, stop. I hold my breath as Susie pushes herself and Claire under the barbed wire to the other side. They start rolling and I crawl toward the gap in the fence. My legs get caught by something. I can't move them. I kick to free myself, turn my head back to see Aldo on his knees, his fingers clasped around my ankles. He drags me away from the fence. I claw at the snow, desperate to find something to hang on to. I can't yell. The guards might come running, start shooting at Susie, who can't be far yet. A hot lava of fury washes over me. I thrash, kick, push myself against him, pummel his chest, sink my teeth into his arm. Aldo lets go of one leg and slaps me hard. I fall back. He moves on top of me, grips me with his knees. I keep kicking.

He opens my mouth and pours grappa down my throat until I pass out.

COMO, ITALY—JUNE 19, 1956

It's late morning in Como—a brilliant warm day. I take a walk along the waterfront to postpone the moment of truth. It only adds to my anxiety, but I find pleasure in that, I don't know why. A rippled sheen covers the lake like an expensive bedcover. The waterbus is filling up with tourists. The sidewalk café tables in the main piazza host more tourists. Locals are having their aperitifs. I walk into the corner café, pay for a cappuccino and a phone token, and ask for the phone book. Standing at the counter, I drain my cup and look for Eva Segalini's number. Lady Eva is not listed in the Cernobbio or Como section. She must have moved away or died. I was hoping to find her, apologize in person, explain why we left so abruptly. I wrote to her from Lugano. It was still wartime and she may never have gotten the letter. I wrote to her from Rome too. She never answered, but the letter didn't come back with *addressee unknown*. I assumed she wanted nothing to do with us.

For a moment I wonder if this disappointment is a harbinger of what's to come at Villa Faro. The baby stirs inside me, tells me she's hungry, and I shake the thought away. I buy focaccia filled with prosciutto, eat it as I make my way along the lake to the funicular for Brunate.

A flower stand stops me. I fill my arms with yellow and orange roses, purple cornflowers, white delphiniums, daisies. To make her happy.

Happy? I drop down on a nearby bench and hide my face in the flowers. Can you be sick and happy? Because if she is up there, at Villa Faro, then she did not abandon us, walk away in anger. Sickness made her stay. If she is up there, I am not guilty of her death or her disappearance. Instead of giving me relief, that possibility fills me with a sadness that immobilizes me. The moment of truth. Is she there? Not there? If she is, if, if, if. What will be? The past dissolving into a haze, the future a bright coin to be spent with joy. I want to sit on this bench forever.

A ferocious kick from the baby gets me walking again. She likes movement. I wait a few minutes in line, then buy my ticket. The baby settles down. In the funicular I sit with my back to the view of the shimmering lake, the far shore with its cluster of buildings that make up the town of Cernobbio, of Mount Bisbino, now free of barbed wire. My eyes follow the funicular tracks, parallel lines climbing up the steep slope. I place the flowers on top of my belly button and tell the baby to take a long deep sniff. The thought, crazy as it may be, helps, and as I climb, I become convinced that I will find Mama. I am as certain now as I am that the baby inside me is a girl. A fragile certainty that can be shattered with the blink of an eye, and yet I cling to it.

How will I approach her? She might be in her room, looking out on the garden. I'll wave, call to her. She'll make the sign that I should wait, she'll come down. When she does, we run to each other and hold each other tight. For a long time. So tight we can barely breathe. When we finally separate, I see that the flowers have left pollen on her cheek.

Or she is sitting in the garden, her face raised to the sun. I say, Hi, Mama, may I sit with you? These flowers are for you.

Or I just say hello, kiss her cheek, and point to the ladybug nestled on one of the roses, tell her how it brings good luck, and wait for her to recognize me. She might smile and say you look like Chipmunk, Susie, my daughter, my oldest. Sit with me and tell me your name.

She might turn away, uninterested, her mind wiped clean by her sickness. Maybe she will let me sit with her anyway, let me hold her hand, maybe even hug her. Unbidden, a hope drops into my head and blossoms into a scene. My baby is born, the three of us, three generations of women, sit together on a garden bench. "What's my granddaughter's name?" Mama asks and the sun swings over the trees to light us all. Once would be enough.

I have twelve years of telling to offer her, family history that I will turn into stories if she doesn't know me. I have all my love to give her. Best of all I have twenty-eight weeks of baby nestled inside me to show her. I'll press her hand on the swell of my belly and baby will tap her foot against Mama's hand and she'll flush with pride. I will say, Forgive me, Mama, for not having loved you enough. Can we start over? She'll answer the baby with a few pats, a Morse code that I take to mean, Yes, we will.

BRUNATE, ITALY—JUNE 19, 1956

I sit in the garden, in the shade of a fat chestnut tree, my head firmly planted in this beautiful, sunny day. I'm knitting a baby sweater with an intricate pattern that makes me cross-eyed. Well, my fault, I picked the pattern. I felt a sudden desire to show off my talents to the baby's mother, whoever she may be. Maybe this fluff of a sweater will make the mother smile, if she's got any smiles left in her. Someone cares, that's what I want to show her.

Someone is ringing the gate bell, quite insistent about it too. Sister Perpetua, with her heavy gait, takes her time down the path. She opens the gate. I slip off my reading glasses. We don't get many visitors on weekdays. A young woman with lots of flowers is standing there, almost as big as Sister Perpetua. Two, at most three months to go, I'd say. Her belly is still high.

Seeing all those flowers, a nursery rhyme pops in my head.

> Ladybug, ladybug
> Fly away home
> Your house is on fire
> And your children will burn.

Whenever we were near flowers, I'd try to find ladybugs for the children. They're pretty and bring good luck. But then I'd start reciting that nasty rhyme. I don't know why. Doesn't even rhyme, for that matter. "Your children will burn." Terrifying.

A raven thought drops down from one of the branches above, black as could be. Unbidden. Marco's treachery, my children must never know of it. I'll be tempted. He came to visit every year after the war to check my progress. That much I know. Dying, he sent me a letter I keep in my pocket. I have read it so often, the creases are tearing.

You needed to stay in Villa Faro and be cured. It was the best thing for you and the girls. I was going to come back for you once the war was over, take you home. That was my plan. I was sure you'd be well by then. That's what the doctor told Lilli. She came to visit you before taking the girls down to Rome. You kept screaming. The doctor said you weren't going to get better.

When I saw the girls at the train station, they looked so vulnerable, so needy. I wanted to hold them forever, wipe the war away from them forever. My role as a father was to protect them.

Your death came easily, far more easily than telling them their mother was insane. Death is final. You mourn, you comfort yourself with good memories, you go on with your own life. Insanity is a stain that deepens, that shames you, that makes you wonder if you too will one day succumb. That is what I believed.

Your new doctor believes there is a good chance you will soon be well enough to walk away from Villa Faro. I wish it for you with all my heart and include the children's addresses. I don't have much time left and want to tell them the truth. I tried after the operation but failed. I am in a great deal of pain and their love and respect is my daily and only bread. I am not sure I will have the courage to see their feelings for me turn to hate and disgust. Forgive me.

There is still an ocean full of anger roiling inside me. Anger and pain sent me spinning, blasted my brain into little bits that wouldn't come together again. Not for years. I admit the war and worry had punched a few holes in me before that night. Crazy came later.

Marco has been their lighthouse the years I've been gone. Susie's lighthouse always. Claire's only parent. Knowing would only poison their future. Burn them.

He's dead now. That helped. I walk a straight mental line now. I take my pills. I keep the anger at bay. The doctor says I'm ready to leave this mountaintop with the lighthouse that scans across the lake to the other mountain, where I lost my girls. I know I'm ready to find my children. I have their addresses. Marco's parting gift, his act of contrition—their addresses and the freedom to tell them the truth.

I will say this: I was too sick to follow. Too sick to want you to know where I was, to burden you, to shame you. I let the Nazis kill me. There's no shame in that. You have lodged in my heart through the madness, the shock treatments, the insulin shots, the talk cure. I never stopped loving you. I ask you to forgive me.

They may not. They may want nothing to do with me, but at least I will have seen them at least once, seen the way they have grown, maybe be with them long enough to discover who they have become. I know I will be proud of them, and if they walk away from me, I will still have the new, bright, clean picture of my grown children to keep me going.

The gate slams shut. I look up and see that the young woman has stopped halfway up the path. She's looking at me above her flowers with a pretty, welcoming face. I smile at her. She walks toward me and, as I watch her, my heart starts racing to catch up to all that was lost, to all that is waiting to be found.

ACKNOWLEDGMENTS

This novel is charged with the memories of many. Where recollection failed, I strove for an emotional truth, which I hope betrays no one's life. Some of the people who allowed me a glimpse into their past have passed away. I will always be grateful to Elena Camiz, Virginia Tagliacozzo, Mario Sarti, Dr. John Gens, my sister Franca Camiz, and my mother, Cathleen Reeder Trinchieri. I hope I have honored their memories and helped keep them alive.

I thank my sister Carolita Sutherland, my brother, Paolo Trinchieri, and Claudio Vismara for sharing their wartime memories. I thank Franca Di Castro for letting me read her family's collection of Roman newspapers. I thank Anora McGaha, Marina Tartara, Judith Keller, Maria Nella Lombardi, and Dr. Barbara Lane for their careful readings.

Special thanks go to Susan Spafford for encouraging me to write from two points of view, to Joan Meisel for her editorial expertise, to Erika Bianchi for sharing what it is like to be pregnant, Joanna Clapps Herman for pointing the way to SUNY Press, and Judy Moskowitz for her constant support.

I send a heartfelt *grazie* to my Italian editor, Claudia Tarolo, and MarcosyMarcos publisher Marco Zapparoli for being such strong supporters. To SUNY Press editor Amanda Lanne-Camilli, all my gratitude.

Of the countless books I read for research, I am most indebted to Miriam Mafai's *Pane Nero* (Arnoldo Mondadori, 1987) and Paolo Monelli's *Roma 1943* (Arnoldo Mondadori, 1948).

To Stuart, my love always.